Love's Grip

Love's Grip

Nika Michelle

www.urbanbooks.net

Urban Books, LLC
300 Farmingdale Road, NY-Route 109
Farmingdale, NY 11735

ISBN 13: 978-1-945855-94-8
ISBN 10: 1-945855-94-0

First Mass Market Printing March 2019
First Trade Paperback Printing July 2018
Printed in the United States of America

10 9 8 7 6 5 4 3 2 1

Distributed by Kensington Publishing Corp.
Submit Orders to:
Customer Service
400 Hahn Road
Westminster, MD 21157-4627
Phone: 1-800-733-3000
Fax: 1-800-659-2436

Love's Grip

Nika Michelle

Chapter 1

Daisha

Damn. He was leaning against my car, waiting for me. My heartbeat immediately increased. There was going to be a confrontation, and I knew it, so I prepared myself for the bullshit.

"Didn't I tell yo' mu'fuckin' hardheaded ass you can't work here? I don't want no thirsty niggas lookin' at my bitch! Didn't I tell you dat!" Spit flew in my face as he yelled at me. "Up in that bitch, like you single and shit!"

His breath reeked of alcohol mixed with Kush, and his eyes were bloodshot red. That physical attraction I'd once felt for him was long gone. His smooth, caramel-toned skin, and brooding dark brown eyes, which had once stirred my emotions, no longer affected me. Well, not in a good way.

I'd been with Raekwan for almost two years, and I was already sick of his shit. He was so possessive and jealous. Not only that, but the nigga was also stingy as hell. That was the reason I was working as a waitress at the hole-in-the-wall strip club in the first place.

"I'm so damn sick of you, Rae! You're the one who won't help me the fuck out, and then you wanna trip 'cause I'm out here takin' care of myself! The reason I ain't taking classes anymore is that you don't want me around other niggas. Well, you know what? I can't avoid bein' around other niggas. Okay. Men do exist! I can't take it anymore, and I want you to pack your shit and get outta my spot! It's over! Now, move out of my way so I can leave!"

He simply smirked at me before wrapping his thick lips around the filter of a Newport. Taking a deep pull of the nicotine, he stared menacingly into my eyes. "Fo' real, yo? You think it's gon' end just 'cause you say so, shawty? Pack my shit?" His laugh was sarcastic. "Nah, it don't work like that. I ain't goin' nowhere. I love you, babe. I just don't want my woman out here like that." He tried to hug me.

Rolling my eyes, I tried to shove him to the side so I could get in my vehicle and leave. That nigga wasn't having it. He didn't even budge.

"Chill out, yo. Every time I put my hands on yo' ass, you gon' think I did you wrong! Now, like I said, I ain't goin' nowhere, and you ain't, either. You gon' quit that fuckin' job and be a good bitch for your man." His tone of voice was threatening, but it didn't faze me one bit.

"Move, Rae! I'm done wit' you! Get that through your thick fuckin' skull! It doesn't matter what you wanna do. You're so scared that I'm gonna meet somebody better than you! Which won't be hard, since you don't do shit for me. All you wanna do is get high all damn day and play video games like a little boy! You need to grow the fuck up. I'm a grown woman, and I need a grown-ass man. And just so you know, I ain't your fuckin' bitch." I was hoping he'd finally get the point and just leave me alone.

He didn't say anything, so I kept going in on his trifling ass. "I don't want you! First of all, when was the last time you paid a damn bill? Huh? What? You think some nigga's gonna come along who don't mind helpin' me?" At that point I was all up in his face. "Fuck your no-good ass. You ain't shit, and you ain't never gon' be shit!"

When he stared at me with narrowed eyes and threw his cigarette on the ground, I didn't expect what came next. Suddenly, his fingers were wrapped around my neck and I couldn't breathe.

"Shut up, bitch, 'fore I shut yo' ass up for good!" He squeezed harder, and I could feel myself blacking out.

Next thing I knew, I saw something that looked like lightning crashing when his strong hand struck my face. My skin stung as he slapped me over and over again. Tears burned my eyes as I tried to protect my face from his assault. Next thing I knew, he was using his fists and I was on the ground. Then I felt a crushing kick to my ribs.

"Please stop! Stop, Rae. I'm . . . sorry." I coughed up blood and tried to stay conscious, although he was beating the shit out of me. The pain was excruciating, and I found myself praying for my life. He was going to kill me right there in that parking lot.

Just as I was about to lose consciousness, I heard somebody say, "Leave her the fuck alone, before I blow yo' fuckin' brains out, nigga!"

I tried to open my eyes to see who he was, but I felt so weak. His voice sounded familiar, but I couldn't place it.

"Nigga, who the fuck you s'posed to be?" Rae asked, then let out an evil laugh.

That was when I heard the sound of a gun cocking. "The nigga that's gon' end yo' mu'fuckin' life if you don't get the fuck up outta here. Now!"

I was out of it, but I hoped that nigga had scared Rae away. By the time I felt my body being lifted from the hard asphalt, I was going in and out of consciousness. My eyes felt like they were glued shut, and my mouth was dry as hell. Pain was radiating all over my body, and all I wanted was for it to stop.

"It's gonna be okay," I heard the strange man say. "I'm gon' take care of you, Ma."

Pistol

Earlier that night I'd spotted her fine, thick ass inside the club, and after that, my eyes had been on her, instead of on the dancers who were twerking and working the pole, buck-ass naked. After I'd sipped my third Corona, I was tipsy as hell, but I ordered another just to have a reason to talk to her. A smile lit up her honey-colored eyes when she saw that I'd left her a hundred-dollar tip. It was priceless.

That shit made a hard-assed mu'fucka like me feel all mushy. It also made me wonder why a woman like her was even working here. I'd frequented the spot for the past few weeks just to see her. She was obviously beautiful and smart. I could tell from our short conversations. Shawty just seemed out of place to me here.

After she'd walked out of the strip club on this particular night, I headed outside to ask her for her number. But instead of getting in her car, she was on the ground, and this dude was punching and kicking the life out of her. I walked up on that nigga who was kicking her, and after I scared him off, I lifted her up off the ground and put her in my car and drove her to my place.

After I cleaned the blood from her face, she was still out of it. I held an ice pack against her swollen eye, and she started to groan and stir on my bed. Her almond-toned skin was starting to bruise, but I needed her to come to so I could check her ribs. I didn't want her to regain consciousness while I was checking them, since she might think I was trying to take advantage of her in such a vulnerable state. When one of her eyes finally opened—the one that wasn't swollen shut—and locked on mine, she looked startled.

"You're okay. Don't be afraid. I got you," I told her in a soothing voice.

"What? Where am I?" She sat up, cringing, and then tried to look around with the one eye that wasn't swollen shut.

"This is my place, and you . . . your . . . I don't know who he is to you, but he . . ."

"My boyfriend . . . Rae. I remember what happened." A tear fell from her open eye, and I continued to hold the ice pack in place on the other one. "Ex now."

"Why're you with somebody who'd do something like that to you?"

"He ain't never done no shit like that to me before."

That was hard for me to believe. "You ain't gotta be ashamed. I mean, I ain't judgin' you."

"No, really." She cleared her throat. "The warnin' signs were there, but that was the first time he actually put his hands on me."

"Wow. Why would you be wit' a nigga who got you even thinkin' he'll whup your ass? From what I see, you deserve better."

"You don't know me," she said defensively, as if I'd said something to offend her. "How the fuck do you know what I deserve?"

"I ain't gotta know you to know you don't deserve to get the shit beat outta you by some fuckin' nigga." The look on my face had to let her know that I meant that shit. "If you don't think you deserve better, you just selling yourself short."

"I'm . . . sorry. Uh, thank you . . . for helpin' me. If it wasn't for you, I'd probably be dead." She closed her open eye, and a tear spilled out. "I can't go back home. He's gonna kill me."

"Not if I can help it. You'll stay here for now, and I'll make sure you get somewhere safe when the sun comes up. I'll take you wherever you wanna go. I'm sure your family's—"

"I ain't got no family . . . ," she mumbled. "I only got one so-called friend, and I don't even know if I can trust her. I think she's the one who told him about me takin' that job. Shit. How do I know that I can trust you?"

"No family?" I looked down at the beautiful battered woman. For some reason, I was unusually concerned about her. I usually didn't give two fucks about anybody other than myself, but I wanted to make sure she was good. That indifferent shit was part of who I'd become during my twenty-five years on this earth. It wasn't really a choice, but a means of survival. If I gave a damn, it would be the death of me. I had learned that shit the hard way. "That's fucked up, and as far as trustin' me, what choice do you have?"

"Since we're havin' such a deep conversation and you saved my life, I guess we should officially introduce ourselves," she said. "I've seen you at the club, but I never got your name. Thanks for the tip, by the way."

"I'm Pistol, and you're welcome."

"I'm Daisha, although I use a different name at work."

"Yeah. I know you as . . ."

"Punkin," we said at the same time.

"It's a childhood nickname," she explained with a slight smile. "I know Pistol ain't your real name, but I'll let you get away with it for now."

Knowing that she was in pain and I could still make her smile was like vindication for a fucked-up-ass nigga like me.

"I like Daisha," I told her in a soft voice as I grabbed a pill bottle from the nightstand. "These are Lortabs that I got when I was in a car accident a while back. I'll break them in half and shit. You know, for the pain. I wanna see if you have any broken ribs, but I didn't want you to feel like I was . . ."

She nodded. "It's okay."

I lifted her shirt, checked her ribs, and saw that they weren't broken, but I wrapped her up with an Ace bandage, anyway. "From what I can tell, they don't seem broken, but you still might need to get an X-ray, just in case." I opened the pill bottle, broke a Lortab in half, and handed it to her, along with a bottle of water I'd placed on the nightstand.

She nodded, took the pain pill, and drank the whole bottle of water before falling asleep. Of course, it was quiet as hell in my bedroom now, and I glanced at my phone to see that it was after five in the morning. With a sigh, I covered her with a blanket and walked out of the room. I left the door open so she wouldn't freak out when she woke up. The light from the hallway would make it so that she could see her surroundings. I walked into the living room, and after turning on the TV, I settled on the sofa. Sleep didn't come easy for me. Shit. It never did.

Chapter 2

Pistol

The sharp pain in my neck was what woke me up. I instinctively rubbed the cramp out, realizing that it was the result of my awkward position on the sofa. Then the memory of the night before flooded through my mind. Glancing at my watch, I saw that it was after 9:00 a.m. I had fallen asleep late as hell, which was quite unusual for me. Normally, I was doing something to make money by this time of morning. Then I thought about it. For the past six months, I'd been on the run. I was wanted for a bunch of federal charges in Virginia and North Carolina, so I'd fled to Atlanta to get away from the heat. Protecting Daisha was a risk I was willing to take, despite all of that.

I stood up and stretched, thinking of the woman I had left sleeping in my bed. Where was her family? She was a mystery to me, and I wanted to know more about her. I made my way to the bedroom of my downtown condo, and I couldn't help but notice that the door was closed. I'd left it open, so I wondered if she'd closed it for some reason.

"Daisha," I called out as I knocked. "You okay in there?"

She didn't respond, so I twisted the knob to see if the door was locked. It wasn't. Maybe she was taking a shower or something and didn't want me to walk in on her naked. But that didn't explain why she had closed the bedroom door. I mean, all she had to do was close the door to the master bathroom. *Damn*. She didn't know me, though, so I understood. Maybe she felt uncomfortable. *Hmm*. Most women didn't care and would be happy to flaunt their body around a man. Instead of busting in on her, I decided to chill out for a minute and wait for her to come out. In the meantime, I decided to make a phone call. I went back into the living room and plopped down on the sofa.

"What up, my nigga? You got that for me?" I asked when he picked up the phone.

"Hell yeah," he shot back cockily. "Don't I always come through, nigga?"

I let out a chuckle. "Right, right. I'll be through there in a few, a'ight?"

"What's a few, man? I got some plays I gotta make."

He was about thirty minutes away, and I had to make sure that old girl was all good. She would probably need me to take her to get her car first, and that was about twenty minutes out of the way.

"Handle your business and call me later, then. I don't need that shit till tomorrow, anyway," I told him.

"Bet. That'll work. Later."

"One." I hung up and looked up at the TV. It was on ESPN, of course. Although I loved sports, I was a gambler first. Life was all about making a dollar, in my mind. Even when it came to a basketball or football game, I had to make a bet. It wasn't just about enjoying the moment. To me, it was all about making a profit, even when it came to my hobbies. A nigga like me could turn anything into a hustle.

The sound of silence made me get up from the sofa. I went back to the bedroom and turned the doorknob again. But this time I opened the door. Before I walked into the bedroom, I closed my eyes, in case Daisha wasn't decent. As much as I wanted to see her naked, I wanted her to invite me to do so.

"You good?" I asked with my eyes closed. "I ain't lookin'."

There was silence. Nothing. I turned around, thinking she must've been startled by my entrance.

"I ain't mean to barge in. I ain't see nothing. My eyes are closed, and I got my back turned to you. Say something, yo."

Nothing.

I opened my eyes and then turned around. There was nobody in the room, and the bed was made. No sounds were coming from the bathroom, either, but I decided to knock, anyway.

"You in there?" I asked. "You okay?"

I turned the knob on the bathroom door, and the door was unlocked. I peeked in, and she wasn't in there, either. It was clear to me now that she had left, but why hadn't she let me know she was leaving? I let out a sigh as I wondered about her. Would that dude come after her? What if my protective nature had got her in more shit than she was already in? If she went back home, would he be waiting for her?

Damn. My head was all fucked up about a woman I didn't even know. All I could do was hope her dude came to his senses and left her alone. Her lack of family had to make her vulnerable to a man like him. I felt the need to keep her safe, but I didn't know where she lived or where to find her. All I knew was she worked at the Blue Flame, and I seriously doubted that she'd go back there after what had happened.

***

A few hours later I was at a pool hall in the hood with my cousins Mike and Dank. They were brothers and had helped me with my retreat to the A. Mike was the oldest, at twenty-six years old, and the most responsible. Dank, who was twenty-two, was reckless as hell, but that li'l nigga knew how to make money. The thing was, with how he handled shit, would he be able to keep it?

"So, you got the heat?" Mike asked me as he chalked his pool stick. "It's gon' happen in less than twenty-four hours, so we gotta be ready."

"I'll get it tomorrow, man. I already talked to Steel, and he got that shit ready. I'm ready."

Mike nodded as Dank hit the cue ball and sent the colored balls rolling across the pool table. "A'ight. 'Cause we ain't got time for fuckups."

"I know that. I got this shit," I said. "Don't forget this shit's goin' down 'cause of me. I know what the fuck I'm doin'. You handle the drug shit, and I'll handle what I'm good at."

One thing about me was, I wasn't a dope boy. It took too damn long to make any real money that way. There were also too many risks. I liked fast money. I'd started out as a jack boy and graduated to a professional crook. I was a master of disguise who could break into anything and had a sure shot. That explained the name Pistol. I'd robbed a few banks in VA and NC, and now I was wanted by the Feds because my partner Flex had snitched.

Mike looked pissed off at my remark, so Dank spoke up to dispel his bad mood. "You playin' pool this round, man?" Dank's eyes were on me.

I sipped a Long Island Iced Tea as I sat there, and shook my head. "Nah, man. Y'all play. I'm chillin'."

When I looked up, I spotted this bitch named Niya, whom I had fucked with about a month ago, walking toward me. I'd cut old girl off because her hygiene wasn't up to par. She was also one of those nasty chicks who didn't keep her crib clean. She'd get her nails and hair done, but she didn't clean up or cook. What the fuck type of shit was that? Her hand was always out, and she was always offering to give some head, but she had no ambition. After a while that shit got old.

"What's up, mu'fucka? I figured I'd find you here." She stood there in front of me with her hand on one of her wide hips.

"Why the fuck you lookin' for me?" I asked before sipping my drink again.

"Are you seriously askin' me that right now?" She looked back at her two friends. "This nigga can't be serious."

"Oh, I'm serious, shawty. We fucked and all that, but I told you what it was. Walk away 'fore I embarrass your ass. I don't even wanna do that shit."

Niya laughed and shook her head. "Please don't act like you wasn't all up in this pussy like you wanted to be reborn. Miss me wit' the bullshit." She batted her fake lashes and tossed her long, wavy black weave over her shoulder.

Why the fuck did I always go for her type? I loved those thick-ass bitches with the fake hair, lashes, and nails. They'd have on a glob of makeup like a damn mask. Now that I thought about it, those hoes obviously had something to hide. Her outfit was worth more than anything in her mom's crib, where she laid her head. The ho was ratchet, and I didn't want shit to do with her ass.

Niya went on. "Nigga, bye. You can't embarrass me. I don't give a damn what none of y'all buster-ass niggas think about me. I stay on fleek, face is always beat, and my pussy is fiyah." She waved me off and proceeded to talk shit. "Fuck you, Pistol. You frontin' for your boys, like you don't be checkin' for me and shit."

"Let's not go there, Ma. You don't wanna go there," I told her. "I don't know. Yo' musty ass don't even bathe every day, so I moved on. I like fuckin' clean bitches."

My niggas laughed.

Dank had to butt in. "Damn. I think you better walk on off, shawty. I know cuz, and shit 'bout to get real."

Niya sucked her teeth. "I ain't scared of that nigga."

"I don't want you to be scared of me, shawty. All I want you to do is leave me the fuck alone. You can do that, right?" I eyed her as she turned beet red.

She bit her bottom lip, and I could tell that she wanted to cry because I'd called her out. "Nigga, I don't fuck wit' you like that any fuckin' way. All I wanted was yo' fuckin' money. You tryin'a play me to the left and shit, but . . ." As if sensing something was up, her homegirls walked over to us.

I shook my head. "Y'all bitches just don't know when to stop these days. Go 'head on, Niya. For real, yo. You didn't get no money, and you ain't gettin' no money."

One of Niya's girls eyed me, with a smile on her face. Was that bitch flirting? I ignored her.

"Fuck this nigga!" Niya told her homegirls and then looked up at me with a devilish grin. "I got something for your ass."

"Whatever." I nonchalantly gulped my drink. "Get the fuck on, yo."

She turned and walked off, and her girls were on her heels. I could only imagine what they had to say.

"Damn, nigga. She bad. You didn't tell me she was funky and shit," Mike blurted out as he wore an amused expression.

I couldn't help but laugh. "I didn't want to tell y'all that shit now, but shawty asked for it."

Dank spoke up. "Shit. You better be careful, man. Ole girl's pissed off."

"That bitch don't move me. She's just some pussy that I ain't tryin'a get wit' no mo'. Even if I'm just fuckin' a bitch, she gotta come better than that. At least keep clean sheets on your bed and use deodorant. Damn. She need to get outta her feelings."

My phone vibrated. I took it out of my pocket and saw it was this chick I'd met about a week ago. I sent her to voice mail really quick, and she sent me a text.

Kendra: Hey. I was hoping to see u.

Me: I just wanna fuck. If u ain't down, don't text me no more tonight.

Kendra: I'm down.

"I'm 'bout to leave. I'll holla at y'all niggas tomorrow," I said as I stood up.

Mike flashed an anxious look my way. "Yo, call me early, nigga."

"For real," Dank said. "We gotta know what's up, man."

"I got y'all. Damn." I pounded them up as I shook my head, and then I left. Once I was outside, I texted Kendra.

Me: Your address?

Kendra: 135 Creek Court, Lithonia, Georgia.

Me: Be there in twenty.
Kendra: Okay.

"You are one sexy-ass mu'fucka," I announced
when Kendra opened the door.

Kendra was looking all hot in a short-ass pair
of shorts and a tank top through which I could
literally see the nipples of her D cups. She was
brown skinned and thick as hell, like I liked. Still,
all I could think about was Daisha. Where the
fuck was she, and was she okay? That was all I
wanted to know, but I hadn't busted a real nut in
weeks. Shit. A nigga needed to get his rocks off.

She pulled me into the bedroom and pointed
to the bed. "Lay back, baby," she purred seduc-
tively as she removed her clothes.

I undressed and did as she said. My eyes
were roaming all over Kendra's curvy frame, but
Daisha was still on my mind. All I could envision
in my head was her beautiful curly locks and
her flawless, smooth skin—minus the bruises
from that nigga. Her facial features were perfect,
and I especially loved her nose. It was wide but
prominent at the same time, which spoke of
her African and Native American heritage. Her
natural beauty spoke volumes. Every time I had
seen Daisha, her makeup was at a minimum. All
she wore was lip gloss in a shimmery color and

eye shadow. Although she wore the uniform of a corset and short shorts at the strip club, it didn't seem whorish on her. Instead, I saw her as a woman who was doing what she felt she had to do.

"What's on your mind, baby?" Kendra asked as she straddled me on the bed.

"You," I lied as she slowly made a trail down my abs with her tongue.

When her warm tongue wrapped around my hardness, I closed my eyes, trying to ward off thoughts of Daisha. Damn. I needed to cum to relieve some pent-up stress.

"Mmm," Kendra moaned as she played with my balls.

My dick was literally down her throat now, and that shit felt good as hell. I held on to the back of her head, and then the sound of her ten-month-old baby crying fucked up the mood. Kendra just kept right on sucking, like she didn't hear that shit.

"Um, yo' kid's cryin', shawty. You don't hear that shit?" I knew from experience that mothers knew how to tune out their children, but that shit was loud as fuck.

"Uh-huh, but she'll stop." That bitch kept right on sucking and slurping on my dick.

I wasn't feeling that shit, so I pushed her away. "I'm good, yo. Tend to yo' baby." I stood up and started to get dressed.

"You act like you ain't never heard a baby cry before." That chick had the nerve to grab my dick.

"I have, but cryin' babies that ain't mine make my dick soft. Specially when the mama ain't got the decency to make sure her baby's good. Later, yo."

I left her standing there in her bedroom, naked and horny as hell, but I didn't give a fuck. Women like her needed to get their priorities straight. Chasing a nigga and a nut was the reason she was in that position in the first place.

I left her place and got behind the wheel of my ride and put the window down before I turned the key in the ignition. Thoughts of Daisha flooded my mind as I started the engine, hit the gas, and peeled out of that bitch's neighborhood. Finding Daisha was on my mind, but damn, I didn't know where to start looking.

Chapter 3

Daisha

That nigga Pistol had been nice as hell to me, but I had had to leave his place. One thing I'd learned during my twenty-two years was that when a man did something nice for you, he expected something in return. No matter how genuine they seemed to be, men did whatever they had to do to get what they wanted.

As grateful as I was to him for helping me, I knew what he was up to. He flirted with me every time he came to the club, and the hundred-dollar tip was his way of showing off how much money he had at his disposal. It just so happened that he walked up on me when I was getting stumped out by Raekwan, and that was his moment to play "captain save a ho." What he didn't know was that I didn't want to be saved. Well, at least to a certain extent. It was a good thing that he'd intervened, but I didn't want to take things any further.

Damn, he was fine, though, with his flawless dark chocolate skin and nice full lips. When he did smile, it lit up his menacing hazel eyes. Such light eyes looked sexy and exotic against his beautiful dark skin. He also had perfect, straight white teeth. I could tell by the way his clothes fit him that he had a nice cut-up body to go with his tall stature. He had to be at least six feet tall. Not only that, but his hair was close cut, and his facial hair was nice and neat too.

Even with his clean-cut looks, I knew that he was a thug-ass nigga. I had a weakness for dudes like him, though, which had been my downfall. The thing was, I was done with the bad boy type. And after what I'd just gone through with Rae, I was done with men for a while. It was time for me to focus on myself.

I had been taking classes toward a BA in psychology when I met Rae. It had been my second year as a part-time student at Clark Atlanta University. When I first saw him, there had been an immediate attraction, but there'd also been a feeling of uneasiness. It was like I could sense something about him, but I'd put the physical over my common sense. That had a bad idea.

Less than a year later, I'd withdrawn from school because Rae was so over the top with his jealousy. That nigga had accused me of fucking everybody, from the professors to the damn janitors. It was ridiculous, and the last straw had been when he came up to the school and punched a random dude whom he saw talking to me. It wasn't even anything like he'd thought. Dude had simply been asking me where the admissions office was, because he was a freshman.

After that, I couldn't risk anybody else getting hurt. I decided to just be the dutiful girlfriend and let him be the breadwinner, like he'd promised. Besides, it wasn't like I really had anybody who was there for me like that. And so instead of just leaving him, I decided to tough it out. I thought I could change him. Well, obviously I couldn't. And the stories of how his father had physically abused him made me feel pity for him. Whenever I threatened to leave, he'd throw it up in my face that everybody left him. That made me stay, because I knew how it felt to be neglected and abandoned.

Then, suddenly, he started cutting me off financially. He even stopped paying the bills. In an effort to make ends meet, I went to work at Wendy's while he hustled, but he was spending his money only on weed, Jordans, video games, and other bitches. Wendy's didn't pay enough, and that was why I ended up working at the Blue Flame.

"Damn! What happened to your face, bitch?" Kevia asked as she stared at me in the dim light of my black Honda Civic. We were parked down the street from her building.

I had contacted Uber when I left Pistol's spot and had gone to get my car. After that I had ridden around, had got something to eat, and had chilled in my car until the sun went down. I couldn't go back home, and my only close friend, Kevia, was my only option. The thing was, I didn't really trust her, because she was Rae's first cousin. They were very close, and she was the one who had introduced us when he moved to Atlanta from Macon three years ago. If only I had known then what I knew now.

"Your fuckin' crazy-ass cousin happened to my face."

She looked surprised. "What? No the fuck he didn't!"

"Yes the fuck he did. He found out about me takin' the job at the Blue Flame. Did you tell him?" I just came out with it.

"Hell no! I can't believe you asked me that shit. Rae's my cousin, but you're my best friend. I can't believe he put his hands on you like that. What you gon' do? I know you ain't gon' stay wit' him after that shit."

"No, I'm not, but I gotta get my shit outta the crib. I don't care 'bout breakin' the damn lease. You gotta go get my stuff for me. I don't wanna run into his crazy ass. He already threatened to kill me, and I ain't chancin' it."

"Where you gon' go? I'd let you stay wit' me, but what if Rae pop up and shit and . . ."

"I'll figure that part out. I just need you to get my shit and put it in storage. I'll give you the money. Can you handle that for me?" I still didn't know if I could trust her, but who the fuck else did I have in my corner?

I hadn't spoken to my mother in over four years, and I definitely didn't plan on going back to Decatur to stay with her. Hell no. It had been a disaster when I was younger, so I could only imagine how it would be now that I was an adult.

She nodded vigorously. "I got you." After that, she lit up a blunt and took a long pull. "My cousin's really lost his damn mind."

"Tell me about it. I mean, he's always been crazy, but I never expected him to try to kill me."

"You think he really would've?"

"I know he would've."

She cringed. "So, what stopped him?"

After she passed me the blunt, I took a hit before answering. "This dude saw what was going on, and he pulled out a gun on him."

Kevia's eyes were wide. "Oh shit. What happened after that?"

"Nothing," I lied. "He helped me, and I spent the night in my car."

"You know the dude?"

I shook my head. "Nah. He was just some nigga who was at the club."

"Well, it's a good thing he was there. You sure he didn't shoot cuz, because I ain't heard from him all day."

"Nah, he didn't shoot him. I wish he had, though."

Kevia gave me a funny look and then narrowed her copper-brown eyes at me.

"What?" I said. "You see what he did to me."

She sighed. "Yeah, but he's still my cousin."

I rolled my eyes. "I got shit to do. I'll holla at you later."

"Damn. It's like that? You mad 'cause I don't want my cousin to get killed? I mean, I don't want you to get hurt, either, but—"

Cutting her off, I said, "You good. Just handle gettin' my shit, and don't let him know that you saw me."

She nodded. "I got you."

Damn. I really hoped I could trust her. I was still in pain and was glad that bottle of Lortabs was in my bag. "Okay. I gotta go. I'll holla at you tomorrow."

"Where you gon' go?" Kevia asked, wearing a concerned expression on her caramel-toned face.

She didn't need to know, so I kept it vague with her. Besides, it was possible that she'd tell Rae, and I didn't want that. "I'll probably just get a room somewhere for now."

Kevia hugged me. "I love you, girl. You know that. Be safe out there."

"I will. Love you too."

After she finally pulled away from me, she stepped out of the car and closed the door. She made her way down the sidewalk to her building, and before I pulled off, I watched as she walked inside.

I'd learned to hide my money, because I had had my suspicions that Rae had stolen from me before. That was why I had a stash spot in the trunk of my car. Rae had never driven my car, because he'd said it was a chick car. That had turned out to be a good thing, given that I had two stacks in the stash. I headed to an extended-stay motel on Memorial Drive in

Stone Mountain. Rae wouldn't have any clue that I was there.

When I got there, night had fallen. I parked and headed to the lobby. With my oversize dark shades on, I booked a room with the front desk attendant, who flashed me curious looks. It was clearly dark outside, and I was at a seedy motel. Although I knew that she had put two and two together, I didn't want to reveal the bruises around my eyes, so I kept the shades on.

"Will you be paying monthly, by the week, or by the day?" she quizzed.

"Let me pay for a week for now," I simply stated.

The ho just kept staring at me and shit. "Okay, that'll be four hundred fifteen dollars."

I pulled out four hundred twenty dollars in cash and passed it to her. My patience was wearing thin by now. All I wanted her to do was hurry the fuck up. Finally, she gave me the five dollars I was owed.

"Here is your key. Your room number is three-twelve," she informed me, holding out the key.

After snatching the key from her, I got my ass up out of that office in a hurry. I had made a trip to Walmart earlier in the day and had bought a few pairs of jeans, some shirts, underwear, toiletries, and snacks. The struggle was real, and

I longed for my belongings. I couldn't go back to my apartment, though, because I just knew that Rae would be there waiting for me.

I found my room, and after popping a whole Lortab, I took a quick shower, turned on the TV, and got under the covers. My mind drifted as I thought about my situation. What the hell was I going to do? I couldn't go back to work at the Blue Flame, and I knew that fifteen hundred dollars wouldn't last long. At the moment my face was all busted up, and I couldn't go looking for a job like that. Then I thought about going back to Pistol for help, but I couldn't. When I finally drifted off to sleep, my slumber was filled with nightmares about Rae.

"Where the fuck you at, bitch?" The sound of Rae's voice on my voice mail made me quiver with fear the next morning. I deleted the message and then listened to his second voice mail.

"You fuckin' that nigga? Why the hell he feel the need to step in our business? I knew you was up to no good, you fuckin' sorry, thot-ass bitch!"

He'd left me ten threatening messages since yesterday, and I deleted each one, then plugged my phone in to let it charge. I also decided to block his number.

It was crazy that I was once again in a position where I was all alone. Becoming attached to the wrong men was my problem, and I had to learn to be by myself rather than with a fucked-up-ass nigga. This habit stemmed from my childhood, I guessed. My parents had been married when I was born, but then my dad had left my mom for another woman when I was four. He'd visited me frequently at first, but then his visits had become rare events. Eventually, he'd stopped coming around completely. Rumors had circulated that he wasn't my real father. After my father left, my mother had changed for the worse. It was like she had had a midlife crisis.

My mom had been the manager of a nice Courtyard Marriott in downtown Atlanta, but eventually, she was fired because of her drinking. After that, she was just reckless as hell. She was locked up for DUIs and was always fucking around with a different man. Not only that, but she dressed inappropriately and was all loud and wild.

We had to move to the projects when I was seven, and then shit got even worse. There were times when my mom wouldn't come home for days, and when she did, some man would be with her. That shit made me feel so uncomfortable. My mother never, ever cooked, so I had to learn to fend for myself early as hell. In no time I was running the streets with Kevia at all times of the night, getting high and shit. My mom just didn't give a fuck, and neither did I.

When I would bring a boy over, she would flaunt herself around him and flirt. It got to the point where I stopped bringing my guy friends around her. Then my senior year in high school, I dated this guy named Anthony. He was twenty, and I was eighteen at the time. One day he dropped me off at home after school. My mother happened to be outside, and she started acting a fool, like always.

"Damn, baby. Who is this fine-ass mu'fucka!" she asked. She had on the shortest shorts that I'd ever seen. They were like jeans underwear. My mom had a banging body, though, but she was a mother, and I felt that she should dress accordingly.

"Mom, this is my . . . friend Anthony. Please—"

She cut me off. "Calm down, bitch. I ain't tryin'a take yo' man." Her speech was slurred. It was only four o'clock in the afternoon, and she was sloppy drunk already.

I felt so ashamed, but Anthony had a sly look on his face. His eyes were glued to my mother's breasts.

"I'll call you tomorrow, Anthony," I told him. I actually had to hint that it was time for him to leave.

"Oh yeah," he said, looking preoccupied. "Uh, it was nice meetin' you, miss . . ."

"My name's Jackie, baby," my mother told him.

"Jackie," he repeated as he grinned in her face.

"Bye, Anthony," I stated firmly.

I shook my head at my mom as he turned to leave. "Why do you have to always be drunk and disrespectful?" I snapped. I shook my head again and then stormed off to our apartment.

Less than a week later, I came home from school early because we had a half day. When I walked in, I caught my mom on her knees, sucking Anthony's dick right there in the living room.

After that, I couldn't trust my mother anymore. I vowed that as soon as I graduated from high school, I was leaving. It didn't even take that long. Kevia's apartment was my sanctuary, and I spent more time over there with her family than with my mom. She didn't seem to care for me, anyway. In her eyes, I'd been only a hindrance in her life. She reminded me of that often.

I got a job and my own place after graduation and never talked to my drunken whore of a mother again. Knowing people in the hood had come in handy. I had someone make up some fake documents for me to get approved for my apartment. Not having any siblings, aunts, uncles, or living grandparents made it easy for me to pull away from my mom. Last I heard, she was in Decatur, but I had never bothered to contact her. I didn't want to. That bitch had ruined me.

Chapter 4

Pistol

"I'm on my way to get the heat," I told Mike over the phone.

"Good, 'cause we gotta make sure everything's in place within the next few hours," he said.

"Oh, believe me. Shit's gonna go smooth. I'll be over there in an hour or so. Then we can really talk."

"Bet. Later, man."

I hung up the phone and looked at my GPS. My destination was only five minutes away. I tried to clear my head, but it was hard. Daisha was all I could think about. Where had she run off to, and why hadn't I got her number when I could? Damn it! I wanted to make sure that she was okay and that that nigga hadn't harmed her again.

My phone rang. It was that nagging ho Niya, so I sent her to voice mail. She was only good for one thing, and at the moment, I didn't want my dick sucked. The way she had acted the night before, I didn't want to have shit to do with her crazy ass.

Of course she sent me a text message.

Niya: I know you see me callin' you, nigga.

My frustration with her was building. I didn't have the time or patience for that bitch. Responding to her would only add fuel to the fire. A nigga in my position had more important shit to think about. Like the lick that would be going down later that night. Or the fact that I was on the run and about to risk my freedom once again. Not only that, but I hadn't seen my mother in months. I loved her with all my heart and knew that she was worried about me.

The thing was, I couldn't even let her know where I was. I'd called her when I touched down in the A to let her know that I was okay, and I talked to her on a regular basis, but she had no idea where I was. All she knew was that I'd caught a case and needed to get away. I was sure that she believed that I was in Atlanta with Mike and Dank, but I hadn't confirmed it, and neither had they. She was down for a nigga and constantly told the cops she didn't know where I was.

That was why I didn't tell her where I was. She didn't need to lie to the cops for me. That would result only in a perjury charge for her. My mother had always been there for me, and in return, I'd only disappointed her over and over again. I felt horrible, because she had two sons who were younger than me. There was no way I'd been a good example for them. You would think after my father was shot to death doing street shit when I was eight that I'd be a good role model for my brothers, but instead, I had done the opposite. I had decided to follow in my father's footsteps.

The only difference was that I wasn't a drug dealer. I robbed the drug dealers instead. I'd keep the money and give the product to my homies to sell. They'd give me a cut, of course, so a nigga was in the money. Later on, my operation evolved into more complex jobs. I began robbing banks, and I even did a few jewelry store heists. I loved the rush that I felt when I took something that was valuable in no time. It was like in a matter of five minutes, I could have a year's salary. Shit. I even loved the way a gun felt in my hand. It was like second nature to me, and even if I tried to defy it, that shit would just call me back.

"Your destination is on the right," my GPS said, interrupting my thoughts, and I pulled up in the driveway of a small wood-frame house. It was painted an off-white and looked innocent enough. However, I knew what was going on up in that spot. It was definitely nothing nice.

Walking up the walkway, I surveyed my surroundings and kept my guard up. My strap was in the waist of my black True Religion jeans, and I was ready for war, if need be. Honestly, I didn't really trust that nigga I was about to do business with. There was something sly and sneaky about him. We'd done business before, but there was just something about dude. Then add the fact that I wasn't from the A and really didn't know what to expect from these niggas out here.

Shit. I couldn't even trust my best friend and partner in crime. We had run the streets together, robbing motherfuckers, for years. With one promise of less time, he'd rolled on me like a damn pair of skates. That shit was fucked up. If I couldn't trust that rat-ass nigga, who the fuck could I trust? Nobody but my damn mama.

I rang the doorbell and waited. As I tapped my foot impatiently, I checked my black-face Rolex. It was a little after ten in the morning, and I was hungry as fuck. I'd been running around all morning, handling business. When that nigga finally cracked the door open, he looked around like I had the cops or some jack boys with me. He just didn't know that I was just as paranoid as he was, since I had just as much to lose.

"C'mon in, man," he said. He was still looking around outside after I walked in. After he was sure that the coast was clear, he closed the door and then secured about ten different locks and dead bolts. Okay, he had that shit secure as hell.

I took in my surroundings as he led me downstairs to the basement. That was where he kept all the high-powered weapons that we were going to need.

"So, what you lookin' for?" He glanced up at me, with a thick cigar in his hand. After he lit it, I immediately smelled the sweet, robust aroma. "Want one?" he asked, referring to the cigar.

"Nah, I'm good. Uh, I need some heavy-duty shit and a couple of handguns."

With a nod, he pulled a white bedsheet off one of the tables that displayed the range of guns he had. He also had knives, ropes, first-aid kits, chloroform, wire cutters, and all types of shit that niggas in the crime business needed. I was going to need a little bit of everything, but the weapons were first on the list.

Despite the tension, that nigga wanted money, and I needed the necessary tools to do the job.

It was mind over matter for both of us, and we continued the transaction, because business was business. After deciding on three AKs, three .45 caliber handguns, a hot-ass silver Glock nine-millimeter, ammunition, and a bunch of miscellaneous shit, I paid that nigga and waited as he put my merchandise in a huge black duffel bag.

"Damn, man. You 'bout to do some grand shit, ain't you?" he said. He seemed impressed, because I'd bought only one tool from him before today.

I chuckled, then didn't give him too much information. "I'm just makin' sure I'm good. It's real in them streets."

He smirked at me like he didn't believe that shit. It was obvious that I was about to rob a mu'fucka or commit a murder plot. That nigga wasn't stupid, and he was in business because of criminal-minded-ass niggas like me.

"A'ight, man," was all he said, having decided to drop the subject.

I walked outside with the duffel bag and looked around nervously, just like he had before. If the cops were around, they sure had enough shit to lock me up for life. After making my way to my car without any incident, I opened the trunk and threw the bag inside. Then I got behind the wheel and peeled off. *Shit*, I thought when my stomach rumbled. I had a taste for some jerk chicken, rice and peas, and cabbage. Oh yeah, the Jamaican spot up the street was where I was headed. A nigga had to eat.

Instead of getting my food to go, I decided to eat at the restaurant. That was because I knew that I wanted my food to be hot and fresh. And I also knew that if I drove to my cousins with takeout, I wouldn't have any time to grub. So I was nice and full when I got to Mike and Dank's trap spot at about one.

"Damn. What the fuck took you so long, nigga?" Mike asked. He looked pissed off.

"I got hungry, nigga. Damn. What the fuck is your problem? We still got time before the shit goes down," I replied.

"I just want everything in place, man." He had calmed down. "Where the shit at?"

"In the trunk. So, what you need me to come over so early for?" I stood there waiting for my cuz to fill me in on why he needed to see me over eight hours before the lick was going to go down.

Dank spoke up instead as he broke up some Kush in a Swisher. "We need you to do a hit for us."

Another hit, huh? It was like those niggas were good only for moving dope. They obviously didn't have the killer instinct. Did I really want to do a lick with them? To be honest, since I'd been there, it was like I was doing all their dirty work. In six months I'd done at least five hits for them.

"For y'all to have the operation that you do, you seem mighty damn amateur," I had to admit. "Don't y'all got mu'fuckas in place for that shit?"

Mike really looked like he was mad as hell then. "It's just that the nigga don't know you. That's all. We gon' have your back, like always. We just need you to roll up on him so he won't suspect that shit."

I shook my head. "You know I ain't scared to dead a nigga. I'm just sayin'. Y'all niggas don't think cats'll get suspicious when they see a strange-ass nigga rollin' up on the block? Y'all ain't new to this street shit, but you sho' actin' like it."

Mike stepped closer to me, and Dank stood between us. "Look, man. To be honest, you're a better killer than both of us," Dank said. Shit, I already knew that. Dank looked back at Mike and then at me. "And yeah, we got mu'fuckas in place for that shit, but this time, we need you to do it. Blood is thicker than water. Right?"

That made me think. "So, what the fuck am I really doing, and why didn't y'all mention this shit earlier? Somebody else owe you money? Stole yo' shit?"

"Dank, you can move, man. We straight," Mike said before looking at me. "Nah, this is different."

That really sparked my interest. "Different how?"

Mike scowled. "He's fuckin' wit' my baby mama and—"

A sarcastic chuckle escaped my lips. *What the hell?* That was some personal shit. "Why the fuck should I kill the nigga that's fuckin' your baby mama, man? I mean, damn. Did he do something to you?"

Mike cleared his throat. "You didn't let me finish."

I nodded. "Go 'head."

"My baby girl told me that he's been . . . touchin' her."

"What? He's been molestin' your daughter, my nigga?"

"Yeah, and I need you to run up on him," Mike told me. "If he sees me, he gon' know what it is and start shootin' before I can. We was beefin' way before my shawty told me 'bout that shit. If he see me or Dank, he gon' start bustin'. If you do that shit, it'll go down smooth and shit. We gon' be wit' you. I need that nigga to bleed. This is the best time to do it, 'cause that nigga by hisself. He ain't never by his fuckin' self when he in the streets, so this the best time to get him."

Damn. Mike's daughter, Mikayla, was only six years old. *What the fuck?* Why did grown men think it was okay to violate a child? I was ready to dead his pedophile ass, but he was only one nigga. Why were they afraid of him shooting at them first? If it was my daughter, I'd want to do that shit myself.

"Let's get that nigga," I said. Then I led him and Dank to my car without even asking.

Chapter 5

Daisha

"Where you at, girl? You good?" Kevia asked as I literally inhaled a chicken wing from Popeyes.

There was a small kitchenette in the motel room, but I didn't have the strength to cook, so I'd gotten some Popeyes and taken it back to the room. It felt like I'd been run over by a big-ass truck. The Lortabs were running low, and I knew that I was going to need more painkillers soon. Shit, maybe my ribs really were broken. I had a little bit of weed left, but eventually, I was going to need to go back to the hood. I didn't know anybody where I was, and I was not about to ask a strange nigga for shit.

However, I didn't want to run into Raekwan or any of his homies. So I'd decided it would be best if Kevia just got me what I needed and met me somewhere to give it to me. I couldn't take the chance of Rae finding out where I was staying, so I'd come up with a place to meet Kevia.

"Uh, I'm at the Courtyard Marriott on Lavista," I lied. "Can you come meet me here? I need some pain meds and some weed. I'll pay you. Oh, and I need to give you the money to put my stuff in storage. Did you find out how much it'll cost?"

I stared at my face in the mirror across from the bed and cringed. My eye and cheek needed to be iced again. The swelling was going down, but the bruises were getting even darker. It crossed my mind to get my ribs checked out, like Pistol had told me to, but I didn't want anybody at the hospital to ask me what had happened. I was just grateful that Rae hadn't found me.

"Okay, girl. What kinda meds you need? Oh, and don't worry 'bout that or the storage. I feel like I owe you for introducin' you to my bastard-ass cousin." Kevia's boo, Rock, was the go-to nigga for OxyContin and shit like that. That wasn't really my thing, but I was desperate for the pain to go away. Not only the physical pain, but the mental pain too.

"Look, get whatever you can from your boo. I don't care."

"You sure?" She sounded hesitant. "That shit's addictive."

"Uh, I'm not really in the position to go see a doctor and shit, so . . ."

"Okay. Okay. I, uh, I need the key to your apartment. I still ain't seen Rae, and he wasn't there when I went over earlier."

"Well, he damn sure been blowin' my damn phone up," I complained.

"Well, from what I heard, he's been fuckin' wit' his baby mama, Capri, again. My brother told me he was over there. Maybe she got him all wrapped up and he'll forget all about what's goin' on wit' you," she said.

Why the hell was she just telling me about that shit? When I really stopped to think about it, it really didn't matter. I didn't give a damn about what he was doing with other women.

"Hmm. I hope it'll be that easy, and I honestly don't give a fuck who he's messin' wit'. Better her than me. Let her take his bullshit," I said. "He ain't took care of that li'l boy since he been wit' me. She is dumb as hell to take him back." When I had found out about their son, we'd already been together for over a year.

It had been a turnoff to know that I was with a deadbeat, but still, I had stayed with him. I guessed I was just as bad as his baby mama. What kind of man turned his back on his own child? Hmm. It made me think about my father. Was I really not his? My mother had always avoided the question. Now that we weren't talking, but I was sure I'd never get the answer.

"I'll call when I'm on the way to you," Kevia said, her voice cutting through my thoughts like a knife.

"Okay. Thanks, boo."

"Anytime."

I ended the call and lay back on the bed. My hunger pangs were gone, and I couldn't do anything but think. Pistol was on my mind, and I couldn't help but wonder what he was doing at the moment. Did he think of me as much as I thought of him? I knew that it was best for me not to get involved with him, but why did I want to go back to his condo? Why did I have this overwhelming urge to see him again?

I had to shake it off. I was damaged goods, and he was a nigga who ran around with guns. One thing I did know was, if I ever got into a relationship again, it would not be with a nigga like him. True, he had rescued me from Raekwan's wrath, but it was best for me to avoid him.

Instead of dwelling on what I knew was not meant to be, I decided to take a quick nap while I waited for Kevia to call me back. All I wanted was a little bit of peace, and lately, I got that only when I was asleep.

Damn. The cops were behind me, and I had just been blowing some strong-ass Kush. My instinct was to put the window down, but that was probably not smart. It was best if they didn't smell that potent-ass smoke. When they cruised past me, I didn't even bother to look. I turned the music up.

Kevia had awoken me from my nap to tell me she was on the way to the hotel on Lavista Road, and I had quickly hopped in my car. I had to hurry and get there before she did. I had an eerie feeling that Rae was going to be with her. Would she do that to me, knowing that I didn't want to see him? She'd seen my face for herself, so if she did that for her cousin, it would tell me a lot. It would mean that she wasn't my real friend, and that her loyalty didn't lie with me. Blood wasn't always thicker than water, and I just hoped she could see that.

After I pulled up into a parking spot at the hotel, I called her. "Where you at, boo?" I asked.

"Right around the corner from you."

"Okay. I'm in my car. I had to come out to smoke a blunt. They only got nonsmoking rooms and shit. I ain't wanna take no chances."

"A'ight. I'll be there in, like, two minutes."

I hung up, hit the blunt again, and waited.

Damn, my body radiated with pain. I wasn't trying to judge, but I didn't see how women stayed with men who beat them. Pain wasn't my forte, and I wasn't going to live like that. There was no way. The thing was, I had to get my money up so that I could come up with a game plan. I had to get away so that Rae would never find me, but I couldn't do that shit broke.

Kevia was standing on the passenger side of my car, waiting, when I looked up. *Damn.* I'd been so deep in thought that I hadn't even seen her approach. I unlocked the passenger door, and she got in the car. She passed me a bag of pills, and I put them in my purse.

"You can't keep livin' like this, Punkin. I mean, damn. You can't stay in this hotel forever. It's gon' get expensive. Look, Rae's on the phone. He wants to talk to you. He's really sorry 'bout what he did." She held her phone out, and I looked at her like she'd lost her mind.

"Are you serious right now?" I shook my head in disbelief. "I should've known better. Get the fuck out of my car!"

It was a good thing I hadn't given her the key to my crib or my money. Shit. Rae had probably sold everything already. I was okay with the fact that I was going to have to just start over. That was fine with me as long as I didn't have to deal with Rae's abusive ass.

Kevia didn't budge. In fact, she called Rae and, apparently, put him on speakerphone, because his voice was suddenly loud and clear in the car. "I'm on my way there, Punkin. I'm so sorry, baby.

I never meant to hurt you, and I wanna make it right. Just gimme the chance to do that. I lost it. Okay? I had smoked some fucked-up shit. I think them niggas on the West Side laced me." His desperation was clear.

I wasn't buying his lies. "Fuck that shit! I don't wanna hear it, Rae! Fuck you, and fuck you too, Kevia! Get the fuck out of my car now!"

It was a good thing I'd gotten my hands on the gun I'd locked in my trunk. If I'd had access to it that night, Rae's ass would've been dead. I wouldn't have needed Pistol at all. As a matter of fact, if I could've taken the piece in the club with me, none of that night's events would have even happened.

When Rae kept talking and Kevia kept sitting there, I knew that it was time to pull that shit out on her conniving ass. She was all about family, and I was all about my survival.

"If you don't get the fuck out of my car, bitch, I'll pull this fuckin' trigger."

The look of surprise on her face when I put the gun to her head was priceless.

"This bitch just pulled a gun on me," she told Rae just as she opened the car door.

My eyes were glued to hers, and my look was stern. All I wanted to do was get out of there before Rae arrived. She stepped out of my car and slammed the door.

"This shit ain't over, Punkin!" she yelled as I pulled out of the parking space.

"Fuck you, bitch! You and your cousin can kiss my black ass!" I screamed back and then hauled ass up out of there.

Right then and there, I realized that I was alone in the world.

Once I was back in my motel room, I was able to relax. I had the munchies, so I'd picked up some food from a spot called This Is It! It was supposed to be real Southern cuisine, but I wouldn't know any different, since I couldn't remember the last time my mother had cooked for me. That shit was good to me either way.

As I ate, I cried, which was weird as hell. It was like my emotions were all over the place. All I could envision was the homeless people who littered downtown Atlanta. Would I be just like them? I was sure they had nobody if they'd ended up in a position like that. The thing was, at that point, I realized that I didn't have anybody, either.

As strong as I was, there was a threshold for everyone. I'd reached the point where the dam had been broken. The tears wouldn't stop, and as much as I tried, they just kept on coming. Kevia had been my friend since I was eight years old. We'd always been close, and she'd always been the one I loved and trusted. All of a sudden, after all those years, I didn't have her anymore. She had sold me out for Rae, and that was unforgivable.

There I was, hiding out in a seedy motel room. What kind of life was that? It was no way for a young woman to live. I was supposed to be out enjoying life, but I was battered and bruised. Not only that, but I had been used and abused. It was time for me to focus on myself, and I was determined to do that.

The last of my money was going to go toward my makeup and wardrobe. It was time for me to get that good job that I'd always wanted. I had college courses behind me. *Fuck waitressing at a strip club*, I thought. It was time for me to do something more professional, so I could afford to go back to school.

Suddenly, the tears were gone. I was going to have to make the best of my situation. At least I had only myself to worry about. Not bringing a kid into my situation had been a good idea. I'd felt bad about the abortion that I had a year ago, but it had been for the best. I'd cried plenty of tears, but I'd known that a child didn't deserve to be subjected to Rae's abuse too.

Chapter 6

Pistol

When we pulled up in a parking spot close to the entrance to Westview Cemetery, I flashed Mike a confused look.

His facial expression was serious as he read mine. "Inside intel let me know that nigga's routine. He comes here by himself once a week, at the same time, to visit his brother's grave. Usually, he'll be by himself, but if there's some shit poppin' off in the streets, he'll have his yes-men watchin' his ole scared ass. It's the only time he's by himself, which is the best time to pop that mu'fuckin' pedophile."

I was confused. "Now that I know what that nigga did, I'm a'ight wit' killin' him, but if it's so easy, why the hell am I doing that shit instead of you? You had me thinking you didn't want to do it, 'cause that nigga and his crew'll start bustin' like we were gonna pull up on the block. What's really goin' on, yo?"

Mike pointed toward a black BMW that was a few yards away from us. "You see that car?"

With a nod, I said, "Yeah."

"That's his henchmen. He goes to the grave by himself, but they watch the entrance," Mike explained.

Shit. Who the fuck was that nigga? He was obviously in the position to have henchmen, so he had to be connected to some illegal shit.

Dank spoke up. "If they see us, they gon' react, but if they see you, it'll be nothin'. Just go pop that nigga and come back to the car." He passed me a bouquet of flowers. "Pick a random grave near him to put these flowers on, and then do that shit. We'll be here to make sure them niggas can't get to you if they become suspicious."

Mike was unusually quiet as he stared out the window. I couldn't help but feel like something was off with him. Maybe it was the thought of somebody violating his baby girl. I needed to know that they weren't just feeding me bullshit to do their dirty work. Killing wasn't a hard task for me, but killing somebody for no reason was. Even if he hadn't molested my cousin's daughter, I would've merked dude if he'd crossed my fam in any way, but I didn't want to be tricked into it.

"A'ight." I grabbed my Smith & Wesson pistol and twisted the silencer on.

Mike then showed me a picture on his cell phone. "This that nigga." He was light skinned, with a thin mustache and wavy, close-cut hair. That nigga looked like a pretty-boy pussy and was nothing like I'd imagined.

"This cemetery is huge. How the fuck am I supposed to find him?" I asked, making a mental note of his facial features.

"After you walk through the gate, go down seven rows. He'll be there on your left," Mike replied, filling me in.

Damn. Those niggas had been as thorough as hell about that shit. They knew exactly where the grave was.

"What if he's expecting this?" That shit had just popped up in my head.

There was a chance that he knew these niggas were watching him. Maybe he was ready for the attack and knew that he'd be targeted when he was the most vulnerable. That might be why he had his henchmen with him.

"Nah, he don't know. My baby girl said he threatened to kill her if she told me or her moms. He knows there's animosity between us, 'cause he fuckin' my baby mama, but he won't expect us to make a hit on him here. He don't even know that I had him followed," Mike explained, with an anxious look in his eyes.

"A'ight." I nodded and concealed the gun in the waist of my jeans.

The tinted windows made it so that dude's niggas couldn't see inside of my vehicle. They probably just thought some random nigga was here to pay his respects to a dead loved one. I slowly got out of the car. The flowers that I held in my hand sold that shit that I was here to pay respects, because when I looked at dude's car, I noticed that those niggas looked like they were asleep. My target must've been in there for a long time.

Maybe somebody had already popped them and that nigga I was supposed to knock off. I was sure that he'd made plenty enemies, that my cousin wasn't the only one. Instead of assuming everyone had been knocked off already, because those niggas might just be taking a nap, I walked through the gate and counted the rows. When I got to row seven, that nigga was standing there, with a pair of dark shades on. I stopped at the grave right next to him.

As I laid the flowers down, I read the engraving on the tombstone. MARGARET LYONS, BELOVED WIFE AND MOTHER. AUGUST 10, 1968–JUNE 27, 2013. She was the same age as my mother. Shaking my head, I discreetly placed my mark in my peripheral vision and was about to grab my gun.

Suddenly he turned and stepped closer to me. My instincts screamed, *Go ahead and shoot his ass*, but he had a huge grin on his face, which threw me off. When he stopped just mere inches from me, he spoke.

"I been comin' here for the past two years, and I ain't never seen nobody visit her grave. Who was she to you?" he asked, trying to find some sort of common ground with me, a complete stranger who was there to kill him.

Where the fuck was his street sense? Did he think getting killed in a cemetery was unlikely, and if so, why were his niggas waiting for him in the car?

"My favorite aunt. I don't live here," I lied quickly.

Common sense told me that he was strapped too, so I had to finesse that shit the right way to keep my own life intact. If I didn't, my fleeing to Atlanta would be in vain.

He nodded. "Word. That's real shit. You mind me askin' how she died?"

"She was sick for a long time. Diabetes." I cleared my throat.

"Word. That's tough." I couldn't see his eyes, so I couldn't tell if he was really as sincere as he sounded.

"Yeah, but at least she ain't suffering no more." I watched his hands to make sure he wasn't going for a weapon or anything.

"Yeah. I guess it's different when somebody you care about is sick. None of us want to see a person we care for suffer and shit. But when somebody you care for gets murdered, that's a totally different story." He balled his fists up at his sides. "My brother was shot to death . . . because of me. I visit him all the time. People keep tellin' me that he forgave me, but I can't forgive my damn self."

"Hmm . . . That's gotta be a fucked-up feelin'."

Dude removed his shades and shook his head. "I'm a street nigga, but when it comes to blood, I'm all about loyalty. I guess my big bro was just tryin'a protect me, but . . ." He shook his head. "I ain't want shit to turn out like it did."

I didn't understand why that nigga was still talking to me. Maybe he just felt the need to get some shit off his chest. There was a chance that he had to be strong for everybody around him, but he felt he didn't have to do that shit for me. If only he knew that I wasn't just some stranger. I was there to use his weakness to my advantage. It was time to end that shit, so I could get to the real task at hand, the lick that would be going down in a few hours. A mu'fucka needed some money and fast.

My hand was on my strap again. "Well, things don't always go as planned."

"You got that right," he muttered as he pointed a silver-plated nine at me. "Who sent you?"

Fuck! I should've just shot that nigga. He had got me with the small talk.

I flashed him a confused look. "The fuck you mean, nigga? You must be on some paranoid shit."

"I'm gon' kill them niggas for not watchin' out. They probably fucked up and shit!" His face was all balled up in a mean, ugly scowl that distorted his pretty-boy features.

All I did was pretend like I didn't know what the hell he was talking about as I pondered how I could get control of the situation. It looked like I was going to have to wrestle the gun out of that nigga's hand. He needed to think I was some docile-ass mu'fucka. Which I wasn't. There was no way I was going to be the one who got killed.

"That nigga Rae's mu'fuckin' punk ass. I know I should've left him on the block. He ain't no real thug. All he and Shyne wanna do is smoke and get pussy." He shook his head as he literally talked to himself.

While he was distracted, I decided to make my move. Without even second-guessing myself, I kicked that nigga hard as hell in his nuts. As he dropped to his knees, I kicked his gun to the ground and then punched him hard as hell in the face. As blood gushed from his nose like a geyser, I pulled out my gun and let off two shots in his head before getting the fuck up out of there.

Making my way back to the car, all I could think about was the fact that I'd heard the name Rae recently. With the chaos of the moment, my mind couldn't recall when and where I'd heard it. Just when I'd been about to clap his ass, he had wanted to hold a damn conversation. That nigga was just as good at acting as I was.

Damn. It was a good thing I'd disarmed him before he shot his loud-ass strap. If that had happened, hell would've broken loose after that. That would've left a few more fresh dead bodies at this graveyard. As I walked out of the cemetery, I noticed that those niggas in his car were still laid back, chilling.

Shaking my head, I headed to my car. Then I got in and drove off.

"It's done?" Mike quizzed me from the passenger seat.

"What you think?" I said, answering his question with a question.

After that, it was silent in the car. I didn't even want to talk about how I'd almost been the one who got killed. When I was a few miles away from the scene of the murder I'd just committed, it finally dawned on me. All of a sudden I knew exactly who the fuck Rae was.

"Nigga, what the fuck you doin'?" Mike spat as I whipped the car around, making an illegal U-turn.

"Goin' back to kill all them niggas," I said. I pressed the gas and sped back in the direction of the cemetery. I didn't know if this was the same Rae who had tried to kill Daisha, but if so, it was the perfect opportunity for me to kill him. It had been dark that night, but I had got a good look at his punk ass. If I saw him again, I'd know exactly who he was. Being that I'd run up on him, he probably had no idea what I looked like. Even if he did, he would not be expecting me to come for him.

Dank tried to talk some sense into me next. "Look, man. If you go back, we might all get killed."

"Y'all all scared and shit for nothing. Even that nigga . . . What the fuck was his name, any fuckin' way?"

"G," Mike said.

"Even that nigga G said those niggas were flakes, so they ain't shit to be scared of."

Shaking his head, Dank said, "Ain't nobody scared. The shit's done. You ain't gotta go back for the rest of them, man. At this point they don't even know who did that shit, but I'm sure they've found his body by now."

"It ain't even been a good fifteen minutes. There's a chance they haven't found him yet," I said.

Mike was quiet at that point, and I wondered why.

"What you gotta say, Mike? Those niggas can identify us, so they gotta die too."

"Identify us?" Mike's voice told me he was skeptical about this, and the look in his eyes reaffirmed this. "Them niggas believe in street justice, like us."

I laughed sarcastically at that statement. "And that's why we gotta kill them. Why didn't y'all niggas think of that shit? You should've been killin' them niggas while I was poppin' G. Once they find that nigga's body, they won't stop till they find out who did it. They know what I look like and what kinda car I drive."

"If we go back to do that shit, it's gon' cut into the time we need to do the lick," Dank reminded me. "You can always get a paint job, and we'll take care of that shit."

"I don't give a fuck 'bout cuttin' into the time to do the lick, and I don't wanna get a fuckin' paint job," I snapped, pulling into the same parking space at the cemetery. "Let's handle them niggas like we should've done."

The relief on Dank's and Mike's faces was evident once I saw that the BMW was gone.

"Shit!" Those niggas must've got tired of waiting, gone to look for G, found his body, and got the fuck up out of there fast as hell.

Did I really want to do a lick with Dank and Mike? I thought my cousins were all hard and shit, but they were looking more and more lame by the minute.

Chapter 7

Daisha

Those damn pills had knocked me out. Honestly, I didn't even know what the hell Kevia had given me. It was already 9:30 p.m., so that meant I'd been out for over six hours. What the hell did I take? I took a look at the pills, and they were long white bars. They were probably some Xanax or something. If they were pain pills, why was I still in pain?

The sound of somebody banging on the door had been what woke me up. If it hadn't been for that, I'd still be out like a light. *Damn*. But who the fuck was at my door? Nobody knew where I was. Had Kevia followed me here? If not, had Rae found me? *Damn it*. I knew he wouldn't give up.

I tiptoed to the door and pushed the flip bar lock against it before looking through the peephole. Pistol was standing there. How the fuck had he found me? *Should I even open the door*? I wondered. I didn't want to, but I did.

"Wow. I found you." He looked relieved. "This is some crazy shit. For real."

Paranoid, I looked behind him. "Come in." He walked inside my room, and I closed the door behind him. "How'd you find me?"

"I wasn't even lookin', but I spotted your car when . . . Shit. I tried every door on this side, until you answered."

What? I thought. There were all types of fucked-up-ass people here. The motel was known for drug sales, prostitution, and all kinds of criminal activity. That was very brave of him.

"So, you wasn't tryin'a find me? This was just a coincidence?"

"Yeah. I mean, I wanted to find you, but I didn't know where to look. I just happened to be over here to . . . Anyway, I saw your car. You need to grab yo' shit and get out of here, Ma. This place is even more dangerous than that nigga you fuckin' wit'."

"Thank you for your help the other night, Pistol, but I'm good—"

He grabbed my arm. "No you ain't. I just did a lick on the first floor. This nigga be keepin' mad kilos and cash out here and shit. He, his girl, and another mu'fucka are dead right now, 'cause I don't give a fuck when it comes to money, like every other nigga out here. This place ain't safe for a woman. Not even if she's wit' her man. You feel me?"

I yanked my arm away. "So you robbed and killed three people in this motel and you still here? Are you fuckin' crazy?"

"Nah, but when I saw your car, I knew I couldn't leave you here. I killed them niggas, but my cousin shot the bitch."

I nervously tapped my foot against the floor. For some reason, I wasn't afraid of him or threatened by him. But damn. Why would I leave with somebody whom the police or more goons may be coming after? Did he think I was fucking crazy?

"How'd you know it was my car?" I narrowed my eyes at him. "And why would you stick around to see, after what you just did?"

"I pay attention to details. Okay. It's part of my lifestyle. And . . . I ain't scared of shit. I needed to know for sure it was your car," he explained. He stared at me. "Now that I do, get your shit and c'mon, yo," he demanded.

"Do you really think I'm gonna leave with you now? What if somebody called the cops and—"

That nigga literally laughed in my face. "Really? You think the cops are comin' here? Why the fuck you think all types of shit go down here? Ain't nobody 'bout to call no cops."

He was right. It occurred to me that I was in the most unsafe place possible. If Rae did show up to kill me, I had no chance of surviving. Once again Pistol was there to rescue me, and so . . . I decided to be saved.

I got my stuff together in a hurry, and Pistol and I ran to our cars in the parking lot. We both got behind the wheel and hightailed it out of there. Pistol drove as fast as hell, bending corners and shit, like he hadn't just committed a few crimes already. It was a good thing that I was driving my own car. By the time we pulled up to his condo, my nerves were even more shot than before.

He walked over to my car, and I put the window down. "You okay?" he asked as he glanced at me.

I unbuckled my seat belt. "Barely."

"Look . . . Daisha, I didn't mean to scare you, but shit is way more real than you could ever imagine."

"What you mean by that?"

"We'll talk when we get inside." His eyes were on mine, and for some odd reason, I trusted him.

With what I'd been through with people, my trust was rare, so I was questioning myself. I didn't say another word as I got out of my car and we walked inside the building. All I did was wait, which was agony. He seemed to be my knight in shining armor, but damn, he was a killer. When I thought about it, though, maybe I needed a killer on my side. The thought actually made me feel safer.

Once we were inside his condo, he turned to look at me. "You hungry?"

I didn't expect that question, but my ribs were touching. I hadn't had anything to eat since earlier. "Kinda," I said, not letting on that I was ravenous. As hungry as I was, I wanted to know what he was talking about when he said that shit was more real than I could imagine. But I didn't ask.

He nodded. "Cool. I'll order something. Chinese or pizza?"

"Pizza. I don't do Chinese anymore." I smiled at him, and he smiled back.

"Good. Me either. I can't identify anything other than the wings." He let out a chuckle. "What you like on your pizza?"

"It don't matter. Whatever you eat. I'm sure you're hungry too."

He sat down on the sofa and patted the spot next to him. "I would've stopped to get something, but . . ."

I nodded and sat down. "I understand why you didn't."

"Good."

He pulled out his phone and dialed. When someone answered his call, he said, "Yeah, I want to order a medium pizza with grilled chicken, onions, peppers, black olives, and extra cheese. Hold on." He looked at me. "What do you want on yours?"

"I can't eat a whole medium pizza," I protested.

Pistol shrugged. "And?"

"Uh, pepperoni, sausage, extra cheese, onions, peppers, and ground beef." *Shit*. I was hungry.

He relayed my order, then looked at me again. "What kind of crust?"

"Thick. For all those toppings."

We both laughed.

"Pan for both," he said into the phone as he grinned at me.

Damn, that nigga was too fine. My pussy was suddenly wet as hell, which was badass timing. Suddenly, my smile faded, but he didn't seem to notice as he wrapped up the order.

"Cash." He paused to listen. "Thanks. Bye." He ended the call and then turned to look at me. His stare was intense.

"Uh, can you talk to me now? I know that the pizza's gonna take a while," I said. My heartbeat had increased from his stare.

Pistol's stare didn't falter as he nodded. "Do you know a nigga named G, this dude that your *boyfriend* fucks wit'?"

"Yeah, I know G. We grew up together. His real name is Greg. He's my . . . well . . . he's my ex–best friend's older brother." The thought of how Kevia had betrayed me made my skin crawl.

"Ex–best friend?"

"Yeah, it's a long story. Kevia introduced me to Rae. G is her brother. Earlier today she tried to get me to talk to Rae, but . . . How do you know G?"

"Look, Ma, that nigga G's a fuckin' perv. He touched my cousin's daughter and shit."

"Ew!" I frowned.

Greg, aka G, wasn't one of my favorite people, but at that point Kevia and Rae weren't, either.

"So, I killed him earlier. . . ."

"How many mu'fuckas have you killed?" I stood up.

"Calm down. Please. Just hear me out. Please. Sit."

Shit. What else was I going to do at that point? It wasn't like I had anywhere to go.

He continued. "My fam told me that old boy was fuckin' with his daughter's mama, and his daughter told him that old boy had touched her. That shit went down at the cemetery today, while he was visiting his brother's grave."

"Shit," I gasped. "Why would you do the hit there?"

I remembered Kevia and G's brother Kevin. He was the cool and compassionate one, but G was different. I wasn't surprised at all that he was a perv. When I used to stay over, he'd be gawking at me and shit. Kevia had told him that I was off-limits to him, and Kevin had made sure that both of us were protected.

"It don't matter, Ma. The fact of the matter is that the nigga's gonna come at me now that I've killed his cousin and shit. Even if he didn't recognize me at first, he'll eventually figure out what happened. That's why I gotta kill him first, and you gon' help me do it."

I cleared my throat and looked at him. "Uh . . . okay, but how am I gonna do that?"

"We'll worry 'bout that later on. It's gettin' late, and we both need to eat and get some rest. Don't you think?" His sexy eyes were penetrating mine.

"You have such . . . beautiful eyes," I heard myself say.

"Thanks, Ma. Shit, you're beautiful. Straight up."

I looked away from him, and the reality of our situation set in. It was a must that we got rid of Raekwan. He was a threat to both of our lives at that point, and he had to be dealt with if we wanted to stay alive.

"I appreciate the compliment, but I can't believe how fucked up things are right now. What's the chance of you saving my life for a second time?" I shook my head as I asked the question.

"Well, some things ain't meant to be explained. It just is what it is."

"Yeah," I had to agree. "You're right about that."

Shit was definitely more real than I could've ever imagined. My appetite was gone all of a sudden, and I felt sick to my stomach.

"Don't worry. I ain't gon' let nothing happen to you."

"Why do you care?" My voice was weak, but I needed to know the answer.

He stared into my eyes without flinching. "'Cause I want to."

Wow. "It's that simple, huh?"

With a nod, he said, "Yup. That simple."

"I gotta use the restroom."

I scurried off, remembering where the master bathroom was. On the way there, I thought about how sparsely furnished his spot was. It made me wonder why such a nice place wasn't lavishly furnished. Maybe he'd just moved in. We were both quite young, and it was a bachelor pad. The lack of furniture was surely a telltale sign that he didn't have a girlfriend. If I was his woman, that shit would've been laid.

A sliver of moonlight shined through the blinds in the bathroom, creating a glow that allowed me to see the light switch on the wall. I flicked the light on, bent down over to toilet, and waited for the vomit to come up. It never did. I stood up and took a deep breath. Maybe it was just my nerves once again. I'd been diagnosed with anxiety a couple of years ago, but I wasn't one to be on any prescribed medication. I wasn't going to depend on that shit for the rest of my life. I'd just have to deal with my issues on my own.

Maybe my urge to throw up wasn't just anxiety or the thought of being with a complete stranger who was obviously a cold-blooded killer. What if the urge to throw up wasn't related to the fact that Rae wanted to kill me and that Pistol had killed Rae's cousin, who had run Bankhead, one of the most infamous neighborhoods in Atlanta? Then again, there was a chance that I felt sick to my stomach because of these two things, though Kevia's mystery pills might have something to do with my nausea too. Something told me to flush those pills that Kevia had given me. I took them out of my pocket, dumped them in the toilet, and pressed the lever.

After flushing the pills and taking a few minutes to reflect, I was back in Pistol's sexy, but intimidating, presence. There was just something about him that was exhilarating to my senses. It was like everything was in overdrive. My physical attraction to him was so over the top. I played it off really well, though. As we waited for our food to arrive, we talked. The subject of our mothers came up.

I learned that he was close to his mom, and he learned that I was estranged from mine. Neither of our fathers was in the picture. His had been murdered, and mine had just decided to leave. In such a short amount of time, I could tell that he was close to his family, but where were they?

"Your family's here?" I asked as my stomach started to growl.

Pistol smiled. "Nah, they're in North Carolina." He glanced at his cell phone. "It's been over an hour since I ordered the pizzas. I should call—"

At that moment there was a knock on the door.

He stood up and walked over to answer it with as much swag as he would have in the streets. That shit was a true turn-on, because it seemed so natural. I could tell that he was cautious about everything, because he looked through the blinds to check out the car before he even peeked through the peephole.

I waited while he paid for the pizzas. After the transaction was done, he closed the door and locked it securely. When I smelled the cheesy deliciousness, I was ready to dig in. The upset stomach from earlier was gone. Pistol had somehow put me at ease. Maybe it was the effortless flow of our conversation. Then again, it was probably the fact that he was so domineering. For that reason, I wasn't afraid of anything happening to me.

Pistol put the pizzas down on the coffee table, then went off to the kitchen to grab plates and something for us to drink. I insisted on something that was laced with alcohol. When he returned to the living room, I was already indulging in the hot pizza. That shit burned the roof of my mouth, and I hissed in pain.

"That's what you get for bein' all fast. You should've waited for me." He chuckled and sat down beside me on the sofa. "Let it cool off, baby girl."

My dad used to call me that.

Despite what was really going on in our worlds, we managed to share lighthearted, funny banter. I really liked Pistol. He was hard, to a certain extent, but he had a sense of humor. That was something that I hadn't seemed to find in the men I'd dealt with in the past. They had all seemed to have a chip on their shoulders, which they hadn't been able to shake off. It seemed that Pistol, on the other hand, didn't let anything get to him.

"You're as cool as a cucumber," I told him as I grabbed my second slice of pizza.

"Hmm." He glanced at me as he took a sip of Henny and Coke. "You just don't know, Ma. I know how to act around a lady, but I can be a hothead at times."

"Well, I figured that much about you. I'm just sayin'. Most niggas don't know how to draw the line. At least you can recognize a lady when you see one. I like how you don't seem to judge me by my circumstances."

"Who am I to judge?" He shrugged his shoulders. "Shit, I ain't perfect. Not by a long shot."

Damn. The fact that he said that made me want him even more, which was probably going to pose a problem. One thing about me was, I was one of those weak-ass women who didn't know how to separate love from sex. That had been my downfall for a long time. For the most part, I was able to hold my own, but if a man put it down in the bedroom, I became his sucker. Shit, I had to work on that. There was no way that I could let him touch me. His eyes and lips said it all, along with his body language. That nigga wanted me bad, and with my luck, he would be the one to have me all fucked up.

Chapter 8

Pistol

I had been sure to put my cut from the lick in the safe in my bedroom closet. Mike and Dank had kept the coke for themselves. I wasn't trying to fuck with that shit. Daisha was sitting in front of the television, but I was watching her. Her lips were slightly parted as she snored lightly on the sofa. The beauty that she possessed took ahold of me as I stood there and stared at her.

It was like she could sense me admiring her, because suddenly her eyes flew open and she self-consciously wiped her mouth.

"Was I drooling?" she asked.

My expression was serious as I shook my head. "I don't know if you were drooling or not, Ma. All I saw was a beautiful woman who was in a peaceful state. You looked so . . . . content."

"Thank you." Her smile was faint as she sat up. "And it's funny you said that. It hasn't been that easy for me to sleep lately, so I must be comfortable around you. Of course, the first night the Lortab knocked me out. When I'm asleep, it's the only time I have any peace, and I thought I needed something to make me sleep. I guess not."

"You took something else other than the Lortabs?" I was concerned about her being on something heavy.

"Yeah. I don't know what it was, though." She filled me in on what had happened with her so-called best friend, Kevia, and that nigga Rae.

That must've happened right before I shot G at the cemetery. *Damn.* So he *was* trying to find her. It was a good thing she had that gun on her.

"I flushed the pills, though," she told me.

I nodded. "Good. If you're in pain, I can give you something. It won't be Lortabs, though." I smiled. "You took the rest of them wit' you."

"I'm sorry 'bout that."

"It's okay," I assured her. "You needed them more than me."

"Well, the pain isn't that bad anymore. I'm just a little sore. A blunt would be the shit, though."

Letting out a deep chuckle, I left the room to retrieve my smoke stash and a Swisher. Her request was right on time. I was full and buzzing off that Henny, so a blunt full of Kush would be the nightcap we both needed. Well, I could think of a better way to cap off the night, but it wasn't the time.

"So, do you think Rae recognized you?" she asked when I returned to the room.

"I don't think he did. Just like how I didn't know where I'd heard his name at first. It took me thinkin' about it for that shit to click. Them niggas were chillin' and shit and had no reason to really pay me any mind. Once they found G's body, I'm sure Rae thought about it and tried to recall what I looked like. Even if he still don't know who I am, those niggas'll end up puttin' two and two together. That's why we should've put some lead in them too. When I didn't know about Rae, it wasn't such a pressin' thing to kill them. Honestly, I think I wanna kill Rae 'cause of what he did to you more than anything. Even if he don't ever figure out who I am or ever find out that I killed his cousin, I still wanna be the one to make that nigga stop breathin'."

It was quiet as I rolled the blunt. I noticed that Daisha appeared to be in deep thought.

"What you thinkin' 'bout?" I asked before I lit the end of the blunt and took a pull.

"About the fact that G was one of the biggest dope dealers in the city and that nigga Rae is supposed to be his top enforcer. With all the money that nigga gets, he still didn't want to do shit for me. The fucked-up way he treated me makes me question myself. Why the fuck did I stay?" Her voice trembled. "I feel so damn stupid."

"Don't do that to yourself. You made a mistake. You ain't the first woman to stay wit' a fucked-up nigga," I told her. "Shit, to be honest wit' you, I'm a fucked-up-ass nigga. I ain't never been one to wanna commit to a chick, but they always catch feelings. Then I move on. Straight up, I ain't never been in a real relationship before," I explained and passed her the blunt.

She took a toke of the potent-smelling weed, with a contemplative look that changed her features. "Hmm. Something tells me that you were always honest wit' them about that, though."

I nodded in agreement. "Yeah. You right 'bout that. I ain't never been one to play games and shit. I let a bi . . . chick know what's up from the jump."

"So if a bitch caught feelings, that was on her, then. Shit. In my experience, I've always dealt wit' lyin'-ass niggas who pretended like they wanted more when they really didn't. I can respect a man who keeps it one hundred from the beginnin'. No games." She hit the blunt again and then passed it back. "Shit, I wish Rae had warned me that he was a bum-ass nigga. I wouldn't have ever wasted my time."

"I feel you, but part of it, too, is that it ain't been one chick who got my attention to bypass the pussy."

"That's 'cause you go for the wrong type of woman. Just like how I go for the wrong type of man. Maybe if we try something different, we'll get different results."

"Real shit you talkin', baby girl. Real shit." I had just been thinking the same thing.

We puffed some more, but before the blunt was gone, she was snoring lightly again. I couldn't help but smile as I carefully lifted her from the sofa and carried her to my bedroom. After taking off her shoes, I put the comforter over her and left the room. Something told me that she had felt me pick her up but had acted like she was still asleep. I had seen the slight smile that spread across her pretty face. All she wanted was to be taken care of, for once. For some odd reason, which I couldn't quite put my finger on, I wanted to be the one to do that.

"I can't stay here forever, Pistol," I heard Daisha say behind me as I sat on the sofa.

It was a little after eight in the morning, and she just ran up on me with that shit all of a sudden.

My head whipped around so I could look at her. "Uh, I wasn't expectin' that, Ma. I'm just tryin'a help you. I know that you ain't got nowhere else to go and—"

"But I *do* have somewhere else to go. I could've stayed where I was!" she snapped.

"Damn. What's up wit' the attitude? You were cool last night."

All of a sudden she burst into tears, and I didn't know what to do.

"Okay." I stood up and made my way over to her slowly. "What's goin' on?"

"What do you think? I know you ain't helpin' me just 'cause you want to. You don't wanna kill Rae for me! That's bullshit! You probably just plan to fuck me, find out where Rae is, and kill him before he and his niggas can kill you! What do you plan to do wit' me after that? Huh? I'm just your way of gettin' to him! Ain't I? You have an agenda, Pistol! I know it! No man has ever done shit for me without wanting something in return. . . ."

I grabbed her arms and pulled her to my body as she sobbed. "You're wrong, Daisha. I don't want shit from you. All I want is to know that you're gonna be okay. You ain't never gotta give me no ass. You ain't never gotta give me shit."

Her body was stiff, and she tried to pull away from me, but I held on to her. "I know that you're goin' through a lot right now. I get it. I do," I said. "You might think I'm helpin' you for all the wrong reasons, but I ain't. Believe me, if I wanna get to that nigga Rae, I can do it without you. I just figured I'd keep you safe and find out about his whereabouts at the same time. All I was tryin'a do is kill two birds wit' one stone. I'll admit that when I first saw you, I wanted to get wit' you. Now that shit's deeper than that. Your safety means the world to me. It's like I feel some kind of connection to you, and there ain't shit you can do about it. I'm gon' make sure that nigga's outta the way so you can go on wit' your life. Even if it's without me in it. You ain't gotta stay here forever, but stay long enough for your bruises to heal and for me to ensure your safety. Okay?"

Her body suddenly relaxed in my grip, and I could feel her tremble as she continued to sob. "Okay," she whispered, finally letting her guard down again. "I'm sorry."

"Don't be sorry." I released her from my embrace to stare into her eyes. "You got a lot goin' on and shit. . . . I understand why you're so emotional."

She wiped her eyes. "You probably think I'm crazy."

"Nah." I chuckled as I grabbed a ringlet of her curly hair and stretched it out. "I love your hair. It's real, right?"

She laughed and shook her head. "Yes, it's real."

"I do wanna get to know you better, though, Daisha, and that's a first for me."

When she sat down on the sofa, I plopped down beside her, hoping that her crying fit was over.

"Okay, but I need coffee and breakfast so I can think straight," she replied.

I gave her a knowing glance. "Go get dressed. I know the perfect spot."

When we got back to my spot after breakfast, I noticed a familiar-looking car parked in front of the building. Suddenly, my heart leaped against my rib cage. It was adrenaline stemming more from vigilance than from fear. The shit was about to hit the fan.

"Fuck," I said under my breath.

"What?" Daisha looked over at me, wearing an alarmed expression.

"Nothing. Just stay in the car." I got out, and she started to protest.

"Wait. What the fuck is goin' on?" Her eyes were full of fear.

"It's not that nigga Rae, if that's what you're worried about." My tone was a little bit rougher than I intended it to be.

She shook her head, and there was a sort of pout on her face. It was only ten something in the morning. It was too damn early for that shit. I made my way up the steps to the entrance to my building and literally jogged to the elevators. When I got to the door of my condo, I noticed that it was slightly open.

"What the hell?" I pushed the door open wider and walked inside cautiously. My gun was out, and I popped the light on, not expecting the scene that I found in front of me.

"Hey, baby," Niya purred. She was sprawled out on my sofa, buck ass naked. "I know you didn't mean none of that bullshit you said the other night. Shit, last time we fucked, you enjoyed that shit. I could tell."

Damn, she was delusional. "How the fuck did you get in here? Put your fuckin' clothes on, yo." I put the gun down on the mantel over the fireplace.

She only grinned up at me as she spread her legs wide open, exposing her bald pussy. The thing was, I didn't want that ho, and she needed to leave before Daisha saw her. That was only going to make shit worse.

"Oh, wow. Thirsty bitches are takin' over," Daisha declared from the doorway.

Damn. It was too late. Daisha's hardheaded ass hadn't stayed in the car, like I had told her to.

Niya's eyes lit up. "So, that's what it is? You already fuckin' some other bitch."

"Look, you don't know what's goin' on between us, bitch, so don't assume. You just make an ass of yourself. It's clear that you're on some desperate-ass shit. What? You just walked up in his crib?" Daisha shook her head and then glanced at me. "This ho got a key to your crib, and you got me stayin' over here?"

I shook my head. "Nah, it ain't what you think. . . ."

"You explainin' yourself to that bitch? It's that serious? Wow." Niya looked at Daisha and then at me.

Without even a second thought, Daisha ran up on that bitch, but I grabbed her.

"If you call me one mo' fuckin' bitch, I'm gon' cut your fuckin' tongue out!" Daisha screamed. Then she glared at me. "Let me go! Who the fuck is that bitch? Your girl?"

I shook my head again. "Nah, yo. How the fuck you get in here, Niya?"

Niya stood up, rolled her eyes, and started getting dressed. "I ain't gotta tell you shit while your ho's standin' here. I'll just holla at you later. You know you the side chick, right?" Her eyes were on Daisha.

"The side chick?" I sighed and shook my head once more. "She ain't the side chick, and you ain't shit to me." I turned my gaze to Daisha. "Go in the bedroom while I handle her, yo." I was still holding on to Daisha, in case she tried something.

"I ain't goin' no fuckin' where!" Daisha snapped defiantly. "If that bitch keeps it cute, I will too."

Niya rolled her eyes. "Keep it cute? Bitch, bye! It look like that nigga been whuppin' your ass. I didn't know you got down like that, Pistol. Hittin' on bitches and shit."

I shot Niya a confused glance. "Oh, hell nah. I ain't do that shit."

"I don't give a fuck 'bout none of that. Call me when you get tired of that. . . ." Niya looked Daisha up and down. "You a stupid-ass nigga. She ain't got shit on me." Then she picked her pocketbook up off the sofa and headed for the front door.

Shaking my head, I walked ahead of Niya quickly in order to block the door. "How the fuck did you get in here?"

"I got a key made, nigga. What you think?" Niya's arms were across her chest as she smirked at me.

"You what?"

"You deaf now, fool? I got a key made." She said it like I was slow or something.

"How . . . When the fuck did you do that? Give it to me now."

Niya laughed sarcastically. "When you was asleep, I took your keys to Lowe's, and they made a spare of each one. I ain't givin' you shit, nigga. You want that shit, take it. I bet you can't find it."

That crazy bitch had made a spare of all my keys? Why the fuck had I fallen asleep around that psycho heifer? What the fuck had I been thinking?

She grinned slyly at me. "Yeah, nigga. This good pussy knocks a nigga out every time."

I rolled my eyes, annoyed. "Your pussy ain't all that. I was just drunk as hell."

"Give him his fuckin' keys, bitch, before I take 'em from your ass!" I heard Daisha snap, like she was getting tired of our heated exchange.

"Take 'em, bitch. You bad. Do it! I fuckin' double dog dare your walkin'-dead-lookin' ass!" Niya snapped back.

Niya held up a key ring, and I dived for it just as Daisha grabbed her by the back of her head and started punching her in the face. *Damn.* I really didn't want Daisha fighting. Her ribs were already badly bruised, and I was sure that she'd also suffered a concussion during the attack. My arm was around her waist in a flash, and I effortlessly pulled her off Niya.

Daisha was swinging wildly in the air, and Niya was kicking and screaming.

"Get your crazy-ass bitch away from me!" Niya yelled as she picked up her pocketbook, which had fallen on the floor during the scuffle, and pulled out a small handgun. "Nigga, you just don't know a good thing when it's right in your motherfuckin' face. I was willin' to ride for you, and you played me to the left like I ain't shit."

She wasn't, but I couldn't say that out loud with a gun in my face. Obviously, her plan had been to seduce me and then kill me.

"Put the gun down, yo," I ordered her. "What the hell? Is it that damn serious?" *Damn.* My gun was on the mantel behind her, and if I tried to get to it, I was sure that I'd be shot.

Niya nodded. "Oh, it's so serious. Especially now. I had planned to shoot only you, but it's a good thing your bitch is here. I can just get her outta the way too."

"You already knew what it was when we fucked around. Why you actin' like I sold you a dream or something? I kept shit all the way real wit' you, and here you are, wit' a fuckin' gun in my face after you literally broke into my spot. You ain't no killer, Niya. You on some other shit right now. You all in your feelings and shit, but you need to go on and get up outta here, for real." I had tried to talk her down, but she hadn't even flinched.

"Nigga, miss me wit' that bullshit. You don't know shit 'bout me and what I'm capable of doin'. If you'd taken the time to get to know me instead of just fuckin' me, this wouldn't be happenin'!"

"You said you was down for just fuckin'! What the hell, yo?" I shouted. "Why the fuck y'all bitches always claim you down for whatever when you really want more? You didn't have to deal wit' me after I let you know that I don't do that love shit! You set yourself up to just get fucked. Now get that damn gun outta my face!"

"Shut the fuck up, nigga! I got the upper hand now! You don't think I'll really shoot your ass, do you?" She put her finger on the trigger. "Well, I will. Right in your pretty-ass face!"

Pow! Pow!

Chapter 9

Daisha

I stood right there behind that crazy-ass bitch, taking it all in. While she concentrated on Pistol, she paid no mind to what I was doing behind her. I'd seen the gun sitting on the mantelpiece when I first walked in, but I hadn't thought she'd pull one out.

Pistol's eyes were gauging her movements, and he wasn't paying me any attention, either. In the heat of the moment, I slowly crept to the mantelpiece and grabbed the gun, hoping that bitch wouldn't look back. She was so busy trying to scare that nigga with that gun that she saw nothing but him. The thing was, I didn't know if she was really going to shoot him. If so, she was definitely going to shoot me too.

Right when she threatened to shoot him in his face, I let off two rounds. One hit her in the back of the head, and the other one hit her in the shoulder. When some of her blood and brain matter splattered across the room and hit Pistol, I knew that I'd killed that bitch.

"Oh shit!" I gasped as I dropped the gun.

I'd never killed anybody in my life. That shit was fucking with me hard, and my body shook from the realization of what I'd done.

"Calm down. Don't panic," I heard Pistol say as he closed the distance between us. "Damn. I should've put the silencer back on that shit."

I was sure that somebody had heard the gunshots. "Oh God. What if . . . ?"

"Shhh." He put his finger to my lips. "I said, 'Don't panic.' The shots were loud, but it's early. Maybe everybody's at work or something."

That was wishful thinking. *Oh shit*. I'd gone from fearing for my life to fearing prison time. I didn't know which was worse.

"I . . . What . . . ?" I said.

Pistol looked me in the eye as he spoke sternly. "I need you to go in the bedroom and pack up some necessities for me. Grab your shit too. I'm gon' take care of the body, and then we'll pack up your car. Okay. There's a duffel bag in the closet in the master bedroom. Just grab some of my clothes and my toothbrush while I handle this. A'ight?"

I nodded and then scurried off to do as he'd said. My heart was beating so fast, and I knew instantly that I was having a panic attack. Once I was in his bedroom, I sat down on the bed and tried to calm down. If I hadn't killed that bitch, she would've killed both of us. There was no way I'd survived the shit I had for that bitch to just take me out. No fucking way.

When my breathing was back to normal and the pressure in my chest had gone away, I got up and opened the master-closet door. After grabbing pants and shirts off the hangers, I threw them on the bed. Then I grabbed some of his underwear and socks from a dresser drawer. After I located the duffel bag he had referred to, I threw his things inside. Then I gathered my own things.

Just then he barged into the room. "You finished?" he asked.

I nodded. "Where we going?" My voice was low.

He pulled out his cell phone. "What's your number? We gotta hurry. This ain't the hood, so I don't know what's gon' go down."

Damn, that was crazy as hell. That nigga didn't even have my number. I recited it, and he was silent as he did something on his phone.

"I just texted you an address. Drive your car there, and when you get inside, set the alarm. The code is nine-eight-four-seven-one. I'll be there after I handle . . ." His voice drifted off. "Don't stop for shit. Go straight there."

"Okay," I agreed with a nervous nod.

He changed his bloody shirt, grabbed our bags, and led me to the front door. My eyes lingered on the dead body, which he had wrapped up in an Oriental rug. My mind was focused, though, and I couldn't dwell on what I'd done. It was either me or her, and I chose me. Well, part of this was to save Pistol too. Damn if I was going to let that ho shoot him.

"Thanks, Ma. You definitely returned the favor," he said before he opened the door.

All I could do was nod. I wasn't a killer, either, but I'd been pushed to that point.

We left his condo and walked to my car, and he put the bags in the trunk. The cops weren't there yet, apparently, which was a shock.

"I gotta hurry up and handle that. I gotta clean up and whatnot, so it might be a minute before I get to you. Make sure you don't speed or do anything that'll keep you from getting where you need to go. You have enough gas, right?"

I hadn't seen the address, but I had almost a full tank. "Is it far?"

"Nah. 'Bout thirty minutes."

I nodded. "I'll be good."

"Okay. Be careful." He kissed me on the fore-head gently and then watched as I got in the car.

He just stood there as I put the address in my phone's GPS and drove away. All I could do was hope he'd make it to the address too. I wouldn't be able to relax until then. The possibility of the police arriving at his place, or Rae and his boys, sent chills up and down my spine. At that point Pistol and I were forever bound, and his hold on me seemed to be tight and secure.

When I pulled up to a brick mini-mansion in Fayetteville, Georgia, I was in immediate awe. Pistol had texted me while I was on the road to let me know that the cops did end up coming, but they didn't know where the shots had been fired from. They came to the door, and he told them that he hadn't heard any gunshots. By that time Niya's body and her car were long gone, and the crime scene had been washed clean. Still, he felt the need for us to get away from there for a few days.

Once I got our bags inside the mini-mansion, I made myself right at home. I gave myself a tour of the place, and at every turn, there was expen-sive furniture and artwork, even sculptures. I especially loved the floor-to-ceiling windows and marble floors. The spot was laid. His uncle had some moola. By the end of my tour, all I wanted to do was get in the upstairs Jacuzzi bathtub. There was also a steam room up there. And the infinity pool on the huge second-floor patio had sold me. Damn, that shit was original. Most pools I'd encountered were on the first floor, not the second floor. *If only I could afford to live somewhere like that*, I thought.

When my tour was over, I realized that I was starving, so after checking the refrigerator, which, surprisingly, was filled with food, I made a turkey sandwich. I also grabbed some grapes. It was clear that somebody lived here, and I was hoping that they weren't going to pop up. While I was eating, I called Pistol.

He picked up immediately and cut right to the chase. "To be honest, we don't need to be in Atlanta right now. Shit is hot, and if we both want to survive and stay outta jail, we gotta do what we gotta do. Know what I mean?"

"Yup, I know exactly what you mean. This place is . . . gorgeous, by the way. Who lives here?"

"It's my uncle's spot. He's out of town for a couple of weeks, so he don't mind if we stay there for a li'l bit."

"Oh." I turned the flat-screen television on in the kitchen, feeling safe and secure for the first

time in a while. Maybe it was the mansion's
alarm system.

"I'll be there soon. Okay?"

I nodded, as if he could see me, as I took a
bite from my sandwich. "Okay," I answered, my
mouth full. It was a surprise to me that I had an
appetite after what had happened. Shit, to be
completely honest, I was just glad to be alive.

"Get comfy and make yourself at home. You're
good there," he said.

If only he knew that I'd already done that.

"A'ight. I'll see you soon, then."

"Bet."

We hung up, and I felt better knowing that
he was okay. It seemed like that bitch really
didn't mean shit to him, because he was glad
that I'd popped her ass. I was sure that I'd find
out what had really gone down between them.
After what had happened, I was ready for him
to spill the tea. But first, I was going to get in
that damn Jacuzzi and relax my aching body.

I finished my sandwich, took a bottle of chardonnay out of the refrigerator, and poured myself
a glass. Then I headed up to the master bath, with
the glass in hand. After I walked in the bathroom,
I examined my face in the mirror. My swollen
eye had finally opened and was looking much
better. The bruising on my face had lightened up,

too. It was a good thing that I healed pretty fast, I thought. After a quick shower, I put on a little bit of makeup to cover the bruises. Then I turned on the water in the Jacuzzi tub.

While the tub was filling, I placed my glass of chardonnay on one edge, then climbed in. As the water rose up my body, my mind drifted to what lay ahead. After Pistol and I took care of Rae, I was going to get back out there and get my life straight. As much as I appreciated Pistol, I didn't plan on depending on him or getting too close to him. *Shit. Who the hell am I fooling?* I thought. *Damn.* I wanted him bad, and it had been only a few days since my "situation" with Rae, but I couldn't go there.

The thing was, he'd shown me more concern than any man I'd dealt with in my whole life. To think that it was unconditional on his part really made me feel something for him. The man hadn't even touched me in an intimate way. He didn't have to, though. The way he looked at me alone was enough to set my soul on fire. He'd looked at me like that from the first moment our eyes met. I knew in my heart that he was feeling me too. But it was too deep too soon. And the timing was just wrong as hell. Which was just my luck. Why the hell couldn't I have met him sooner?

I aligned my sore muscles with the Jacuzzi's jets and felt my whole body relax amid the bubbles. This bath was so therapeutic. I was buck ass naked, but I didn't give a damn. It wasn't like I'd packed a bathing suit. If Pistol walked in, it wouldn't faze me one bit. It wasn't like he'd never seen a naked woman before. From what I knew about him, he'd seen plenty.

I took a sip of chardonnay and then leaned back with my eyes closed. Okay, maybe I was taking a note from that dead trick Niya. I'd even shaved my pussy and shit. Damn it, I wanted to fuck Pistol, but I didn't want to admit it. Shit, I wanted that nigga to come on to me. I wanted to entice him and finally make love to a man. Fucking was all that I was used to, and I needed something more. He needed something more.

"Mmm. Well, I see that you found the Jacuzzi."

I sat up and spun around. There was Pistol's fine ass. He was standing there, with a cute little smirk on his face. That mu'fucka literally took my breath away. I was playing hard, but I had felt an attraction to him from the first moment he graced me with his presence. He was just too much for me to take. It was like he was too complex for me, and I still didn't know enough about him. Yet I wanted to fuck the shit out of his fine, sexy ass.

"Yeah. It's good for the pain." I smiled up at him, not caring that my full C-cup breasts were exposed.

His eyes lingered on them, and he wasn't trying to hide it. "You, uh . . . you *naked* naked?" He scratched his head and licked his lips from lust before turning around. "I'm sorry."

I laughed. "Is there any other way to be naked? Don't be sorry. Take your clothes off and get in with me."

"For real?" His eyes were glazed over, and I knew that he wanted to get up in my good good.

I nodded as I sipped my drink. "For real."

That nigga came out of his clothes fast. Damn it, his dick was perfect. It was smooth, dark, circumcised, long, and thick. Still, he didn't touch me as he lowered his body in the warm, titillating water.

"Oh, that feels so good." He looked at me and smiled. "You good?"

"Yeah. You?" I looked him over, and of course, his body was smooth and ripped like he was a boxer or something.

"I'm good, Ma. Just ready to get that nigga. So far shit's been quiet as hell. Mike and Dank owed me one, so they came and got old girl's body and the car while I cleaned up. I'm just glad you thought fast and shit. I checked her gun, and that shit was loaded. She was serious 'bout killin' me. You saved my life. Now we even. You ain't gotta think you owe me."

I shook my head. "I still owe you. If it wasn't for you, I'd be on the street."

The scent of his cologne had permeated the air, even though he was engulfed in water. He smelled so good that I almost lost my morals and started to climb on his dick. Instead, I held my composure and drained my glass of wine.

"Let's not think about that right now," he said. "How 'bout we just take advantage of the moment? I can't even pretend no more, Ma. I want you. I don't wanna just fuck you and use you to get to Rae. I wanna make love to you and appreciate a real woman for once. You're definitely a real woman. Not the plastic, fake shit I'm used to."

His warm, soft lips were on mine in an instant, and then our tongues became intertwined. I invited the intimacy. Shit, I needed that feeling, although I knew better. I was vulnerable as hell, and I knew that giving him my body was only going to make me feel so many emotions that I wasn't ready for. Honestly, it was more than I needed to feel, but my body went against my better judgment.

His hands found their way to my breasts and then my nipples. Then he stopped kissing me. "You okay?" he asked. His voice was a soft whisper.

All I did was nod, and then his mouth was on my hard nipples. Fuck, he had me right where he wanted me to be. Even if I didn't want to, I couldn't help but let him have his way. It was like I lost all control of myself. *Damn it.* I was his fucking puppet. All he had to do was keep doing what he was doing, and I was putty in his hands.

Suddenly he stopped. "Earlier today you was all mad at me 'cause you thought I wanted to fuck. What's different now?"

"I returned the favor. I don't owe you shit now, so I'm givin' you the pussy." My eyes were on his, challenging him to go for it, despite what I'd said earlier.

Still, my defenses were up, because of my vulnerabilities. Honestly, I was just sick of getting hurt. Now all I wanted was for him to make me feel good.

When he lifted me up out of the water and sat me down on the edge of the Jacuzzi, I couldn't help but get caught up in the moment. He spread my legs wide, shook his head, and then leaned over to indulge. The way his warm, soft tongue felt on my pussy made my insides instantly turn into mush. My overstimulated sex had me trembling all over. At that point I felt no pain, only all pleasure.

"Ohhh . . . fuck!" My mouth was wide open as I watched him continuously suck and lick my swollen clit. "My . . . damn . . . Pistol . . . shit." It felt like I was going to explode into a million little pieces.

His sexy hazel eyes shot up to meet mine. Thick, long lashes hooded his eyes, adding to his seductive aura. That nigga winked at me, showing off, as he used his tongue tricks to take over my entire anatomy.

I involuntarily started rolling my hips as warm tingles started to take over my senses. With my hand on the top of his head, I gyrated and moved my pelvis around greedily. It had been a while since a man had eaten me out like that. Shit, Rae had tried, but he wasn't nearly as good at it as Pistol was. He may not have ever loved a woman with his heart, but his actions with that tongue told another story. That nigga had clearly loved *somebody* if he knew how to eat pussy like that.

"Mmm, you taste good as fuck. Just like I knew you would. Mmm . . . mmm . . . mmm . . . mmm . . ."

My eyes rolled back in my head as he expertly slurped, sucked, and licked. He held my legs behind my head while his tongue deliberately traveled from my pussy to the crack of my ass.

"I love this shit." He stopped for a second as he pushed his pointer and middle fingers deep inside of me. His eyes were on mine, making eye contact again. An instant shiver traveled all over me. "Not only are you fine as hell, but this voluptuous-ass body of yours is so sexy. Mmm." His eyes slowly roamed over me as his fingers explored my wetness.

The sound of my pussy popping turned me on, so I could imagine what it did to him.

"Fuck. I got this pussy wet as hell." He smiled down at me, exposing white teeth and dimples. "But, like I was sayin', you're fine, your body is amazing, you taste good as fuck, and your pussy smell hella good. I'm so ready to feel you, Ma, but let me make you cum first."

He must've known what I was thinking, because soon he had me literally climbing the fucking wall. See, that was the shit I was talking about. That nigga had me fucked up, all damn ready. After he sucked me into oblivion, giving me an incredible orgasm for the third time, I was trying to get away from that lethal tongue of his.

"Fuck me . . . please," I literally begged.

He slid a condom, which he'd had stashed on the edge of the Jacuzzi, down his masterpiece of a dick before positioning his perfect body over mine.

"You know what, Ma? I done fucked plenty of bitches, but this . . ." His eyes were penetrating my soul. "This here is different. You're different, so I wanna do something different. I'm gonna make love to you."

The way he entered me was so gentle, and I just loved the way he kept his eyes on mine.

"You okay, baby?" he whispered.

I nodded as his length and width took my breath away. Soon I was used to his size, and I held on to him as he gently ground deep inside of me. Instantly, he found my spot, and he stayed there. He covered my body with kisses and constantly fed me his sweet tongue. Soon my body was trembling under him from the best orgasm I'd ever felt in my life.

"Oh shit . . . damn. Uh . . . Pistol . . ."

His hands were on my hips as he spread my ass cheeks open. His dick was so good. I had no words for how that shit felt.

"Mmm, damn, Ma. This pussy is . . . in . . . fucking . . . credible."

I held on to his ass cheeks and squeezed as he made me cum again.

For the next hour, he took me there over and over again, before my wet-ass walls came crashing down on his ass. He had stamina, but the pussy was too good. I knew because he told me, and given what I knew about Pistol, I believed him.

"Shit!" His body jerked uncontrollably as he held on tightly to my ass. "Fuck, Ma. Damn!"

That nigga's dick was lodged deep up in my shit at that point, and he'd been going in on it before he came. Damn, my pussy was still throbbing as he got soft inside of me.

"Oh . . . mmm. Hell fuckin' yeah," he whispered in my ear as he slapped my butt cheeks. "You got me hooked, Ma. Best fuckin' pussy I've ever felt in my life. Shit."

Chapter 10

Pistol

Shit, baby girl's pussy was good as fuck. I hated the word, but that shit was on fleek. That mu'fucka was snapping and literally biting my dick like nothing I'd ever felt before. It was no wonder that nigga Rae was acting crazy over her.

I mean, no woman deserved to be beaten, but it made sense why he'd lost his damn mind. If I wasn't a rational-ass-thinking nigga, I'd never want her out of my sight. The thought of another nigga touching her had me seeing red, and I'd had the pleasure of feeling the pussy only one time.

The early morning sun was streaming through the venetian blinds, alerting me of a new day. I jumped up and smiled down at the woman who'd finally gotten my attention and given me the desire to surpass the pussy. All I wanted to do was get up and make sure that she was fed, that she was well taken care of. Even deeper than that, I wanted to make her feel happy and secure. I longed to give her something she'd never had.

When I got in the kitchen, I whipped up a couple of omelets with cheese, turkey sausage, tomatoes, onions, and peppers. I even popped some bread in the toaster. Then I found some sliced pineapples and strawberries in the refrigerator. The coffee was brewing as beautiful Daisha made her way toward me, rubbing her eyes.

"Mornin', gorgeous," I greeted her warmly. It was the first time I'd ever made breakfast for a woman other than my mother.

With her eyes still closed, she stood on her tiptoes and kissed my lips. "Mmm. It smells good in here."

Damn, that was the feeling I'd longed for. That familiarity and comfort with a woman. We hadn't known each other long, but I already felt that shit. Damn, that had to be as close to love as I'd ever come. What shocked me even more was how soon it had happened.

"For the first time in my life, somebody scares me," I told her honestly as I stared into her pretty eyes.

"What?" She looked taken aback. "Who?"

"You." I grabbed her and kissed her again.

She smiled. "How do I scare you?"

"You got me feelin' shit I ain't never felt. I don't know how to feel about that shit, but I'm gon' let it happen." I kissed the tip of her nose.

"You sound confused to me. You sure it ain't the sex talkin'?" she teased.

"Sit down while I fix your plate. And no, it ain't the sex. I done had plenty good pussy before. Don't get it twisted. Like I told you, I'm interested past the pussy, and that's what's scary to me."

Daisha sat down at the table. "I'm scared too." She let out a sigh and continued. "I didn't want to go from one relationship to the next. To be honest, though, I can't even call what I had wit' Rae a relationship. And it's been over for a while."

"Well, regardless of what's goin' on outside of what we doin', I ain't lettin' you get away again. That's for damn sure," I replied.

Neither of us said a word as I fixed our plates. I put her plate in front of her, I placed mine on the table and sat, and she said grace before we dug in. The fact that she always blessed her food said a lot about her. I'd never seen any woman do that other than my mom. She would love Daisha. I knew it.

Daisha's voice suddenly cut through my thoughts. "There's so much that I don't know about you, Pistol. Like your real name, for starters."

"My real name is Tyreek Gordon."

She giggled. "Pistol suits you better."

"I agree."

"Are you from North Carolina? I mean, I heard you mention that that's where your family is."

"Yeah, that's where I'm from."

She shoveled food in her mouth before she continued with her questions. For some reason, I didn't mind this inquiry. If we were going to pursue something, she needed to know the truth. After what we'd been through so far, there was no way the fact that I was on the run would make her turn her back on me.

With a nod, she asked, "So, how long you been in Georgia?"

"Six months . . ."

"Damn. Only six months and that bitch was actin' like that?" A sly smile spread across her pretty, thick lips. "You did put it down last night. I ain't even gon' lie. I kinda see why that ho was actin' like that."

I was feeling myself as I smiled, but I had to give credit where it was due. "Shit. You know you got that comeback, Ma. You got a damn gold mine between yo' thighs. If I was a shiesty-ass nigga, I'd pimp you out."

"You're silly." She giggled.

"I'm glad you know that was a joke. Ain't no way I'd let another nigga even think about gettin' that. That's all mine now. Just know that shit, shawty. I don't play 'bout mine."

She looked up at me. "Oh, I wasn't plannin' on lettin' another nigga get this. It ain't 'cause you said so, though . . . shawty."

We both laughed, but then I got serious.

"Look, baby girl. Like I said before, I'm a straight-up nigga. I need to tell you something. You need to know exactly who you fuckin' wit'."

When she put her fork down and gave me her undivided attention, I told her all about the fact that I was wanted by the Feds. Not once did her facial expression change.

"Damn." She shook her head, and her eyes misted over. "I don't care 'bout that, though. I mean, as long as you stay outta trouble . . ." Suddenly her voice trailed off as she thought about it. "I guess that's impossible."

"Right," I agreed with a sarcastic laugh.

"Shit. Just don't get caught. You ever thought about leavin' the United States and goin' some-where where they can't extradite you? Like Cuba. They hate this mu'fucka. Castro'll be ready to defend you."

I glanced at her and shook my head. "You ain't like no other chick I ever met. I always thought about goin' somewhere and just givin' up my life here. That's hard to do, though, since I'm so close to my moms."

"Take her wit' you."

"It ain't that easy. She . . . she's sick. She was diagnosed with cervical cancer over a year ago. That's why I robbed those banks and shit. She needed surgery, and being that it was a pre-existing condition, her insurance didn't cover that shit. I did what I had to do to make sure my mom could live, yo. She got the surgery two months ago, but she still gotta get the chemo and radiation and shit. Until they say she's cancer free, I ain't goin' nowhere. You feel me?" I almost choked up, but I held it together.

Daisha's warm hand was on top of mine, and her eyes were on me. "I can tell that you really love your mom, Pistol." Tears filled her eyes and then spilled down her cheeks. "Makes me wanna make shit right wit' mine."

"I think you should."

"She don't deserve it." She shook her head as she squeezed my hand. Then she suddenly let go and continued to eat her food.

"She's your mother. She gave you life. What could she have possibly done to make you resent her so much?"

After she filled me in, all I could do was say, "Oh, damn. That's fucked up, Ma."

"Tell me about it." She stood up and grabbed both of our plates. "And that's only half of it."

I watched her as she rinsed our dishes off and put them in the dishwasher. Before she could sit back down, I grabbed her by the waist and sat her on my lap.

"You smell really good." I nuzzled her hair.

"Thanks. Must be that shampoo I use. It has argan oil in it."

I had no idea what that was, but that didn't keep me from inhaling the scent of her hair over and over again. What I was feeling was so new, and it actually felt good. Then reality set in. Both of us had separate issues that could keep us apart. There was nothing that I wouldn't do to ensure that we ended up together. Even if it meant leaving the country. There was no way I was going to let them lock me up for over twenty years. Hell nah. They'd have to kill my black ass first.

"What you thinkin' 'bout?" She rubbed the top of my head as she asked.

"Us . . ."

"What about us?"

"This shit happened so fast, Ma. I mean, don't get me wrong. The shit feels good, but damn . . . our timing is all wrong."

"I understand how you feel about the timing, but we don't have control over what the heart wants. We can either indulge or decide to leave it alone. I hope you choose to indulge, because I don't give a damn about timing anymore. This is our time, Pistol. Together, there's no tellin' what we can do."

Let me find out that I'd snagged my ride-or-die, I thought. When I'd heard folks talking about having a soul mate, I had thought that shit was ridiculous. Now that I had connected with Daisha, I could kind of see what they meant. It was like we were opposite ends of a magnet. We just seemed to pull one another in.

"I didn't wanna bring it up now, Ma, but first thing's first. I need to know where that nigga Rae be at."

"I heard from Kevia that he's fuckin' with his baby mama again. Her name's Capri."

"Hmm." I rubbed my chin thoughtfully. "You know where she live at?"

"Of course I do. Me and Kevia used to fuck wit' her back when I first got wit' Rae. She wanted to come to my job and harass me, so I had to go to her house and harass her ass. I don't play them scary-ass games. Don't no bitch put fear in my heart." I could tell that she meant that shit.

"And from this day forward, as long as you got me in your life, no man will put fear in your heart, either. I'll always protect you. Just know that," I told her.

Daisha looked down at me with so much gratitude in her eyes. "Thank you." Leaning over, she kissed me sweetly. "I know you're not used to this, but I'll always protect you too. In any way I can."

It was a first for me to trust a woman other than my moms, but I did. Who would've ever known? Daisha had proven that she was trustworthy. Shit, she'd killed for me. I hadn't even done that for her yet, but I planned to merk Rae. His days were numbered, and the sooner I got that nigga, the better.

"You proved that you got my back, shawty. Now I just gotta handle that nigga, so we can at least get him out of the way."

She nodded as she held on to me. Her head rested on top of mine. "Yup, but that'll be only one obstacle out of the way."

Her words resonated with me. She was right. Getting him would rid us of just one obstacle. We had many more to surmount if we wanted to be a real couple. The only thing was, would we both survive, and even if we did, would I still have my freedom? The prospect of prison loomed over me like a dark cloud. I *would* find the woman for me when I was threatened with years behind bars. *Oh well.* That was the story of my life. The hand I'd been dealt wasn't the best one, but I was going to stay in the game. As a matter of fact, I was going to ride that shit till the wheels fell off. Shit, what the fuck did I have to lose?

"I gotta make a few runs, baby girl. I'll be back." It was about three o'clock in the afternoon, and I needed to handle some shit.

Daisha looked up from the repeat episode of *Black Ink Crew* that she was so into. I hated that reality TV bullshit, but I wasn't tripping. It was good to see her enjoying herself. The smile she'd been wearing all day was infectious.

"Okay, but you ain't going after Rae right now, are you? I kinda wanna enjoy . . . us first." There was a disappointed look on her face.

"Nah, I ain't no reckless-ass nigga. That shit's goin' be planned out right. I don't want no fuck-ups or mistakes. That's why I'm gon' do it myself.

I ain't even involvin' my cousins. They act like they scared of that fuck nigga, anyway."

It made my head hurt just thinking about how sloppily we'd handled G's murder. Honestly, I must've been caught up in the heat of the moment. The thought of that nigga molesting my little cousin had made me go about shit irrationally. It wasn't like me not to think shit out and make sure nobody was left to seek revenge or snitch.

"I don't really think it's that they're scared of Rae. It's the fact that G was the head nigga, and his niggas gon' be ready for blood now that he's dead. I think they're more afraid of the Bankhead Mob."

"The Bankhead Mob?" Damn, I'd heard of them before. "G ran that shit?"

Daisha nodded. "Your cousins didn't tell you that?"

"Hell nah." Those niggas were the most infamous, ruthless crew in Atlanta, other than the Cue Boys.

"I guess they left that bit of information out for a reason."

The wheels in my head really started turning then. I had a bone to pick with my cousins. It had been clear to me that G had a crew, but I hadn't thought he was on the top tier of the

Bankhead Mob. Now I knew why Mike and Dank were so nervous. Had my cousin fabricated the story of his daughter being molested by G? What if the motive behind G's murder was something else?

Shit. It wasn't like me, but deep down inside, I felt like that shit could wait. Daisha had done something to me that no other woman had been able to do, and she had become my priority.

When I got back to the house, it was a little after six o'clock. That was perfect timing for what I planned to do. Our reservation was for nine o'clock, so we had plenty of time. I wasn't one to plan a romantic evening, but I knew that Daisha probably hadn't been spoiled in a while, if ever. After popping the trunk open, I jumped out of my ride and grabbed the bags inside the trunk.

There were over ten bags, and they were full of designer clothes, shoes, and bags for Daisha. She hadn't asked for anything, and I knew that she wasn't high maintenance. One thing I was sure of, though, was the fact that every woman out there liked to look good. Even if Daisha wasn't feeling the best on the inside, at least I could help enhance the outside. Then, when she'd look in the mirror, she'd be a little bit less insecure.

When I walked inside the house, I could smell the aroma of something good cooking. Damn, let me find out that she could burn too. My stomach was surely one way to my heart, because I loved to eat. Now that I thought about it, I'd never eaten a woman's food other than my mother's. Well, with the exception of when I went out. The chicks I normally fucked with didn't cook. I followed the smell to the kitchen, and Daisha was standing over the stove, stirring up something in a pot.

"Hey, good lookin'. What you got cookin'?" I asked playfully as I walked up on her. Damn, her ass looked so good in those tights she was wearing. I pinched it softly, and she giggled hysterically.

"I'm cookin' oxtails, rice, and cabbage."

"Smells good, Ma. For real. But it kinda cuts into the plans I had for us later."

She turned, wearing a curious look on her face. "What plans?"

Right on cue, the doorbell rang, and I smiled down at her cute ass before kissing her cheek. "Looks like I should've called you first, huh?"

She looked at me like I was crazy. "Who is at the door?"

"Uh, you relax. I'll go see."

"My nerves are bad as hell, Pistol. What's goin' on?"

I laughed. "Nothing, Ma. Chill. I'll be back."

She shook her head and went back to cooking.

When I returned to the kitchen, I had this chick named Megan in tow. She was a professional makeup artist. I had met her at Lenox Square, in the mall's MAC store. I had wanted to get Daisha some makeup to cover her scars, but I'd had no clue what to buy. That was when I'd asked a random makeup artist if she made house calls, and she'd told me that she did. Then I'd found out that she was about to get off work, which was perfect.

"Daisha, this is Megan. She's a MAC makeup artist. I, uh, hired her to do your makeup because I made dinner reservations for us tonight. Not that you need it, but I know that you're a woman who cares about her appearance. After what you've been through, I just want you to feel good about yourself."

There was a huge smile on Daisha's face. "Thanks. Wow. Dinner . . . I guess we can eat this tomorrow."

I grinned. "Of course. Now, I'll tend to the food while you get dolled up."

She left the kitchen and led Megan to the dining-room table. I'd already lugged the bags of clothes, shoes, and purses upstairs, to surprise her with later. For the first time ever, I had planned a date and was looking forward to it. This was not just meeting up with some chick to fuck, but a real damn date. *Shit*. What the hell had Daisha done to a nigga? Whatever it was, I was damn sure feeling that shit. Straight up.

Chapter 11

Daisha

That chick Megan was actually cool. We were the same age, and so we decided to exchange numbers. It was a breath of fresh air to meet a chick who was positive and ambitious. I think I needed that influence. Once she was done with my makeup, she passed me a handheld mirror.

Shit, I almost cried. My face was finally beat in a good way. "You did that," was all I could say. But, damn, I couldn't help but smile. It didn't even look like Rae had ever put his hands on me. If only this makeup job would last.

Pistol came in the room just then and took a look at me. "Well, damn, Megan. You the shit for real, yo. Let me buy everything you used on her. For real."

I gave him the side eye. "What you tryin'a say, nigga?"

He chuckled. "I'm just sayin' she did the damn thang, Ma. That's all. You know you're gorgeous with or without that shit."

I'd filled Megan in on what had happened to my face, so she wasn't looking at Pistol all sideways. "Well, everything I used on her, including the brushes, comes up to about three fifty," she said.

Three hundred fifty dollars, I said to myself.

Pistol just reached in his pocket and pulled out four hundred-dollar bills. "Thanks again, Megan."

I was stunned as he walked her to the door and then joined me in the dining room.

"Okay, it's almost seven o' clock, and our reservation is at nine. I put the food up, so all I need you to do is get dressed," he announced.

There was a cute little pout on my face as I pointed out a known fact. "I don't have anything to wear for a fancy dinner date, Pistol. All my clothes are—"

"Did I say anything about you havin' something to wear?" he asked, interrupting me. He shook his head. "You're definitely used to fuckin' with bum-ass niggas. I got you covered, Ma. Follow me."

My heart leapt in my chest as he led me to the bedroom. When I first saw the numerous bags on the bed, I was ecstatic. Then that feeling was

replaced by something else. I'd never been the
type of woman who worshipped material things
or expected a man to buy them for me. All I had
ever wanted from a man was love, loyalty, and
for him to help me out with my bills. My smile
faded, and Pistol could tell that something was
wrong.

"Why don't you take a look in the bags?" he
said.

"Uh, I expected one outfit for tonight. Not a
shopping spree."

His face was contorted from confusion, and
his hazel eyes suddenly dimmed. "What . . . ? I
thought you'd be happy."

"I'm not *unhappy*. I mean, you just spent four
hundred on my makeup. Are you tryin'a buy me?
If so, you don't have to do that."

I didn't want him to think I wanted him to
do things like that for me. I'd be fine with him
simply being there for me, like he'd been so far.
Shit, that money could've gone toward rent at
another spot. He just didn't know that my priorities weren't like those of most chicks my age. I
wasn't into spending money on unnecessary shit.

Pistol shook his head. "No, I ain't tryin'a buy
you. . . ."

"Is all of this out of pity, then? Do you feel
sorry for me?"

He let out a deep sigh and sat down on the bed. "I feel a lot of things for you, Daisha, and none of them have anything to do with pity. As far as feeling sorry for you, why should I? You seem to be a strong woman who's makin' it through her situation just fine. All I wanted to do was make you feel better. It was just a gesture to show you that a man can do something other than fuck you. Believe me, what I spent ain't even enough for you to be worried about. I'm good. I had some extra to spend. Okay. No agenda. Just me tryin'a be a good nigga for once."

Damn, I felt awful as I stared into his sincere eyes. The man was just trying to show me something different, and there I was, shitting on his efforts. I was so damn fucked up that I couldn't appreciate a genuine act of kindness.

"Thank you. I'm sorry. I—"

"If you tell me you're sorry again, we gon' have a problem." His voice was serious, but he was wearing a wary smile. "You're a strong woman, but you're also fragile. I get why you're defensive. You gotta protect yourself, but not from me. Just let yourself go, Ma. I ain't gon' do nothin' to hurt you. That's my good word. I'll never lie or mislead you. I'll always keep it one hundred wit' you. Trust me."

He stood up and pulled me to him for a tight bear hug. I felt my body melt against his. Damn, he was so damn solid, and his chest was hard and chiseled. When he pulled away, he stared down at me with those damn eyes.

"Now, I want you to choose something to wear. Preferably the short black Prada dress," he said. "I'm 'bout to go get dressed. We've already wasted enough time wit' your nonsense."

I laughed it off, but he was right. A bitch was tripping. *Enjoy the man*, I told myself.

"Okay," I replied. I smiled at him right before he leaned over to give me a sweet kiss.

Once he was out of the bedroom, I tore into those bags like a kid on Christmas morning. Who the fuck was I fooling? All women liked nice, expensive shit. Especially when somebody else bought it.

Dinner at Chops, a top-notch steak house, was amazing. Pistol had pulled out all the stops and had made reservations for us in a secluded private room. It was set up all romantic, with low lights, candles, champagne on chill, and a violinist. Who would've ever thought? And Pistol had gone all out in terms of his clothing and was decked out in a charcoal-gray Italian suit, with a tie and nice leather dress shoes. I was impressed that he'd dressed all up and shit. I didn't even think a street-ass nigga like him owned a suit.

The food was good as hell. My ass was full as hell after I ate a super-tender filet mignon that melted in my mouth like butter. It was so delicious. The steak, grilled asparagus, and creamed potatoes were enough for me. There was no room in my belly for dessert. However, Pistol ordered cheesecake and some caramel sauce on the side, and I kicked off my leopard-print Jimmy Choo stiletto-heel pumps so that he could put some caramel on my toes and then lick it off. Oh, that shit felt good.

"You're such a freak," I teased him when he went back to eating his cheesecake.

"Well, you got pretty-ass toes, so I figured, *Why not*? I mean, shit, we can do anything we want to in here. Look around. Nobody's here but us."

The violinist had left us alone, and I was sure that our server wasn't going to return anytime soon. I picked up the small dish full of caramel and got down on my knees.

Pistol's mouth fell open in surprise. "What you doin', Ma?" He laughed. "I ain't lettin' you suck my toes."

I couldn't help but laugh too. "Nah. I got somethin' else in mind that I wanna suck."

His eyes narrowed as he put another forkful of cheesecake in his mouth. "I ain't gon' stop you, Ma. Do what you feel like doing. I told our server to leave us alone for a while, anyway."

"Perfect," I purred, then unzipped his pants and fished inside the slit of his boxers.

Once I found his hardness, I pulled it out and poured some of the caramel down the shaft. He shivered from the chill, but I was going to warm him up in no time. Teasing the head, I had him squirming and staring down at me with sultry eyes.

"Mmm," I moaned, taking him deeper into my mouth.

Soon I was deep throating that shit all sloppy like, and he was loving it.

"Oh . . . fuck . . ." He shook his head. "My fuckin' toes are curlin' right now."

I smiled up at him, although my mouth was full of dick. My eyes were seductive as I continued to please him orally. His hands were on the top of my head, and his eyes were starting to look vulnerable as hell. All clues that he was about to bust. Damn, I wasn't one to swallow nut, but damn, there wasn't anywhere for me to spit it out.

We were in a five-star restaurant, so there was no way I'd feel right spitting that shit in my water glass or on a cloth napkin. *Fuck!* I guessed I would have to take one for the team. Besides, the man had saved me and had spoiled me more in a couple of days than the man I'd been with had over the course of years.

"I'm cumin'. Oh . . . shit!" He held on to my head and literally fucked my throat.

His nut spewed into my mouth, and I quickly took it down like a champ. That nigga looked at me like he was shocked out of his mind. I reached up, grabbed my water glass, and gulped down the water. *Oh well.* I'd read that the protein in sperm was good for you.

"Wow . . ." He stared at me as he put his dick back into his pants.

"Wow what?" I asked, suddenly feeling bashful after getting all freaky deaky on that nigga.

"That was . . . damn . . . that shit was fuckin' stupendous. Shit, I want some of that pussy now. Where the fuck the server at?" He looked around, all anxious and shit.

"Well, you did tell him to give us some private time." I looked up at him and licked my lips enticingly.

"Mmm . . ." He stood up and opened the partition that separated us from the rest of the restaurant's patrons. "I'll be back. I'm 'bout to go find that mu'fucka."

I waited for him, with a smile on my face. After the way I'd sucked his dick, I knew that he was about to rock my fucking world.

The date that Pistol had taken me on at Chops was just the beginning. After that dinner date, we enjoyed a few days of blissful peace and tender lovemaking. I was pampered, and I wasn't complaining. I'd never felt the way Pistol made me feel in my life. It was actually scary. However, I knew that shit wasn't going to last. We were going to have to leave our hideaway soon.

That meant that Pistol was going to put his life in jeopardy by going after Rae. In a way I didn't want him to risk it. I wanted him to run away with me. Maybe we could go on the run together and take his mother and brothers with us. He had plenty of money to make it happen, but I didn't want to push the issue. I was just in a fantasy world. He'd already told me once that he couldn't go anywhere. His mom was sick. Besides, having so many of us with him was a risky proposition.

"We're going back to the city tomorrow," Pistol told me as we sat by the pool, buck ass naked.

We'd just pleased one another for probably the hundredth time in the past few days. I was getting used to living and eating well, with no worries. Going back to the real world wasn't something I was looking forward to.

"So, does that mean you'll be going after Rae soon?" I needed to be prepared mentally.

"Yeah. My cousins said ain't shit happened, so I don't think that nigga know shit. He must not have recognized me."

"Well, that gives you an advantage, right?" I was hopeful that it did. I didn't want anything to happen to him, and especially because of me.

"Mmm-hmm." His fingers were creeping up my thigh, toward my wetness.

"Do you ever get enough?" I shook my head as he teased my clit.

"Nope, and I probably never will." He leaned over and took my nipples into his mouth.

As good as what he was doing to me felt, I just couldn't enjoy it like I wanted to. In the back of my mind, I knew that there was a chance that something so good would be taken away from me. To be honest, from the outside looking in, I knew that it was too good to be true. The man whom I was falling for was going to risk his life to kill my crazy-ass ex, *and* he was running from the Feds. *Damn.* How much more could a potential couple have against them?

"You okay?" Pistol's voice cut through my thoughts like a knife.

"Honestly . . . no. I'm . . . I'm afraid that this . . . us . . . is just too good to be true. I don't believe in luck, 'cause I don't have any. Never have. So, why would I think we'll just be runnin' off into the sunset together? Why get used to this when I know in my heart that some force beyond our control is goin' to ruin it?" Tears filled my eyes, but I willed them away. *Please don't cry, bitch,* I said to myself.

Pistol stopped the sexual stuff and pulled me to him. As he cuddled with me, he said, "The other night at Chops was the first time I've ever planned a romantic date. A lot of what we're going through is a first for me too. I know that we ain't made this official yet, but . . . I know it's coming. The future seems dim for us, Daisha, but I don't think we met for nothing. We ain't goin' through what we're goin' through for nothing."

His eyes met mine, and it was clear to us both that the chemistry between us was like a wildfire. It had just happened out of nowhere and couldn't be contained. The passion was just spreading all over us, like nothing we'd ever experienced in our lives.

Pistol went on. "So, regardless of what happens, there's a reason behind it all. I'm just glad to know that I'm actually capable of feeling something other than a good nut. I knew you were going to change my life the moment I laid eyes on you. Take it for what it is, baby girl—whether it be temporary or something that will last a lifetime. Only time will tell."

"But what do you *want*?" I stared into his eyes as I asked this question. "This . . . thing between us is movin' along in dog years. It's like there are too many feelings too soon, and I don't know what to do with them. I mean, I'm lovin' this . . . probably too damn much."

Pistol caressed my cheek. "What's gonna happen is gonna happen, Ma. We ain't got no control over the future. All we can do is take advantage of what's in front of us right now." There was a sly grin on his face. "'Cause I sure do wanna take advantage of you."

I shook my head. "You're a mess."

One thing I could tell about Pistol was he had an uncanny ability to live in the moment. I, on the other hand, was more cautious and anxious about the future. Maybe I could take a lesson from him. Like he'd said, it was best to just take advantage of what we had right now and enjoy it. When I thought then about what had happened with Niya, it only reminded me of what a gamble life really was.

Chapter 12

Pistol

Daisha had given me Rae's baby mama's address, and it was only a matter of time before I decided to make my move. I would do it tonight, and I wasn't going to take my cousins with me. That shit was something I wanted to do on my own. The thing was, I was sure a nigga like him would slip up. Daisha wasn't around to give him the pussy, so I was sure he'd be on the late-night creep later on.

"I'm goin' wit' you," Daisha insisted as we sat on the sofa in the living room. The fear in her eyes was evident, but I was sure it was only for my safety. Not hers.

"No. I don't wanna put you in danger."

"But you said you needed my help. . . ."

"To find him. Not to kill him," I told her.

"Okay, but let me be there so I can have your back."

"No!"

She literally jumped when I said that, and she then looked at me like she didn't know who I was. The fact was, she really didn't. I'd never gotten an attitude toward her before, so she hadn't seen that side of me. I needed to know if she could handle the intensity that I often displayed.

"You did what you did the other day because you felt you had no choice," I explained. "In this situation, I'm makin' *all* the choices. I don't want you there. You had my back before, but I don't want to put you in that position again."

Daisha shook her head. "It's not fair that you get to make all the decisions. If something happens to you, where does that leave me? I'd have to live with that shit. You wanna go do that shit alone? Why? At least take Mike and Dank with you."

"Nah, I don't need them to kill one man. I got this. That's why I'm goin' after him at his bitch's crib and not on the streets. I wasn't prepared for Niya, but I'm prepared for him. Nothing's gonna happen to me. I'm gon' pop that nigga, and then it'll be done. Then you can get yourself together and not have to worry 'bout him."

She nodded. "Okay. You're right about one thing. I can get myself together and not worry about him. Just know that I will get myself together. I'm going to find a good job and go back to school to finish my degree."

"Good. I want you to do what you want, Ma."

She just stared at me for a minute. "Maybe . . . uh . . . I think . . . we're movin' too fast. It was the whole thing with Niya. I was feeling like life is too short, so why not just do whatever? The thing is, I don't think I'm ready for anything right now other than a friendship. Which means the sexual side of this has to stop. It's good—don't get me wrong—but I don't wanna be confused right now. Once Rae is gone, I'm gonna get a boarding room somewhere, get that job I've been wanting, and learn to live for me. You understand that, right?"

"I can deal wit' the no-sex part, but what is there for you to be confused about? I'm curious." I turned to look at her.

She leaned back on the sofa and sighed. "My feelings. I care for you, and we have this crazy bond that came out of nowhere. It's just that I lose myself in relationships, whether they be real or sexual. I have to work on me, Pistol. Then you have yourself and your family to worry about. You don't need me being a burden on you too."

"A burden?" I shook my head. "Your brain be workin' overtime, Ma. For real. Who said that my family or you were a burden? I never said that."

"I know, but you have enough shit on your plate."

"And I want you on my plate too."

Damn. Why the hell was she always trying to run away? I mean, I understood why she felt that things were moving too fast, but I didn't get why she wanted it to stop. We could slow it down, but stop? That shit was fucking with me. It wasn't even about the sex. I wanted to know for a fact that she'd stick around.

She sighed. "I don't know if you'll be taken away from me, Pistol. I'm just being honest. Whether it be prison or death. Everything is so . . . unpredictable."

"That's wit' anybody you're in a relationship wit', Daisha. Why did you stay wit' that fuck nigga for so long, but you can't get used to the thought of bein' wit' me?"

"'Cause I'm tired of gettin' hurt. For once, I'm feelin' like I found the perfect man for me, and look at what the fuck we're facing. I can't go through the heartbreak of another failed relationship. It's like once I put my heart into someone, it ends up ripped right out of my chest. That's something that I don't wanna deal with again anytime soon. Don't you get that?"

"Why did you let me make love to you, then? Why didn't you let me just continue bein' the nigga I was if this was just gon' be some fuck shit? I did something different because I thought that's what you wanted." Now I was confused.

True, we hadn't been dealing with each other long, but our circumstances seemed to have made us move along faster than the average. Some people had sex the first night they met, and ended up married and in love. Why the fuck was she overthinking what we had going on? I had noticed that she was trying to make up for the fucked-up decisions she'd made with men in the past. That was no reason to miss out on something that was actually meant to be. My circumstances hadn't been an issue at first, but now, all of a sudden, they were. I was starting to think that Daisha was just a little bit bipolar, and I wasn't trying to be funny.

"Because I wanted you to, but the fact remains that you have never been in a serious relationship before," she said. "How do I know that you're really ready now? How do I know that it's gonna all be worth it? Why fall in love with someone who can end up in a grave or a prison cell? Why set myself up to love and long for a man that I can't touch? Huh? I'm not built for that."

I shook my head at her. "I told you what was going on already, Ma. I kept it real wit' you before anything even happened between us. Okay. Fine. I'll just kill Rae so you can go on wit' your life. If that's all you want, that's what you gon' get!" With that said, I stood up and walked toward the front door.

"Wait. That's not what I meant, Pistol. I'm just sayin'—"

I turned on my heels. "Fuck it, yo! I get it! The shit I got goin' on is too much for you. Just know that there is nothing that keeps me from wanting you. Not your drama with that nigga or the fact that you don't have anybody that you can depend on. None of that shit scared me away, a nigga who ain't never been serious about a woman. Your feelings for me ain't as strong as I thought they were, but mine are damn sure strong enough for you."

She didn't even respond to what I'd said. Instead, she stared at me as tears fell down her cheeks, and then she shook her head and walked out of the room.

It was time for me to put shit in motion so she wouldn't feel like she was obligated to appease me. Damn, I wanted Daisha bad, but she'd been damaged by men before me and by her mother. Because of that, there was nothing I could do to change her state of mind. All I could do was kill that nigga Rae and give her the freedom she needed to do her. Besides, from my point of view, that was all she really wanted. When I was finally open to love a woman, for once, that shit wasn't well received. Was that my karma?

An hour later I was sitting in my car, which I'd parked under a huge oak tree on the street, enveloped by the darkness of the night. That chick Capri lived in a nice house outside of Sandy Springs. So, his baby's mama was living it up while Daisha struggled. I mean, it was good, if he took care of his seed, but damn. On the outside looking in, Daisha was just old dude's sidepiece.

There were no cars in Capri's driveway, but there was a garage. I wondered if Rae had parked inside it. The spot was dark as hell, though, so I figured either there was nobody there or they were fucking. Either way, I needed that nigga to show his face so I could blow it off his damn neck. I didn't care if he was pulling out of that bitch or pulling up.

I despised niggas like Rae. They lived the street life and pretended to be all hard, but they would put their hands on a woman. Maybe he was mad that he was under G's command, and his lack of power made him feel inferior.

I guessed mentally and physically abusing a defenseless female made his soft, lame ass feel more powerful.

The thing about me was, I may not have ever given my heart to a woman, but I hadn't ever ripped a woman's heart out, either. I felt that the least I could do was let them know where I stood. If they didn't want to deal with it, that was cool with me, and if they did, that was cool too.

I'd been sitting there waiting for over an hour, and nothing eventful had happened. I had thought about breaking into that bitch, but I didn't want to chance it, as that nigga might not be there. Capri wasn't my target, and I didn't believe in hurting innocent children. I was aware that a child lived there. I was waiting for Rae, so I could just run up on his ass. If his bitch found his ass lying on the steps, in a pool of blood, I didn't give a fuck about that.

"Fuck it," I said out loud, figuring that I could come back and case the spot again the next night.

It was crucial that I got rid of that nigga, not only for Daisha's sake, but for mine too. I wasn't going to rush it, though. That shit had to be done right, because I couldn't risk my freedom or my life. With my gun in my lap, I hit the gas and pulled out of my secure parking spot.

Shots rang out.

The gunshots were loud as hell and came out of nowhere. They didn't stop. In the pitch-black darkness, I couldn't see where they were coming from. This didn't stop me from sticking my strap out the window. My shots were aimless, but I was hoping they'd make the shooter run for cover. After taking about a dozen shots, I pulled my weapon back in. A few seconds later, the crashing sound of my back window being shot out made me duck down. The windshield shattered as the bullets exited my car. I tried driving erratically to dodge the shots, but they kept coming. I aimed my weapon out the window again as I kept driving.

By the time I bent the corner, I didn't know if my tires had been shot out. I had no clue if I'd shot whoever was shooting at me. It had to be that nigga Rae. He had to have realized that I was out there waiting, stalking him like the killer I was. That shooting shit had knocked me off my square, because I hadn't expected it. I deduced that he was inside the house and his car was parked in the garage. G's murder must've had him on guard, or he wouldn't be bucking at me and shit.

The gunshots finally stopped. I kept on driving, and it became obvious to me that my tires were still intact. Suddenly, I felt something warm oozing down my arm. When I glanced over, I saw blood dripping down to my pant leg. My heartbeat increased. I couldn't see the wound. If I'd been shot, why didn't I feel it? The adrenaline rush must have made me numb. Or maybe I hadn't been shot. Maybe I'd been cut by glass from the broken windows. *Shit*. I damn sure hoped it was the glass. My crib was less than thirty minutes away, but would I make it? Not knowing the extent of my injury made me wonder if I would bleed out first. That thought made me press the gas pedal harder.

"Pistol! Oh my God! You're bleeding!"

Daisha rushed over and grabbed me as I staggered through the door. I think I'd underestimated the amount of blood that I was losing. Her face went pale as she stared at me.

"What happened?" she asked as she led me over to the sofa and sat me down.

I just shook my head. I felt weak as she pulled my shirt off and examined my back.

"You were shot! You have to go to the hospital!" Her voice was frantic. "C'mon. Let me take you. Now!"

"No." I shook my head again. "I can't go to a fuckin' hospital." My speech was slurred, and

I knew that was a sign that I was bleeding too much. "It's probably just a flesh wound."

"No, it's not just a flesh wound! I don't see an exit hole, Pistol. The bullet is still . . ."

"Well, you gon' have to get it out," I said weakly.

"What? Oh, hell no. I don't know how to do no shit like that. . . ."

"It's just a lot of blood, Daisha. I'm still good. I'm sure that the bullet isn't too far in and hasn't messed up anything major. There's a first-aid kit . . . in the bathroom, under the sink. Go get that, and some towels and some ice. I'll tell you how to do it. Okay? Oh, and grab that bottle of Henny out the kitchen too."

She nodded. "Okay. Try to keep pressure on it." Her face looked like she was in pain. Tears filled her already puffy eyes, and I felt awful.

How the hell had I let that nigga shoot me?

Daisha stood there, watching me. "You really should let me take you to a hospital," she said. "I can't do this."

"Go do what I said, Daisha."

The tears fell as she shook her head at me. "But if you don't go to the hospital, you might . . . die! What if the bullet did more damage than you think?"

"If I go to the hospital, I'm goin' to prison," I reminded her.

She scurried off without saying another word. My vision was blurry as I watched her leave the room. A few seconds later everything faded to black.

Chapter 13

Daisha

I returned to the living room after gathering everything that he had told me to. By the time I made it back, he was out like a light on the sofa, which made me extremely concerned. I immediately poured some of the liquor on the wound before applying pressure to it with a towel. It was a good thing his sofa was leather, because he was leaking blood on it.

"Pistol! Shit! Wake up! Wake up! Please!" I yelled.

He was breathing, but it sounded shallow as hell. I wished that nigga had let me either take him to the hospital or call an ambulance. I popped the first-aid kit open as my heartbeat sped up to the max. Damn, I'd never been so nervous and afraid in my life. If that nigga died, I would never forgive myself. I should've dragged his big ass to the car and taken him to the hospital, anyway.

When I poured rubbing alcohol into the wound, he suddenly came to.

"Argh! Oh shit," he yelled and bit down on the throw pillow that he was clutching. "Fuck!"

I looked closely at his wound and could see the bullet glistening right there under his shoulder blade. He was right. It wasn't *that* bad. At least, it wasn't a hollow-point bullet. In that case the damage would've been worse. The bullet was intact and looked like it could be easily removed. The blood just made the wound seem worse than it was.

I relaxed. "I see the bullet. So, what do I do now?"

"Use the tweezers and dig it out." His voice was strained, and I could tell that shit hurt like hell.

He gritted his teeth, and I did what he said. More blood gushed out, but he took that shit like a champ. The bullet wasn't budging, though. It was lodged in his muscle, tight as hell.

"Mmm . . . hold up, Ma." He tried to stop me, but I kept right on trying.

Less than a minute later, I had the bullet out, and he looked like he was in agony. However, he was still taking it well.

"You been shot before?" I asked as I cleaned the wound and covered it with gauze.

Pistol nodded. "Three times." He pointed to a faint scar on his stomach. "The other time was in the leg."

"You're blessed," I told him as I pressed the tape against the gauze to keep it in place.

"Because I've been shot three times?" His eyebrow shot up.

I couldn't help but laugh through the tears that threatened to fall. "No. Because you survived."

He looked relieved. "Give me that bottle of Henny."

I handed the bottle to him. He drank from it, and then he offered me some. Damn, I sure needed it.

As I chugged a shot of the liquor, he asked, "You know how to roll a blunt?"

"Yeah." That shit burned the hell out of my throat, but I took one more shot before passing him the bottle back.

He told me where his stash was and where he had stashed a few Percocet. I guessed he needed everything he could get for the pain.

"So, what happened?" I asked when I got back to the living room.

While I rolled a blunt, he filled me in, and I couldn't believe it.

"What? But . . . ," I said.

"I know. I thought I was prepared for that nigga, but . . . I underestimated him."

"But what if it wasn't him? That bitch Capri is plum crazy too. If she thinks somebody is after her man, she comes for them just like a nigga would. She's s'posed to be part of some crew of chicks who gangbang and sell heroin. That bitch should be thinkin' 'bout her son, but she on that street shit. I know for a fact she carries a gun. That's why I got one. She threatened to shoot me over that nigga so many times. I had to let her know that I be strapped too."

He looked shocked. "Why didn't you tell me that?"

"Number one, because I didn't think this would happen, and number two, you left pissed off at me." I finished rolling the blunt and then lit it.

"I wasn't pissed off at you. I was frustrated. You don't know what you want, Ma. You flip-flop all the time. One second, you good wit' me, and the next second, you actin' like a nigga kidnapped you."

"And you act like I asked you to kill that nigga Rae for me," I countered. "You left talkin' 'bout you gon' kill him for me so I can move on wit' my life. It's like you act like you're only doin' me a favor. To be honest, if you kill him, you will be, but it would be to your advantage too. I feel like you're holding it over my head, like I asked for your help. I don't want to go into another situation feeling obligated. I just need some time before I jump into something else. . . ."

"You already jumped into something else, Ma, whether you wanna admit it or not. The way you feel for me is clear in your eyes. I don't give a fuck what you say."

He stared at me, and my whole body quivered. *Damn.* He could see right through me. It was a shame that I was that transparent to him.

I decided to change the subject as I passed him the blunt. "Are you sure you're good, yo?"

He popped two Percocet and then took another sip of Henny. "I'm straight, Ma. The bullet's out, so I'm good."

"But that doesn't mean . . ."

He used all his strength to lean over and kiss me. The kiss was deep, and the soft sweetness of his tongue literally made me dissolve into a puddle of mush. How was he doing that to me? Why was I so damn weak for him? His lips were so plush and warm against mine. Just the way my body seemed to weaken at his touch was enough to let me know that I was losing the battle.

"Stop fightin' what you feel, Daisha. I know that you're down for us one minute and against us the next, because you don't wanna repeat history. Well, I don't wanna repeat history, either. I wanna give love a chance."

His arms were around my waist now, holding me tightly. He laid his head on my breasts like a little boy and drifted off to sleep. The moment was so pure, honest, and sweet. I just sat there for a while, enjoying the masculine scent of his cologne. The rhythm of his breathing was like music to my ears. Thank God he wasn't killed. If he hadn't come back, I would've lost it completely.

Eventually, Pistol seemed to get heavier and heavier on me by the minute. His snoring was getting louder too. I somehow managed to crawl out from under the crushing weight of Pistol's body without waking him. I cleaned the blood off the sofa and then covered him up with a blanket before I headed to the bedroom and got in his bed. It wasn't like I could lift him up and carry him to the bed. I also knew that the pain pills mixed with the alcohol and the weed would have him knocked out for a while. The thing was, I was worried about him. What if the wound got infected?

That nigga was hardheaded as hell. He wasn't willing to go to a hospital. I understood why, though. Hospitals reported cases involving gunshot wounds to the authorities. Pistol couldn't afford to get caught. He had told me before that he'd rather die than go to prison for the rest of his life. The thought made my eyes sting with tears.

I had to turn the television on to distract myself from my nagging thoughts. Every bad scenario had played out in my head when Pistol was gone, and I was starting to revisit them now. To think that I was falling in love with someone who I knew would be taken from me one way or another. It was like I was a glutton for punishment, but life was too short not to experience true love. Like Pistol had said, whether it be temporary or for a lifetime, I should take it for what it was. That nigga's grip on me was something serious.

The next morning, I was up early and set about whipping up breakfast. Pistol was still snoring lightly on the sofa, and I wanted to make sure he had something hot to eat when he woke up. He would need to get his strength back up. After his plate was made, I put it on a tray and poured him a huge glass of water and a small glass of orange juice. I put the two glasses on the tray and then carried it into the living room.

"Wake up, handsome." I sat the tray down on the coffee table. "Pistol!" I gently shook him, and his eyes fluttered open.

"Mornin'." He frowned as he tried to sit up.

"Take it easy." Once he was sitting upright, I picked up the tray and put it on his lap. "Eat this."

He looked up at me. "Thanks, baby girl. I'm starvin'."

"Well, you did lose a lot of blood. I cleaned everything up. When you're done eatin', I have to clean your wound again and change the gauze."

He nodded. "A'ight. Uh, thanks for last night."

"You don't have to thank me, Pistol."

I turned and went back to the kitchen to fix my plate. By the time I got back, his plate was empty and the television was on.

"That was good," he said before gulping the water down.

"You want more?"

He smiled and then winced as he stood up. "Nah. I'm good. If I eat more, I'm gonna just go back to sleep." With a chuckle, he rubbed his belly. "I'm gonna go take a shower, and then you can change the gauze and shit. I need to get out there and find out if that nigga's still alive. There gotta be a way for me to get to his ass if he is. It ain't like I got a crew out here, and I don't really know if I wanna involve Mike and Dank."

"Do they know that you went after Rae last night?"

"Nah. I didn't tell them shit."

I nodded. "Okay, well, just be careful. Like I said, that bitch Capri'll shoot too."

He shook his head. "They definitely won't catch a nigga slippin' this time. I gotta go get a car too. If you see all the holes in that mu'fucka . . ."

With that said, he walked off to take his shower, and I said grace before eating my food. The sound of the television was merely background noise. All I could think about was the fact that Pistol seemed consumed with the thought of getting Rae. I thought it would be best if he took it easy for the day, but I knew that he wasn't trying to hear that.

That still didn't stop me from making up my mind about it. I'd have to talk to him. In my opinion, it was too soon for him to go anywhere. I also felt he should be in tip-top shape when he did go after Rae, as I was sure that Rae was even more prepared after the shoot-out they'd had last night. Whether he or Capri did the shooting, Rae had to know that Pistol was after him. Even if he didn't know who Pistol was, he knew that it was somebody. Rae was a punk-ass nigga who wouldn't fight a man straight up but would beat on a woman. Of course he was going to shoot first and ask questions never.

When Pistol walked back in the living room, his swag was back on in full effect. I had to smile about that, because shit could've really gone left the night before. I cleaned his wound, which looked a lot better already, put a new piece of gauze over it, and then taped it.

"Uh, can you sit down and talk to me for a second before you . . . leave?" I asked when I was done with the wound care. I plopped down on the sofa and patted the spot next to me.

"Yeah. What's up, beautiful?" He sat down beside me on the sofa and then kissed me on the cheek.

"I think you should chill for now. It's like you're obsessed with killing Rae. You need to let me take care of you until you're good. Then go out there and continue where you left off." My eyes were anxious as I looked over at him pleadingly.

"I'm sorry, Ma, but I can't waste any time. I know you'd rather I stay here and lay low, but I can't. I gotta get back out there and find out what's goin' on. One li'l bullet ain't stop no show. I ain't no weak nigga."

I rolled my eyes at his hardheadedness. "It's not that you're weak, but you are human. I bet your mama can't even tell you nothing."

He chuckled good-naturedly. "Nope. I need you to relax and let me handle shit. You don't need to worry 'bout me. I'm gon' be fine. . . ."

"You said that last night but came back up in here literally bleeding to death," I reminded him.

"I got this. Okay? Besides, that shit wasn't that bad."

"Okay." I nodded. "But promise me you won't go after Rae and you'll just get information for now. That's the least you can do for me, since you won't go to a hospital."

"Mike is outside. He's gonna take me to get a car. Somebody will be here to tow the other car a little later." He reached in his pocket and pulled out a huge wad of money that was wrapped with a rubber band. He held it out to me. "Go get your hair and nails done. Get a massage or whatever. Just don't worry your pretty little head about me."

"What you tryin'a say? I need my hair done?"

"No," he laughed. "I love your curls, but I'd love to see your hair straight."

"Promise me that you won't go after Rae tonight, and I'll get it straightened."

Pistol sighed. "I'm just gonna get a car, get some info, and then I'll be back. Okay?"

"Promise."

"I promise."

That pacified me for the moment, so I leaned over and kissed his lips before grabbing the money. Neither of us brought up my rant from the night before or the moment when he laid his head on my breasts. It was just clear to us both that we had no control over what we were feeling for each other. I was having a hard time with it, but I was willing to take a chance on Pistol. My heart was constantly proving that I really had no choice.

Something had told me not to go the hair salon that I always went to, to get my hair done, but I didn't want anybody other than Tonia to do my hair. That bitch knew exactly how to stretch out my naturally curly ringlets so that my hair flowed down my back. Not only that, but she was actually cool. We'd hung out plenty of times in the past, but I couldn't really call her a friend. The catch was, she did Kevia's hair too.

I was so glad that my bruises were finally clearing up, and with the help of the makeup Pistol had bought for me, I was able to cover up what was left of them. Tonia didn't even notice them when I walked in.

"Hey, girl! Where the hell have you been?" she squealed as she hugged me tightly.

I winced, because my body was still a little sore. "I've been around. Workin' and tryin'a maintain. What you been up to?" I kept a smile on my face, because I wasn't one to let folks all up in my business.

I may have been through hell and back, but I was thankful that I didn't look like what I'd been through. Despite the marks and bruises, I was still a beautiful being. Rae had tried to break me and beat me down, but he hadn't succeeded. As long as I had life in me, I was capable of changing my circumstances. I was determined to move on and not let my past keep affecting me.

"You already know." She smiled. "Same thing. Work and takin' care of those twins of mine. They're gettin' so damn grown."

Tonia had seven-year-old twin daughters, Faith and Hope. They were so cute but were mature way beyond their years. I think that was because she worked so much and left them with her fifteen-year-old sister. Teenagers these days were probably the worst people to choose to babysit. With social media and all the temptations out there, kids exposed to them couldn't help but do what they were influenced to do.

"Stop. The twins are adorable, and they're so smart."

Tonia beamed proudly. "You're right. What you tryin'a get done today?"

"Girl, I want you to straighten this shit."

She popped some gum loudly as she nodded. The salon was packed, so the sound of house music playing and chatter was the norm. "Okay. You need a deep-conditioning treatment too and your ends clipped. You're slippin', honey." Tonia shook her head at me.

She was right, but she just didn't know what I had been going through. I played it off. "Like I said, girl, I been working and shit."

"I feel you, but I think it's that nigga you been fuckin' wit' that's takin' up all your time. What's his name . . . ?"

"I ain't wit' him no more."

"Oh, dang, okay."

The silence between us was awkward as she led me to the shampoo bowls in the back. I knew that getting my hair done was a bad idea. All I could do was hope that Tonia would get me in and out, and that there would be no more talk about my ex. When Tonia shampooed me and massaged my scalp, I felt so relaxed. I even drifted off to sleep for a few minutes.

"C'mon, boo. You gotta get under the dryer. I got your conditioner in." Tonia's voice made me open my eyes.

"Okay," I said just as I spotted Kevia at the front of the salon.

Damn, I knew I should've taken my ass to the Dominican salon I went to when Tonia wasn't available. If that bitch Kevia spotted me, there was going to be some shit. See, I wasn't scared or nothing, but I didn't want any drama. I knew that she was still holding a grudge about me pulling that gun out on her. What did she expect, though? She'd betrayed me.

"You good?" Tonia asked as she pulled the dryer's hood down over my head.

I nodded. "Mmm-hmm. I'm straight."

It was whatever. If that bitch spotted me, there was just going to be some shit going down.

Chapter 14

Pistol

"Nigga, you won't believe what the fuck I just heard while I was waitin' for your ass to come out," Mike said before I could even sit down good in the passenger seat of his car.

"What, man?" I tried not to show any sign that I'd been shot the night before, but that shit was still painful.

"One of the niggas that was in that BMW when you killed G is named Rae and shit. His baby mama got killed last night by some nigga. She'd noticed that somebody was lurking outside her house, and she was paranoid 'cause of what had happened to G. That ho went outside buckin', 'cause they found her in the yard, wit' a strap beside her body and shit. That's crazy as fuck," he explained.

Damn. So I'd killed his girl. Daisha was right. She did ride for that nigga, and she'd died for him too. *Fuck*. Well, at least nobody had connected G's murder to us. Of course, at that point, nobody knew that I'd shot that bitch, either.

"Uh, damn. Wish they'd killed that nigga instead."
Fuck!

"Shit. Damn right, man. That nigga Rae is reckless wit' his mouth and shit. Ain't no tellin' who was gunnin' for his ass."

"So, who told you 'bout that shit? I mean, it ain't like you run wit' G's niggas or nothing."

Mike glanced at me and then lit a cigarette. He cracked his car window because he knew that I hated the way that shit smelled. "Man, you know how the streets be. Shit gets around. One of my li'l shawties told me."

I nodded and then changed the subject. "Where's Dank?"

Damn, I had to rethink my strategy for getting to that nigga Rae. Now that his son's mom was dead, he'd be caught up in his feelings, trying to avenge her murder. Maybe I'd catch his bitch ass slipping.

"That's nigga's at the trap, handlin' business. We gettin' off that shit from that lick fast, man. Shit. Ain't nothin' like straight profit."

"How's your li'l one, man?"

I was concerned about my little cousin and how she was adjusting after what had happened to her. Mike was going on like that shit hadn't even happened. What did his baby mama have to say about that nigga G? None of that shit had even come up.

"Oh, she's a'ight, considerin' what she been through and shit. Her mama's all torn up 'bout that nigga, but she'll get over him, just like she got over me."

"Hmm. You right 'bout that, yo. I just hope li'l cuz can get over it."

Mike didn't say anything as he nodded his head to some incomprehensible shit that was playing on the radio. It sounded like that nigga Future. I liked trap music because I could relate to that lifestyle, but half of those niggas who rapped weren't really spitting no real shit.

Mike spoke up after the song on the radio ended. "So, what happened to your whip, man? I saw your windows all busted out and shit. Another one of the bitches you fuckin' done snapped?"

"Oh, nah, man. I was in an accident last night."

"Damn, my nigga. What happened, yo? Glad you good."

"Yeah, I'm straight. Some mu'fucka crashed right into the back of me on I-twenty, my nigga. I wanted to stop and shoot that fool, but I kept going and shit."

"That's fucked up, man. It's all good. My nigga Charlie gon' take care of you. I ain't like that old Chevy, anyway. You need some hot shit."

"Nah, man. That's the last thing I need." I didn't want to call any unnecessary attention to myself.

"Yeah, I forgot. You a nigga who like to stay under the radar. Me, on the other hand, I'm a flashy-ass nigga." He let out an arrogant cackle as he pulled into the car lot.

An hour later I drove off the lot with another old-school box Chevy, with Mike's car in my rearview mirror. This one was indigo blue instead of black. Mike had shaken his head at me when his boy passed me the keys.

"I'm a simple man," I'd said with a smile.

I loved old-school rides. That was my shit. On the way to the car lot, Mike had convinced me to roll to his spot for a few. Dank had just left the trap and wanted to cook on Mike's grill, smoke something, and have a few drinks. It was cool with me since Daisha was out getting dolled up. Earlier, I'd tried to call and check up on her, but she wasn't answering. I'd sent her a text telling her to let me know when she was on her way to the crib.

I arrived at Mike's place while he was parking in his driveway, and I pulled up behind him and got out.

"Damn, nigga. You usually have some pussy on deck, but I ain't heard you talkin' 'bout no bitches lately," Mike said when we walked up the driveway of his two-story brick house.

"Shit, nigga, bitches are the last thing on my mind since that shit happened wit' Niya. I'm 'bout gettin' them dollars."

"I feel you," Mike said as he pulled out his key to unlock the front door.

We stepped inside and then headed straight to the sliding-glass door that led out to the patio. Dank had already fired up the grill and was about to throw some steaks on that bitch. My mouth watered just thinking about it.

"'Sup, Dank?" I greeted him.

He looked up at me with a Bud Light in his hand. "Sup, cuzzo? You want a beer?"

"Hell yeah," I replied.

He reached in a cooler, grabbed a beer, and passed it to me. "The bitches are on the way," Dank announced.

"Oh, hell yeah," Mike said with a smile.

I wasn't really in the mood to be surrounded by chickenheads. One thing I knew about my cousins was that they liked the same type of bitches I had once been into. Those ratchet-ass broads who didn't know the first thing about being domestic, had no ambition, worshipped the Kardashians and Beyoncé, loved to post pictures on Instagram, were saving up for butt shots, and constantly twerked for attention.

For some reason, that shit had been appealing to me at first. Maybe that was because I hadn't wanted to commit. My attraction to that type of woman had only been my way of avoiding something serious. If I'd always gone after women like Daisha, I probably would've fallen in love a long time ago.

"Is that ho Rain comin'?" Mike asked Dank.

"Hell yeah. She wanna fuck you bad as hell, Pistol. That's all that ho talk about." Dank laughed as he put the top of the grill down.

"Who the fuck is Rain?" I asked. That name wasn't familiar to me.

"That ho that was tryin'a fuck you the first night you came over here. You remember that ho, nigga. She's a redbone with a short Halle Berry cut and shit. Her ass is fat as hell, but shawty's breath be funky than a mu'fucka." Mike laughed and lit up another stinky-ass cigarette.

I remembered exactly who they were talking about. It needed to rain in that bitch's mouth, because it smelled like she'd sucked several dicks right before licking several assholes. The bitch was fine, but that shit only got a bitch so far when she couldn't even breathe around a nigga.

That ho needed to stop breathing all together, and when I fucked with a chick, I needed her to be alive and well.

"I wish you'd quit them mu'fuckas, and I ain't tryin'a fuck that yuck-mouth, dragon-breath bitch. Y'all can go on wit' that shit. I ain't impressed by that ho's fat ass. That shit's just more funk to add to her breath. You know if she don't brush her teeth, she don't wash her ass."

Dank and Mike fell out in a fit of laughter.

"You one funny-ass nigga. Shit, I'd bend that thick bitch over and push her guts through her mouth," Mike stated.

"Shit, I'd fuck that bitch and hold my fuckin' breath. She can suck a dick. That's why her mouth smell like that. That ho be lettin' niggas bust in her mouth twenty-four-seven," Dank added for good measure.

"Well, if she sucked your dick, that explains her stankin'-ass mouth," I joked.

Mike pounded me up, while Dank pretended to be mad.

"Good one, my nigga," Mike said.

"That's fucked up, cuz," Dank asserted.

"You know I'm fuckin' wit' you," I said. I had to smooth it over since that nigga was cooking. "I just want my steak before that broad gets here. I don't want her breathin' over my food."

We all laughed again as I rolled up a much-needed blunt full of that strong-ass gas.

Two hours later, there was a bunch of people over at Mike's house, enjoying the free food, alcohol, and weed. The niggas were hooting and hollering, enjoying the sight of half-naked bitches who were glad to flaunt and pop it for a so-called real nigga. Me, though, I wasn't impressed. Instead, I was wondering why the hell Daisha still wasn't answering her damn phone.

"Damn. Why you bein' all antisocial and shit?" That chick Rain was all up in my face once again as I sat in a chair on the patio.

I was trying my best not to cuss her out, but she was fucking annoying me. That ho had been trying to get me to talk to her ever since she arrived, but I had been ignoring the hell out of her ass. Why didn't she get the damn point?

"I ain't antisocial, yo. I just don't wanna socialize wit' you. You been in here this whole time rubbin' your ass on every nigga in this room. What the fuck you think we got to talk about?" I stood up and pulled out my cell phone to call Daisha again.

"Oh, so you all that, huh?" She was still all up in my personal space and shit. It was clear that she was drunk and probably fucked up on some other shit, like Molly. Her body movements were all erratic and shit as she lunged at me.

"Somebody better come get this ho 'fore I punch her in her funky-ass mouth," I yelled.

Next thing I knew, there was chaos. Old girl started throwing whatever she could get her hands on at me. Why was she mad because I didn't want to fuck with her?

"Fuck wrong wit' you, Ma? You ain't gotta be actin' like that 'cause I don't want you to suck my dick. I'm good on that," I said firmly.

Two chicks who must've been her homegirls were holding her back as she went off. "Fuck you, nigga! I would've turned you out, anyway! Ain't nah bitch got shit on me!" Veins were sticking out on her neck as they led her out the front door.

All I could do was shake my head. What the hell was wrong with the women I'd been in contact with lately? They all seemed to be losing their minds. It was time for me to go. I was high as hell, and I was nice and full. I had my ride and the information I needed. And the spot was getting even more crowded, so that was my cue to leave. I also had to find out what the hell was going on with Daisha. Had she run off again?

"I'm 'bout to head on out," I told Mike and Dank.

"Word, my nigga? Damn. We got some strippers on the way. They get down and dirty too," Mike said.

They had no clue about Daisha and the fact that I wasn't interested in any woman other than her. I decided to leave them in the dark about it.

"I'm good on that. I seen enough strippers to last me a damn lifetime."

"Word. Well, do you, my nigga. I'm gon' watch them bitches pussy pop, and then I'm gon' pop some pussy!" Mike laughed and slapped me five.

I pretended to be impressed, but I wasn't. Fuck what he was talking about. The only thing on my mind was Daisha. Had that nigga Rae tracked her down? Maybe he thought she had something to do with his son's mom getting murdered. That shit made my heart drop.

"A'ight, nigga. I'm gone," I said.

I pounded Dank up and headed out the front door to my car. There was a sinking feeling in my chest, and something told me that shit just wasn't right. Something was in the air, and I had no idea what it was or what it meant. The only thing I knew was that shit couldn't be good.

Chapter 15

Daisha

Being that I wasn't in the mood for drama, I realized that I should've followed my first instinct. It wasn't the usual day that Kevia got her hair done, so I hadn't expected to see her here. She was talking to Tonia while I sat under the hooded dryer, trying to remain incognito.

When I saw Tonia look in my direction, with a smile on her face, I knew that incognito shit was in vain. Shit, I should've known better. Tonia had been doing our hair for years and knew that we were supposed to be best friends. The thing was, at that moment, I didn't know what was going to go down. Then I thought about the fact that G was dead. I had no clue what mood Kevia would be in.

Kevia wore a scowl as she walked in my direction. My guard went up immediately, and I was prepared for whatever. Her last words to me were, "This shit ain't over," so if I had to whup that ho's ass, then so be it. It wasn't like she had her big, bad brother G to hide behind anymore. She couldn't whup my ass, anyway. We'd fought plenty of times over the years. That was when we were younger, though. Kevia was a little taller and a lot thicker than me. That didn't matter, though. In my eyes, the bigger they were, the harder they'd fall.

Kevia sat down at the empty dryer beside me. I just stared at that bitch like she'd lost her mind. What the hell was she trying to prove, anyway?

I read her lips as she attempted to apologize. "I'm so sorry 'bout what happened, Punkin. Rae's crazy as fuck. I know that he don't give a fuck 'bout nobody but himself now. The nigga got mad 'cause I didn't get you to stick around to talk to him, and slapped me in my damn face."

I lifted the dryer up so I could hear her better.

She continued. "I know you put that gun to my head because you were afraid of what Rae would do. I know you wasn't gonna shoot me. I was just mad at the time. Rae told me he was gonna kill you, but that was after he convinced me to get you to talk to him. I'm glad I ran into you. You're my best friend, and I never meant to put my fucked-up-ass cousin before you. Please accept my apology."

Staring into her eyes, I couldn't tell if she was sincere or not. It wasn't like she had a good track record lately. There was absolutely nothing that made me feel that I could trust her. Although she had had no clue that I was getting my hair done today, what if she called Rae and told him that I was there? Would he come and act a fool in front of all those people? *Hmm.* Knowing him, probably so.

"I accept your apology, Kevia, but I still don't trust you. What if you're really helpin' that asshole?"

She shook her head. "Well, I'm not." Tears filled her eyes. "You know, my brother got killed the other day. Both of my brothers are gone now."

My heart sank for her. "I'm so sorry, Kevia." Although I knew that Pistol had done it, I couldn't give away what I knew.

"I need you more than ever, Daisha."

She sobbed, and I ended up hugging her. It wasn't what I'd expected, but damn, what was I supposed to do?

Once she had pulled herself together, she wiped her eyes and shook her head. "His funeral is day after tomorrow, if you wanna come."

I nodded and swallowed hard. "You know I want to be there to support you, but I can't."

"Damn, yeah, I get it. Rae's gonna be there."
She sighed and shook her head. "It's fucked up,
though, 'cause Capri got killed last night."

"What?" I was shocked. Did Pistol know?

"Damn, bitch. Where you been? Under a rock?
Everybody been talkin' 'bout that shit. Some
nigga wit' a black Chevy was stalkin' her and shit.
She had called Rae to tell him that somebody
was outside, and she thought it was related to
G's murder. Of course, you know he told her
to stay put, but she went outside and started
shooting. Bullets were everywhere, and she had
a shot to the head. It was obvious what went
down. RJ was in the house when it happened.
Good thing he slept through it, though, which is
unbelievable. Rae found her." Kevia shook her
head. "I didn't like that bitch, but that shit's still
fucked up."

"She was the one who left her house to go shoot
at somebody. Maybe she should've listened to
Rae."

Kevia shook her head at me. "You really hated
that ho, didn't you?"

"It's not that. Forget it."

"Look, I'm 'bout to go. I just came in to talk
to Tonia 'bout doin' me and Mom's hair for
the funeral. I would've just called, but I was
at the Kroger across the street. To be honest,

I'm glad it worked out this way, so we could talk. Maybe we can . . . get together soon. You good? You got somewhere to stay?"

I nodded. "Yeah, I'm good. I'll call you."

She stood up. "Okay." The she turned and walked toward the door.

My nerves were bad, because I didn't know if she had really been genuine or not. What if she'd lied about Rae to get me back in her good graces? I wouldn't be surprised at anything Kevia did. Honestly, I think she'd been cordial only because we were in a crowded hair salon. That bitch hadn't wanted to cause a scene and have Tonia on her bad side. Especially since she needed Tonia to get her and her mom right for her brother's funeral.

My tresses were bouncy and shiny by the time I left the hair salon. I'd also gotten my fingernails and toenails done. It was good to know that Kevia hadn't sold me out that time. The short talk I'd had with her had been on my mind, but then I'd decided to brush it off for the time being. I would just have to get to the bottom of her agenda later. My phone had died while I was at the salon, and I was anxious to get in my car and plug it in so that I could call Pistol. I knew that he was probably worried about me.

A few minutes later I was situated in my car, so I dialed Pistol, and he answered before the first ring could finish.

"Hey, you good, Ma?"

That greeting surprised the hell out of me. "Yeah. My phone died. Sorry."

He let out an audible sigh of relief.

Wow, I thought. Was he that worried? I felt bad and good at the same time. *Damn.* Somebody really gave a fuck about me.

"I'm just glad that you're okay. There's so much goin' on," he said.

"I know, right? Did you know that it was Capri who—"

He cut me off. "Mike told me. That shit is crazy, 'cause that's not what the fuck I expected. I thought it was that nigga."

"That bitch got what she deserved."

"We'll talk when you get here. Just be safe. Okay?"

"Okay. I'm on my way. I'll be there in a li'l while." I kind of wanted to stop at Massage Envy to get a massage, but I had decided against it.

With the volatile shit that was going on, I didn't want to chance running into anybody else I knew, especially Rae. I'd blocked his number, but he'd sent me several nasty text messages. Over the past few days he'd sent me plenty of threatening messages on Facebook. I hadn't mentioned any of it to Pistol, because I knew that he was already pissed off enough.

I pulled up at the house and parked beside what I assumed was Pistol's new whip. It looked a lot like the previous one, but it was blue instead of black. The classic look of the old-school ride told me a lot about him. He was an old soul, and I thought I liked that about him. That shit was kind of intriguing. I also liked the fact that he had no filter. He said what was on his mind, and I loved his honesty.

Then I thought about it. Why hadn't he got a different car? This one looked too much like his old one, and Rae would be looking for a dark-colored Chevy like his. Pistol had to be extra careful when he went after Rae the next time.

Pistol had given me the house key that Niya had made, so I used it to get in. At first I had thought about knocking, but what was the point? He knew that he'd given me a key and that I was on my way there. Besides, what if he was taking a shit or something?

Pistol was sitting on the sofa, smoking a blunt, when I entered the living room. The smell had greeted me at the door, so I knew what was up. When he looked up at me, his eyes widened.

"Wow," he mouthed, but no sound came out. "I mean, I love the curls, but damn, you look like a different woman." This time his words were loud and clear. He grinned and flashed those white teeth. That nigga was too damn sexy for his own good. It was like that shit was criminal.

"In a good way?" I asked as I patted my head and sat down beside him.

He passed me the blunt and ran his fingers through my hair before smelling it. "Yes, baby, in a good way. It's so damn soft and smells so good."

I smiled. "That's the shampoo you like. I made sure she used it."

"Do you have some of that shampoo?" he asked, looking over at me.

After taking a hit and blowing smoke out of my nose, I said, "Yup. I bought some. It's called Moroccanoil."

"Good, 'cause I wanna smell that before I go to sleep and when I wake up in the mornin'."

I read a lot into those words, and my heartbeat increased. Was he saying that he wanted to be with me on a permanent basis? That shit was so heavy that I didn't bother to ask for clarification. Maybe I was reading more into his words than what he really meant.

"Well," I said as I passed him the blunt, "I have a serious question for you."

"What's that?" His stare was so intense that it sent chills all over me.

"If you wanna be careful about goin' after Rae, why would you get a car so much like the one you had? I talked to Kevia today. I saw her at the hair salon. She mentioned that Capri had called Rae to tell him that a black Chevy was outside her house. If he knows that G and Mike were beefin' and he suspects something, he may put two and two together if he sees your car. Just promise me that you'll be careful when you go after him. I'm sure that since G and Capri were murdered, he's gonna want blood."

"Shit, I want blood too, but it's like I just can't get to that nigga. I can't get Mike and Dank involved. I'm just gonna have to go to Bankhead and blast that nigga on his own territory."

"What? By yourself?" I was terrified at the notion. "You can't do that."

The Bankhead Mob was deep, and Pistol didn't have even a small crew. Why the hell was he being so damn reckless?

"I can and I will," he stated stubbornly.

At that point, I was angry. "You underestimate shit, and I don't like that. Are you that damn arrogant, Pistol? Do you think you're fuckin' immortal because you survived three gunshot wounds? What the fuck is your problem? Do you have a death wish?"

He shook his head and took a pull from the blunt before saying calmly, "No, I don't think I'm immortal. Yeah, I'm arrogant. I'm also grateful that I'm still here after three gunshot wounds. I don't have a problem, and I don't have a death wish. All I want is for you to be safe. That's all this is about. I don't want you to think I feel like I'm doin' you a favor. Shit, I'm doin' this for us. It's the least I can do until I can change my situation, so let me do it. Okay?" He was stern when he said this, and so it shut me up.

I shrugged my shoulders. "Okay. Do you, then, Superman."

"A'ight, Wonder Woman." He leaned over and kissed me passionately.

His tongue tasted like Kush, and I sucked it and got just as high as I would have off that blunt.

"Mmm," he moaned into my mouth and then tried to remove my shirt.

I grabbed his hand to stop him. "Wait . . ."

He froze. "Oh damn. My bad. No more sexual stuff? I thought we had got past that."

With a cute little smile, I flirted with him. "We are past that. I just want to go . . . uh . . . freshen up a little."

"Oh." There was a sly grin on his face. "Okay, Ma. Do you. I'll be right here waitin'."

"Okay." I got up and headed to the master suite.

It was hot outside, and the cooch had been sweating. I had to take a quick shower and put on some of the sexy underwear that Pistol had got me from Victoria's Secret. He'd confessed later that he'd checked my pants, shirts, and underwear to get my sizes. That shit was so fucking thoughtful. My heart fluttered as I considered this, letting me know that my feelings for Pistol were getting deeper.

Right after I stepped into the master suite, my phone vibrated in my back pocket. I'd almost forgot that it was there. I pulled it out and looked at the screen and saw that it was Kevia calling. Something told me to answer, although I really didn't want to. I was anxious to get back to Pistol.

"Hello," I said into the phone.

"Hey, girl. Guess what the fuck just went down?"

"What?" I asked, not playing into her guessing game. If anything, I wanted her ass to get to the point, so that I could get some dick.

"The damn po-po done came to the hood deep as hell to pick Rae up. They had already questioned him about Capri's murder, but they just came through again to get him. I think he's a suspect and shit. They handcuffed him and all."

"Do you think he did it?" I asked, playing it off.

"My cousin got some shit wit' him, and I won't really put nothin' past him, but I know he didn't do it. He was wit' Rock that night. I didn't tell Rock about him slappin' me, so they still cool, as usual. I know my nigga would go ham on his ass, so I didn't say shit. He just knows not to do that fuck shit again."

"So, y'all gon' give him an alibi?"

I was hoping that nigga would get locked up for life. That would keep Pistol from having to risk his life by trying to get to him. The mere idea of this was like a weight had been lifted from my shoulders.

"It's the truth. Rock said they were at Dugan's, watchin' the game. He got receipts and all to prove it, and they go there all the time, so the waitress can vouch for him. He my cousin, yo. I ain't got much family left."

I sighed. "So after all the shit he's done, you're still protectin' him?"

"Are you serious right now, Punkin? Damn. I'm protectin' him from something I know he didn't do!" She sounded pissed off.

"Look, you messin' up my vibe for real. I really don't wanna talk about Rae. You don't really know if he did it or not. Just 'cause Rock said he was wit' him don't mean that he was. I gotta go. I'll call you later."

"Yeah, whatever," Kevia said in a frustrated voice before she hung up the phone.

Taking a deep breath, I went into the master bath, put a shower cap on, and removed my clothes. At least Rae was out of the way . . . for now. The way it looked, he was going to get out of that shit. If his alibi stuck, he was going to be back on the streets in no time.

I turned the shower on and tested the temperature of the water before stepping in. Then stood under the showerhead. The water pressure was strong, and the spray felt so good as it kneaded away my stress. I wanted Rae out of the way, but I didn't want anything to happen to Pistol in the process.

My body overheated, despite what I'd just heard. All I wanted was for Pistol to take over my body again and make me forget everything. At that moment I decided not to tell him about what Kevia had just told me. I was going to get all sexy and entice that sexy motherfucka, who was waiting for me in the other room. It was more pressing that I relieve some pent-up tension and not worry about Rae or any of the chaos that was surrounding me. My mind and body were both in need of getting lost in seduction and the bliss of lovemaking. I'd tell Pistol all about that shit with Rae later.

Chapter 16

Pistol

Boy, when Daisha walked in the room, I almost lost all my good sense. Honey had put on that sexy-ass purple negligee from Victoria's Secret. It was all lacy and tight, and it showed off all her curves. Her ass cheeks peeked out sexily from her thong underwear. Ma was thick, and although her body wasn't all perfectly tight, it was perfectly right for me. All I wanted to do was grab her and hold on to her thick ass while I dug deep inside of her.

"Mmm, mmm, mmm." I just shook my head, at a loss for words.

She motioned for me to come to her, and I did. Shit, I was happy to. When I was in front of her, I dropped to my knees. I was at her mercy. I'd do anything for the sexy goddess who stood before me. Before Daisha, I'd performed oral sex on a couple of chicks whom I was feeling a little more than others. But when I did that shit to her, it was different. It was like I was ravenous with it. Her pussy just tasted so good, and I loved how wet and gushy she felt afterward.

My tongue traveled up her leg, and I inhaled the sweet scent of her pussy. I could also sense her arousal. It was definitely something that attracted me to her more than to the average woman. That was the chemistry of it. Sometimes when you put two people together, it was just a natural thing.

"Pistol . . . ," she whispered.

I stood up and pulled her to me. Our lips joined, and then our tongues did a sensual dance. Hers tasted so sweet, but I wanted to taste something else. I wanted to ignite every square inch of her brown-sugar skin with my tongue until she couldn't take any more. Then I was going to bury my nine inches so deep inside of her goodness until we both exploded into bits and pieces of ecstasy. *Damn.* Li'l mama had me thinking poetic, erotic thoughts and shit.

I removed the sexy lingerie from her body ever so slowly, enjoying my own personal little peep show. The way her skin glowed beneath the lights made every nerve ending in my body stand at attention. It was good to see her natural coloring coming back. The bruises were finally going away. I'd been gentle with her at my uncle's, but now that she was healing up, maybe we could go a little harder. Shit, the way she'd walked up on me, I was ready to get freaky.

We didn't have any music on or anything, and there was no talking going on between us. Only pure, unadulterated nastiness was about to go down up in that bitch.

"Shit!" Daisha gasped once I'd laid her down on the sofa and taken her hard clit into my warm, wet mouth.

"I been wantin' to taste your sweetness, baby. Talkin' 'bout no sexual stuff. Shit. This here is my pussy," I said between slurps, sucks, and licks.

That pussy was flowing like a river in no time.

"Oh . . . fuck . . . Pistol!" She grabbed the back of my head and started humping my face.

I loved that shit, and I stared her down, challenging her not to cum yet.

Her eyes were vulnerable as hell as she looked up at me in longing. Baby girl wanted that nut, and she wanted it bad.

"Fingers, baby . . . fingers," she moaned, grabbing my hand. "Mmm . . . shit . . . It feels so good, I can't breathe."

I gently pushed my pointer and middle fingers inside of her. That pussy snapped around them tightly. In no time she had her thighs around my head and her whole body was shaking.

"Fuck! I'm cumin'! Yes . . . fuck . . . yes! Pistol . . . mmm . . . ahhh . . . ohhh . . . shit!"

I didn't let up, though. A nigga kept right on eating that pussy until tears started running down her cheeks and juice was all over my sofa. *The wetter, the better*, I thought. The thought of how tight, warm, and gushy that shit was about to be had my heart thumping against my rib cage.

"You good, Ma?" I grabbed a condom from the pocket of my jeans and then quickly removed my clothes.

"Yes," she said breathlessly.

She'd replaced my fingers with her own, and I watched attentively as she played with her pussy. The way that shit looked, sounded, and smelled had me gone. My dick was so damn hard, and I was hoping that once I was in that good shit, I wouldn't nut all fast.

Her soft hands were all over my back, massaging and squeezing, as I pushed my way inside.

"Ohhh . . ." She bit her bottom lip.

She felt so fucking good, I had to close my eyes. "Am I hurtin' you?" I asked, hoping that I was not, as I leaned over to taste her succulent lips.

That pussy was so tight and wet that I had to do something with my mouth so I wouldn't be moaning like a li'l bitch. My eyes rolled back in pleasure. The warmth and the way that pussy sucked me in and clenched me like a vacuum seal was that shit. It was like that thang was made just for a nigga.

"No . . . It feels good, baby. Mmm . . ."

I grabbed her ankles and went deep. As I long stroked those sweet walls, she stared up at me in awe.

"Ohhh . . . shit . . . ," she whispered. Baby girl started pulling back, but I held on to that ass.

"You ain't goin' nowhere. Gimme that pussy. Damn, Ma."

I didn't beat it up, but I ground up in that pussy with those long, deep strokes. She threw that shit right back at me, like she was saying, "Nigga, what?" She'd been running from it at first, but then she made a comeback. By the end of the first round, though, I had her when I flipped her over on her stomach.

"Put that ass up in the air," I demanded, then slapped those cheeks and went back in.

"Oh, shit!" she screamed as I climbed all up in those guts from the back. "Damn, Pistol! Ahhh . . . fuck!"

A nigga was standing up in that shit, trying hard not to bust. My balls were tingling, and her pussy kept right on squeezing the hell out of my dick. Not only that, but the wet sounds were so loud. Then add the fact that her thick ass looked so good as it bounced and jiggled while my dick moved in and out of her fat pussy. My eyes stayed on that shit as she wound her waist and twerked that ass. I watched in amazement as her glistening pussy lips gripped the shit out of my dick.

My hands were all over her ass cheeks, caressing and massaging. My nut was rising, and I tried to defy it, but I couldn't.

"I'm cumin'!" she yelled, to my relief. "Fuck . . . Pistol! Ahhh, mmm. Yes! Oh my God! You workin' that good-ass dick, nigga! Damn!"

That pussy opened up even more, and I slid even deeper inside, causing my nut to rise quicker than I had thought it would. Her strong-ass pussy muscles were milking my shit, and I was holding on to her waist for dear life.

"Argh . . . fuck! Damn, Ma. Uhhh . . . shit!" My body trembled and jerked as her muscles continued to massage my shit.

Smaller tingles continued to rise to the head of my dick, and it was like I was still nutting. Damn, that shit was fucking stupendous. *Shit*.

I slowly pulled out, and it was like her pussy didn't want to let me go. That tight shit was still clasping my dick and made a popping noise once my dick head was out. I wanted to sleep in it, but I had to throw away the condom. We weren't quite at that level yet.

"That was so fuckin' good . . . ," she said. Her breathing was all hard as she turned over on her back.

"Damn. That was better than good, Ma." I stood up, and my knees were weak as hell.

"I need to change your gauze again. All that work made you bleed through."

She followed me to the bathroom and cleaned my wound. The delicate way she took care of me was so nurturing, and it made me think of how my mom was when I was a kid. Once she was done, I turned around and we kissed.

"You're the only woman I've ever kissed like that," I told her when we finally came up for air.

"Like what? For a long time or . . ."

"Tongue. I never tongue kissed before you," I confessed.

She looked at me like she didn't believe it. "Yeah, right. You're too damn good at that shit." Her expression changed once she saw the look in my eyes. "Are you serious?"

"Dead ass," I confirmed. "I told you. You just do something to me."

"Damn. I must bring out the best in you, 'cause all these firsts of yours are very impressive."

I pulled her naked frame to me and squeezed those fat ass cheeks. "I love this fat li'l ass of yours. You are so fuckin' sexy." It was like I couldn't help just squeezing her tight.

Damn it. It was clear that I was falling in love with Daisha. The feeling was so foreign that I didn't recognize it at all. It had to be that, because the nut was over, but I still wanted her around. I never wanted a day to go by that I didn't see her face. I inhaled the sweet scent of her hair again.

"You ready for round two?" I grinned down at her, and she shook her head.

"Pistol! Wake yo' ass up!"

I woke up to Daisha standing over me. When my eyes focused on her good, I noticed that she was holding my cell phone in her hand.

"What? What you doin' wit' my phone, yo?" I knew that she could be a little emotionally unstable, but was she on some crazy shit? "You goin' through my phone?"

She turned on the lamp on the nightstand and rolled her eyes. "No, I wasn't goin' through your phone. That shit wouldn't stop ringin' and vibratin' and shit. I'd grabbed it to give it to you, and a text from some bitch named Kendra popped up on the screen. She wants you to come over and pick up where you two left off the other night, 'cause she got a babysitter tonight. Are you fuckin' her? 'Cause I ain't got time for this shit. I just killed one bitch and—"

"It ain't what you think it is, Daisha." I sighed as I rubbed the sleep from my eyes.

"What the fuck is it, then? You were clearly just fuckin' some bitch, and you fucked me, what? A day after that?"

"Look, it was the night after that shit popped off wit' you and old boy. It was before I thought there would be anything between us. You ran off on me, remember? I had met Kendra 'bout two weeks ago, and it was supposed to just be a fuck thing. She was suckin' my dick and shit when her baby started cryin'. I left, and that was the last time I saw her or talked to her. We didn't fuck, and now that me and you are doin' our thing, I ain't tryin'a fuck her. Calm down. Shit. It's four in the mornin'."

"That's my point. The ho's been blowin' your phone up since three. You need to let her know that you ain't interested no more. I ain't got time for no more drama than we're already dealin' with. For real."

She was looking at me like she meant business, and so I did what she asked. It wasn't like I was trying to play her. Honestly, I had never expected Kendra to try to contact me again after that night. I started to send her a text, but Daisha shook her head.

"Nope. Call that bitch. She needs to hear your voice," she demanded, with her hands on her hips.

I pressed the button to call Kendra and didn't have to wait long for her to answer. She must've been anxious to taste this dick again. The thought almost made me smile, but I didn't. I wasn't trying to get on bae's bad side. She seemed to be a little bit feisty at times, and I didn't want her to punish me by taking that good pussy away from a nigga. *Fuck Kendra.*

"So, you comin' over or what?" Kendra asked, popping some gum all loud in my ear.

Who chewed gum at four in the morning? Only some thot-ass bitch who was up trying to find some dick because she finally had a babysitter. Knowing her, she got some random person to watch her child just so we could finish our fuck session. What she didn't realize was, I didn't tell her that shit would be continued. I was done with it.

"Nah yo. I'm gon' keep it straight up wit' you, shawty. What we did was what we did, and that's it. It's over wit'. To be honest wit' you, I'm wit' somebody, and we tryin'a work on something. You should focus on your shawty and shit. Ain't no need to check for me no mo'."

"Nigga, fuck you! You just one dick in my call log. As far as my shawty's concerned, don't worry 'bout her. She's well taken care of!" With that said, she hung up in my ear.

I almost laughed out loud at her ignorant-sounding ass, but all I did was shake my head. Daisha sat down beside me on the bed and kissed me softly on the cheek.

"Sorry to wake you up wit' the bullshit. Seein' some bitch send you some shit like that just fired me up. I got something I really need to tell you. Uh, Kevia called me and filled me in on something when you were asleep."

I looked at her and covered my mouth as I yawned. "What's goin' on now?"

"The police got Rae. They think he killed Capri."

"Ah shit. Yeah, her baby daddy would be the first suspect. They ain't got shit on him, though, so they can't hold him. It'll buy me some time, though."

"Yeah, 'cause Kevia said he was wit' her boy-friend during the time of the murder, so he got an alibi. He'll be out soon. Hopefully, you'll have time to come up wit' some other strategy other than goin' to Bankhead to go after him."

"Oh, I'm gon' come up wit' something. I just hope they release that nigga."

Shit. I didn't know anybody in Atlanta other than my cousins and the dope boys who trapped with them. Maybe, just maybe, I could get some inside information on Rae and how the Bank-head Mob moved without raising any suspicions. Then, by the time the police let him go, I'd be there waiting to dead his bitch ass.

"Mario. Just the nigga I was hopin' I'd see," I called through my car window.

That tall, lanky, dark-skinned nigga walked over to my car and pounded me up. I was pur-posely avoiding my cousins, although I was on the block, looking for this nigga. He was Mike's right-hand and was obviously just refreshing a few of the corner boys' product.

"My nigga Pistol. What's good, man? You look high as fuck!" He laughed and then checked something on his cell phone.

"Life is good, man, and I am high as fuck. There ain't no other way to be. You know I ain't from round here, but I'm tryin'a be on some moneymakin' shit. I gotta know what moves to make. My cousins were tellin' me 'bout this nigga Rae who fucks wit' the Bankhead Mob and shit. Now, I don't fuck wit' dope, but I wanna come up on a nice li'l lick. If you help me wit' some intel on that nigga, I'll be glad to give you a cut. I mean, I know you be in the streets more than Mike and Dank, so you'll know more."

See, I was looking for Mario because that nigga had diarrhea of the mouth. He didn't know how to hold shit in and was always ready to prove that he knew something that you didn't. Niggas like him were the worst niggas to have in your crew. They'd do and say anything, and it wasn't just for the money. It was because running their mouths like a bitch made them feel important.

That nigga leaned into my car as he looked around. Then, his voice lowered, he said, "Shit. Your cousins would know more than me. They fuck wit' that nigga Rae when it come to they coke supply. You didn't know they killed that nigga G for Rae? He was the leader of the Bankhead Mob and shit."

What the fuck? Did that nigga just say what the fuck I thought he said?

"What, my nigga?" I said.

"Rae approached them niggas and told them that he wanted to take over the Bankhead Mob, but he needed somebody to kill G for him. He knew that Mike and that nigga G had beef. Of course, Rae couldn't do it himself, 'cause then he'd look like a traitor. Which the fuck he is. Mike and Dank was down to do it 'cause Rae promised he'd let them have some of the Bankhead Mob's territory. Not only that, but he paid them niggas top dollar to do the hit. Them niggas gon' double they profit now 'cause Rae 'bout to be on top. Well, if he don't go to the pen for killin' that bitch. Mike just said this mornin' that if that nigga go to prison for that shit, he gon' try to take over Bankhead his damn self."

Steam was coming out of my ears, and my blood was so hot, it felt like acid was running through my veins. So, my own cousins had played me. They didn't want to include me in their moneymaking scheme. I guessed they didn't want to have to split that shit three ways. That nigga G had never touched Mike's daughter. Why the fuck had he lied to me, and why such a twisted-ass lie at that? I guessed that nigga knew that I'd keep that shit under wraps because it was such a delicate subject. Maybe he knew that was the way to get me to do his dirty work. So, Mike and Dank didn't think they could just tell me the truth about the hit. Then they had the nerve to take the credit for it around Mario. Them niggas didn't want to give me any of the money for the hit. Those fuck niggas.

Then that nigga Rae had just sat there in the car at the cemetery, like he didn't know what was about to go down with his cousin. All those niggas were disloyal-ass traitors. The niggas I'd grown up with had fucked me in the ass raw, with no K-Y Jelly. It felt like that shit with Flex was happening to me all over again. Shit, I was surrounded by snakes and rats. Obviously, Mike's intel had been Rae the whole time. He was probably the one who had called Rae to tell him that his baby mama had been killed. Rae also had to know that I'd done the hit. It was clear that Rae didn't know that I was the same nigga who had intervened between him and Daisha that night. Then I wondered if he suspected that it was my car that was outside his baby mama's house. He'd seen my black Chevy at the cemetery.

"Hmm. Well, damn, man. I 'ppreciate the info," I said.

"No problem, man. I don't like that nigga Rae, anyway," Mario revealed, still leaning into my car. "He got this pretty-ass girlfriend. She work down there at the Blue Flame. That nigga treat her like shit. He treat all his chicks like shit, and he got a lot of bitches. I believe he killed his baby mama. If he get out, kill that nigga and take him for everything he got. Fuck nigga."

I nodded, knowing that Mario was referring to Daisha. "Yeah, man. I'm 'bout to go holla at my cousins. I'll see you around, man."

"A'ight. Be easy, my nigga."

"Oh, and don't tell my cousins what we talked about."

"Already." He stood up straight and watched as I peeled off.

I was mad as pure fire as I grabbed my strap and tucked it in the waistband of my jeans. Shit, there were no words that could express my anger. I'd grown up with Mike and Dank, and to think that they'd cross me like that. . . . The only thing I could think about was the fact that my next hit might have to be on my own blood, and not on that fugazzi-ass nigga Rae. That shit had my mind in a zone that a killer like me knew was dangerous. Shit, as I pressed the gas, all I saw was red. Blood, to Mike and Dank, wasn't thick worth a fuck.

Chapter 17

Pistol

My hand landed on the horn of my car, and it let off a long harsh honk.

"Fuck! Move yo' shit, muthafucka!" I yelled out of the window in frustration.

The fact that some fool wanted to pull in front of me and just sit there only fueled my already hostile-ass mood. The light had turned green, and I was just mere seconds away from getting to the bottom of the bullshit my cousins had pulled. I didn't have time for patience, so I honked the horn again. That time I didn't stop until the driver of the truck started moving.

"Thank you. Damn!"

But by the time my foot touched the gas, I heard the sound of sirens behind me, and then I saw flashing lights. My heart immediately fell to the bottom of my feet as I glanced in the rearview mirror. I was hoping he was passing me, but that pig motherfucker was on my ass. Something told me to make a run for it, but the road was narrow and that slow-ass truck was still in front of me. *Shit.* I had nowhere to go.

According to the driver's license that I had, my name was Darren Hardy. Darren was my homeboy who had died five years ago in a freak accident with a four-wheeler. Gas had leaked from his car after the truck hit him, and he'd been smoking a cigarette while sitting in his car. He'd gotten out of the car after the accident, and when he'd thrown the still lit butt on the ground, it ignited a flame and his pant leg caught on fire. As he tried to stamp out the flames, he fell and hit his head on the ground. Because of that, he couldn't get away from the fire. Nobody else was out there with him, and by the time I got to where he was, it was too late. I had always blamed myself for that shit, because I hadn't been able to save him.

As I sat there waiting for the officer to get out of the patrol car, it felt like I was being engulfed by fiery flames too. It wasn't like I had been speeding or had done anything illegal. I had just been sitting there in one damn spot. But the pit of hell seemed to be swallowing me up, nonetheless, and for the first time since I didn't know when, I closed my eyes and said a silent prayer.

When I opened my eyes, I saw in my rearview mirror that the officer had emerged from his patrol car. *Damn it.* It was a white cop. *Shit. Just my fucking luck. Could a nigga catch a break?* He was young, though, so hopefully, he was a Democrat, I thought. Maybe he was an Obama supporter and had some type of sympathy for the plight of the black man. *Shit.* Then again, he could be an overzealous cop who wanted to slaughter a black man right there in the middle of the street.

The officer walked slowly to my car, with a stride that let me know that he was in no hurry. Sweat started to gather on my forehead, although the air conditioner was on full blast. A voice told me to make a run for it. I had an intense urge to just get out of the car and try to make it on foot. Then I thought about the possibility of having a shoot-out with a cop. Damn if I needed that heat. I'd just have to take my chances. As long as he had no probable cause, he couldn't search me or my car.

I hadn't been smoking, and there weren't any drugs in my shit. All I had was a gun on me, and I had hid it under my seat. When I saw him standing there at my window, I slowly slid it down.

"Yes, Officer?" I said, greeting him politely, trying my best not to rub him the wrong way.

"License and registration please." His narrow gray eyes were on me as I reached in the glove compartment.

After that, I went in my pocket for my wallet. I passed him the license and registration and waited for him to let me know why he'd stopped me instead of the asshole who was holding up traffic in front of me.

"Your taillight is out. Looks like it's cracked. Did you know that?" He sounded like some hillbilly-ass cracker to me.

"No, sir. I, uh, I just got this car, so . . ."

He nodded. "I'll be back."

The pulsating beat of my heart was audible to my own ears. Why the hell hadn't I checked every fucking square inch of this damn car? *Shit!* I watched as he made his way back to his cruiser to check and see if I had any warrants. Of course, I didn't. Well, Darren didn't.

For what seemed like an eternity, I sat there biting down on my bottom lip until I tasted blood. Finally, the officer was back out of his car, and I would soon learn my fate. If there was anything good working in my favor, he'd let me go and I wouldn't have to do anything stupid, like shoot his ass.

"You're free to go, Mr. Hardy. Get that taillight fixed."

"Will do," I said as he passed me the registration and license.

A female voice came from his walkie-talkie. "One-eight-seven on Wesley Chapel Road . . ."

He pressed a button to respond. "En route."

Without saying another word, he rushed off to his patrol car, and I got my ass on.

Shit. I had just been on Wesley Chapel. There had just been a murder there? *Shit.* I wondered what the fuck had happened. That was where Mike and Dank served, but when I'd checked the trap spot earlier, they weren't there. I was heading to their crib when the slow-ass truck held me up and then the damn cop. It was a good thing I had got out of that shit with the cop. Maybe my luck wasn't so bad, after all.

Less than fifteen minutes later, I pulled up to Mike and Dank's crib in Decatur. There weren't any cars parked in the driveway, so I wondered if they were home. There was a chance that they'd parked in the garage: maybe they wanted it to look like they weren't there. I turned the car off and got out. Dank was walking outside just as I was going up the steps.

"Cuz." He stopped in his tracks.

As mad as I was, I decided to play it cool. "'Sup? Where Mike at?"

"He ain't here. I'm on my way out. Gotta go to the trap and—"

"You shouldn't do that, man. I just got stopped for a busted taillight and heard over the cop's walkie-talkie that there's been a murder over there. It's hot as fuck by now."

"Damn." Dank shook his head and pulled out his cell phone. I was sure that he was about to call Mike. While he dialed the phone, all I could do was stand there and pretend like everything was copacetic. It was best if I had both of those niggas there together, so I could get it out of the way all at once.

Dank frowned. "That nigga ain't answerin'."

Well, he wasn't at the spot a few minutes ago, so I was sure he was good. The thing was, I needed his bitch ass to show up soon, so I could get that shit over with.

The sound of a car stereo's vibrating bass in the distance let me know that somebody was about to either pass by or pull up. It was Mike. His tired skidded as he pulled up fast in the driveway, like he was running from something. He was going too damn fast so close to home. Something had rattled his lying ass. Once he hit the brakes and put the car in park, he jumped out like his ass was on fire. When he saw me, he looked surprised.

Dank spoke up first. "Why the fuck you didn't answer yo' phone, man? What's goin' on, on Wesley Chapel?"

Looking daze, Mike ignored the questions, headed up the driveway, used his key to open the front door, and walked inside. Dank and I followed him.

"I had to pop Mario," Mike said, finally filling us in.

What the fuck? That nigga had killed Mario? His so-called right-hand man? Not to mention the fact that I'd just got some very shocking information from Mario.

"Why?" Dank asked, with a frown on his face.

I wanted to know that shit too.

"I went to the trap to pick up the cash, and he popped up. We got into it and shit. That nigga pulled his strap out on me first. I had to shoot him."

His explanation was vague, and I wasn't buying it. "So, that shit *just* happened? What y'all get into it for?" I quizzed him, testing how quick he was on his toes. He must've got to the trap right after I left. It was going to be Mike's story against Mario's, but I wanted to see how far Mike would take his.

"He was runnin' his mouth 'bout shit he ain't know about. He told me you was askin' 'bout Rae and shit."

"Oh really? Did he tell you that he told me everything? Is that why you killed that nigga? Did he tell me too much? Huh?" I questioned.

Before he could even blink or take a breath, I had the barrel of my strap pointed at his temple. "Tell me why you lied to me, nigga!"

Dank was freaking out behind me. "What's goin' on, cuz? Put the gun down, yo! What the fuck is this shit all about?"

My hand was around Mike's neck now, and I was choking him. I turned the gun on Dank.

"Shut the fuck up, nigga! Now that mu'fucka's on you! What you gon' do while I choke your brother out? Huh? You gon' do something?" My eyes challenged Dank, and he backed down, with his hands up.

"What the fuck is this all about, man?" Dank's eyes were full of fear, because he knew that when I pulled a gun out on a nigga, I intended to use it.

"I know about everything, and that's why you killed Mario, ain't it?" My attention was back on Mike now.

Something told me that Dank really had no idea what was going on, but on second thought, I wasn't so sure. From my experience with snake-ass niggas, I just didn't know. From what I could tell, blood didn't mean shit.

Mike's eyes were bloodshot red as he shook his head. "No . . . I . . . I . . . killed him 'cause he's a lyin' mu'fucka. Let me go, man, so . . . so . . . I can explain." His voice was strained as I squeezed his windpipe.

Against my better judgment, I released that nigga's neck. He started coughing and tried his best to breathe.

"Get beside this mu'fucka, Dank," I ordered. "I don't want you out of my sight. I don't trust y'all mu'fuckas as far as I can throw you!" My eyebrows formed a straight line as I scowled at them.

"Look . . ." Dank held his hands out. "Calm down, cuz, and—"

"Don't fuckin' 'cuz' me! That's some fuckin' bullshit! Mario told me y'all niggas planned to kill G wit' that nigga Rae. I know that y'all told Mario y'all killed him and Rae paid you to do it. Not only that, but you did that shit so Rae could take over the Bankhead Mob. You want some of their territory. That nigga didn't do shit to Mikayla. You made that bullshit up to get me to do your dirty work, 'cause you didn't want them Bankhead Mob niggas to come after your punk asses."

I went on. "What? You didn't wanna cut me in on that shit? That's how you do your own fuckin' blood? You already know what the fuck I'm facin'. Talkin' 'bout blood is thicker than water! I see that's some bullshit! The fact that we blood ain't stop y'all niggas from bein' disloyal than a mu'fucka! I guess you rather them niggas come after me! What the fuck did I get out of the deal, huh? I thought I was protectin' my li'l cousin, but I was just helpin' y'all fuck niggas expand your damn territory! I should shoot both you lyin'-ass motherfuckas right now!"

"Hold up!" Dank yelled and looked at his brother. "I'm usually the one who be doin' shady-ass shit, but you ain't even let me in on this one, bro. You told me that nigga touched Kayla. What the fuck, man? You and Rae were in on that shit together? He paid you? I ain't know shit 'bout that shit, Pistol. Straight the fuck up, cuz." He shook his head as he looked me in the eye.

I believed that Dank was in the dark about everything. It was obvious by the way he'd reacted, and his facial expression told it all. He was pissed off, just like I was. Clearly, that nigga Mike had left us both out of his plan.

"Fuck! If y'all would just shut the fuck up and listen," Mike pleaded. "Can you get that gun out my face, man?"

Shaking my head defiantly, I said, "Hell nah. If you wanna talk, now's the time, but I ain't puttin' my fuckin' strap down."

"That nigga Mario made all that shit up, man. He was fishin' for information to see what you knew. He'd been tryin'a get shit out of me since G got killed. It's like he'd been all paranoid for a long time. Mario was not the real-ass nigga you may think he was. Shit. I found that shit out a long time ago. I just didn't think he'd take that shit so fuckin' far. Everything he told you is a fuckin' lie. That nigga was all paranoid and kept comin' up wit' all types of conspiracy theories to explain G's murder. He kept sayin' I was gon' take over Bankhead and I was in cahoots wit' that nigga Rae. A year ago I bought some coke from Rae, and then my baby mama started fuckin' G. It was a one-time thing. I don't fuck wit' Rae, and we ain't plan to kill that nigga to take over shit. If Rae wanted to take over the Bankhead Mob, I damn sure wasn't in on that shit."

Mike continued. "That nigga Mario had all that shit in his head. He thought that I was on some next-level shit and that my plan was to leave him behind. He was talkin' all crazy. I told y'all the fuckin' truth from the jump. Shit! Y'all been knowin' me all my life. It ain't like me to come up wit' some crazy-ass scheme and leave y'all out of it. Mario was on a power trip, and that nigga had a damn head injury from a bullet he got hit wit' a few years back. Can't believe a mu'fuckin' thing that came out of his mouth. He had to go, and I don't even see how you could believe that nigga over me in the first fuckin' place."

What he was saying made sense in a way, but Mario was dead. There was no way to get his side of the story. I couldn't get those two niggas in one spot and interrogate them both to figure out the truth. All I had to go on was my gut, and my gut told me that I couldn't trust my own damn cousin. The only thing about that was, my instincts hadn't been that reliable lately. What if I killed my cousin for nothing? What if I left him alive, he crossed me, and I ended up losing my life or my freedom?

"You been on some fuck shit since I got here, Mike. I don't know what to think," I said. "You got me and your brother standin' here like, 'What the fuck, man?' Why would Mario sit back and make all that shit up? Huh? What he told me actually makes a hell of a lot more sense than what the fuck you sayin' right now. Make me believe you, nigga, or get merked, *fam*." I smirked at him, and he shook his head.

"Hear me out, cuz. I can prove it." His eyes were on mine, but his were empty.

"Yeah, nigga. Prove it." Because I damn sure didn't know what the fuck to believe.

After what I'd been through, giving out trust was like handing over a rare jewel. Once upon a time, I thought I could trust everyone in my family, but now it was clear that I couldn't. I was still on the fence about Dank, but the look in his eyes let me know that he was just as confused as me.

Chapter 18

Daisha

The smoke from the blunt I'd just fired up settled in my lungs, and I felt an immediate rush. Damn, Pistol had some good-ass weed. There I was, sitting on the sofa with his laptop in my lap, searching for a job. I'd vowed that this would be the last time I smoked weed. I was going to clean my system out and do what I'd set my mind to do. Nothing was going to stop me from pursuing my goals this time, not even Rae.

My phone rang, and I looked down at the screen. It was Megan, the chick who had done my makeup, so I answered.

"Hello."

"Daisha, hey. It's Megan."

"What's up, Megan? How're you?"

"I'm good. Off work today. I was just callin' to ask you about your date the other night."

If only she knew that there was so much more going on in my life. She knew about my abusive ex, but not about all the drama that was going on with me and Pistol in our effort to get rid of his ass for good.

"It was great. We had a good time." All that good, nasty sex we'd had came to mind.

"Good. I've been so busy, but I also wanted to ask you if you wanted to go out to get a couple of drinks with me. There's a nice spot in Buckhead I want to hit up tonight. You said you don't fuck with chicks like that, and neither do I. I figured, why not go together?" she said, sounding all convincing.

"Okay. What time? You want me to meet you there?"

Since I was so used to being with a controlling man, my instincts told me to call Pistol to let him know I would be going out for drinks. Then I thought about it. I was a grown-ass woman, and I could do what the hell I wanted to do.

"Uh, yeah, but it's still early. I gotta make a few runs, but I'll hit you up in about an hour with the address. I'm thinking you can meet me there at about ten. Is that cool?"

I checked the time, and it was only a little after seven. "Yeah, that's perfect. Gives me enough time to get ready."

"Okay. Great. I'll talk to you soon."

"Okay."

We hung up, and I went back to smoking and looking for employment. Something still told me to call Pistol, despite the fact that I didn't need his permission to go out. The shit that was going on with Rae and Kevia was what made me decide to tell Pistol my plans. Atlanta wasn't that damn big, as evidenced by the fact that Pistol had killed G and hadn't known that he was connected to me or Rae. What if I ran into that fool? I had no clue if the police had released him.

After pressing the button on my phone to call Pistol, I waited as his phone rang. My call went to voice mail, and I hung up. Something just didn't feel right, but I didn't want to panic. Maybe he was just busy at the moment. It wasn't like I could keep tabs on a grown-ass man. He'd had his life before I met him, so I decided to relax.

"Office manager at a premier upscale salon and spa located in Buckhead, Atlanta. Looking for a professional who is well spoken and has the ability to organize and help expand clientele. If you have office experience and are computer savvy and outgoing, please call . . . ," I read out loud, I stopped when I saw the phone number.

It was a hair salon, so I figured that they were still open. I dialed the number.

"Beauty Land of Oz. How can I help you?" a pleasant male voice answered.

"Good evening. My name is Daisha Bailey, and I'm calling in reference to the office manager position."

"Hmm. Well, don't you think it's kind of late in the day to be inquiring about a job?"

I was taken aback by his question. "Honestly, no. I don't think it's ever too late to go after what you want," I replied. "I figured you were still open, so why not take my chances? What's the worst that could happen?"

He chuckled. "I like you already. My name is Ozzy, and I'm the owner. How soon can you come in for an interview?"

"Anytime is fine with me," I said anxiously.

"Okay. Will eleven o' clock on Tuesday work for you?"

"Yes, that's perfect."

It was Friday, so that gave me enough time to get prepared.

"Great. See you then."

"Yes. Thank you."

"No problem, Daisha."

I hung up with a huge smile on my face. It was like shit was finally falling into place as far as my job prospects were concerned. When I thought about my potential love life with Pistol, it was bittersweet. Then I thought about everything else in the atmosphere that was going wrong, and my smile faded.

Shit. I needed a damn drink and some positive, drama-free company.

It was a little after 2:00 a.m. when I got back to the house after having drinks with Megan at the Suite Lounge in Buckhead. I had had a good time with Megan and was now tipsy as hell. Pistol had attempted to call me when I was at the Suite Lounge, but it was so loud that I'd had to send him a text. I had let him know that I was just getting a couple of drinks with Megan and I'd be there soon. He hadn't responded, so I figured that something was wrong.

I found him in the living room when I walked through the door. "Hey. How was your day, babe?" I asked him after I kissed his cheek and sat down on the sofa beside him. "Why're you sittin' in the dark? What's going on?"

He looked over at me as I leaned over to turn on the lamp. The look in his hazel eyes let me know for a fact that something was up. His aura also seemed off to me, and I could tell that his cool-as-a-cucumber demeanor was out the door. There was some shit that was really bothering him.

"Ma, we need to talk." His voice was calm, but he sounded funny to me. I couldn't figure out what it was, but there was definitely a red flag waving. "We 'bout to take a li'l road trip, Ma. We'll be gone only for a few days, though. I need to regroup. I don't know if I can trust my own damn family."

My eyes widened. Was he talking about his cousins? I listened as he continued to let me in on what some dude named Mario, who was cool with Mike, had told him. Then he explained how he had gone to confront his cousins about that shit and had found out that Mike had killed Mario. That was after a cop had stopped him for a busted taillight. He said that, just like him, Dank hadn't seemed to not know what was going on, and that Mike had claimed to have proof that Mario was full of shit. Then he stopped there, leaving me in suspense about the situation.

"Okay, so what proof does Mike have?" I needed to know that shit. Adrenaline was rushing through my veins, and I wanted some clarity.

Shit, if his own cousin had betrayed him, that was fucked up. It really wasn't surprising to me, though. Rae had always been jealous of G, and his greed had made me think he'd do anything to be on top. I didn't know Pistol's cousins, though. It was hard to believe that his own blood would lie and use him in that way. Then I thought about how my mother had done me, and suddenly, anything seemed possible. Just because you shared the same bloodline as another person didn't mean that they were loyal. That had been evident in my life. However, I also knew that anything could happen.

"Here're the screenshots Mike sent to me." He tilted his phone so I could read the text messages that Mike had forwarded.

Mario: I heard 'bout what happened to G. You was in on that shit, wasn't you?

Mike: Hell no, nigga. Where you get that shit from?

Mario: I know y'all niggas beefin' over old girl, and I know that you wanna take over the BHM.

Mike: I don't even know what the fuck you talkin' 'bout.

Mario: Yeah, right. I know what the fuck you up to. I heard 'bout how Rae wanna be on top. I know you do business with that nigga.

Mike: That was so damn long ago. You know I don't fuck with him like that. We'll talk face-to-face. This ain't the time.

Mario: I'll find out the truth, nigga. Shit don't ever stay a secret for long. Your cousin's here, and now you wanna replace me.

Mike: Whateva.

Mario: I been a loyal nigga to you for years, man. It's fucked up that you makin' plans without me.

Mike: Ain't nobody makin' no plans without you, nigga. WTF? You act like I'm yo' bitch or something.

Mario: Nah, nigga. You carryin' me like I'm yo' bitch.

I didn't know what to make of the texts, but it seemed like Mario was paranoid about Mike doing a takeover of the BHM, the Bankhead Mob, without him. It was also clear that Mario had seen Pistol's presence as a threat.

"Mike claimed that nigga Mario was just fishin' for information from me," Pistol said. "After we talked, Mario went to the trap spot, and he and Mike had a confrontation. He said that nigga pulled his strap out and was all in his feelings about Mike supposedly makin' big moves without him."

I shook my head. "What do you think?"

"That's the thing. I don't know what the fuck to think. I wanna believe my fam, but shit. Blood don't mean shit when it comes to money, for real."

I sighed. "Shit's crazy, but . . . that's the street life for you, Pistol. You know that."

"Yeah, I do. It's just . . . I don't know how to feel right now. I just need to go where I can think, and I can't do that shit here."

I understood that. "So, what you tryin'a do?"

"I just need some sleep, and then we'll talk about that."

"What?" I looked at him and shook my head. "*You* need sleep?"

He didn't respond to that. Instead, he went into how his cousin Mike had tried to prove that G had really molested his daughter.

"That nigga even called Mikayla and told her to tell me what she'd told him about Mommy's boyfriend." He sighed and rubbed the top of his head. "She said that he touched her on her private parts. Mike wasn't coaching her. Well, at least not then. It's hard to believe that he'd get his daughter to lie about something like that. Still, I don't know what to think. It took every-thing in me not to kill my folks, but I couldn't do it. I just couldn't let hearsay make me do that shit. Now that nigga Mario ain't even here to back up his own damn story."

As I rubbed his back, I had to let him know that I was there for him. "I know why you're confused right now, babe. It's easy to be mad at your own family, but it's hard to actually get revenge against them. I know. Shit, I've plotted so many times on how to get back at my moms, but I just can't bring myself to do it."

Pistol looked at me and then laid his head on my shoulder. "I don't even wanna talk about that shit, Ma. When I said that I needed sleep, I really didn't mean actually sleeping."

A sly grin spread across his face, and I shivered. Next thing I knew, he scooped me up in his arms and carried me to the bedroom. His warm, soft lips covered mine, and we kissed with more intensity than ever. It was surprising to me that he was in the mood, being that he was going through so much.

"Uh . . . babe?"

"Yes?" he whispered against my lips.

"You're squeezin' me too tight."

He laughed and loosened his grip on my waist. "Sorry. You just feel so good, Ma. You my stress reliever."

"Aw," I crooned as he gently laid me down on the bed.

"Mmm. Damn, Ma. That was exactly what I needed," Pistol told me an hour later. He slapped my ass and then jumped up to flush the condom.

I waited for him to come out of the bathroom before I went in to wash up. When I returned to the bedroom, he was lying on the bed, smoking a blunt, and had a snack waiting for me. He must've known that I had worked up an appetite from that good-ass sex.

I sat down next to him. "My favorite." I grinned at him and picked up the bowl of tortilla chips. He'd poured salsa in a smaller bowl.

He smiled back. "I figured you'd want something to munch on."

"Well, you figured right," I said, literally gushing at him. "I guess you really do pay attention to detail."

"I told you." He passed me the blunt and then dipped a tortilla chip in the salsa before putting it in his mouth.

Most men I'd dealt with didn't care what my favorite snack was. Pistol didn't even ask me most things. He just knew because he paid attention to what I did. That nigga took notes, and it made me feel like he really gave a fuck about me and how I felt. I'd even noticed that when we had sex, he seemed to just know my body. He had noticed what I liked the first few times, and so there was no question in his mind about how to make me cum.

"Damn. Why didn't we meet years ago?" I wondered out loud after I hit the blunt.

"Like you said before, this is our time. Years ago it wasn't."

After hitting the blunt again, I passed it back to him because I wanted to eat. I looked and saw that he'd put a glass of juice on the nightstand.

"Ain't no alcohol in that, is there?" I'd had enough to drink.

"Nah. I figured you had enough to drink."

"See? Right again." I shook my head.

He chuckled and put his arm around me, then pulled me in closer to him. His nose was in my hair now, and I could feel his breath as he inhaled and then exhaled. "Now I'm all the way good."

I settled into his body and got comfortable. We continued to talk and smoke as I snacked. When the chips and salsa were gone, I felt nice and satisfied. Looking over at Pistol, I noticed that he was knocked out. I leaned over, kissed his cheek, and then got up to take the dishes to the kitchen.

Suddenly, an uneasy feeling washed over me. I tried to ignore it. Maybe it was just anxiety kicking in over the fact that I had no clue where Pistol and I were going. I also didn't know what was going to happen. Rae posed a threat to us, and we didn't know for sure if Pistol's cousins did too.

Chapter 19

Pistol

A nigga was up by 5:00 a.m., packing up some things for me and Daisha. She was still sound asleep, and I was enjoying the sweet melody of her breathing. The sight of her chest moving up and down with the vitality of life was promising to me. As long as I kept her alive, I would have a heart. If anything happened to her, I wouldn't be the same. That I knew for sure. So, I had to make certain that she was safe.

That shit with my cousins was still weighing heavily on my mind. Mike had been blowing my phone up all night, but I had been ignoring that nigga's calls. I knew that he was just checking to see if we were all good. The fact was, we weren't. . ... Just because I had put my gun in my waistband and had walked up out of their spot didn't mean that shit was over. Not by any means. I just needed some time to think and get some clarity on what had really happened.

The fact was, that nigga Rae probably didn't know who I was. Even if Mario had told the truth and Rae had got Mike to get G merked, there was a chance that he still didn't know who I was. Something told me that he wouldn't recognize me from the shit with Daisha or with G. Maybe I'd be able to get away with getting the information straight from the horse's mouth. I was hoping that he'd be released from police custody soon. First, I needed to take a trip somewhere. It was very important that I did.

I checked my phone and saw that Dank had been calling me too. He'd even sent me a text message, which I didn't bother to check. Those niggas could wait. Shit, I had other things to do.

"Wake up, baby. We gotta get ready to go." I gently shook Daisha, and she moaned and groaned, with a frown on her face.

That made me smile. Baby girl loved to sleep.

"C'mon, babe. Get up. You can sleep in the car." I leaned over and softly kissed her ear before whispering, "I'll eat your pussy."

Her eyes were wide open now. "Okay." The smile she wore was big as hell, too, as she stared up at me.

"I figured that would get you up," I said and chuckled.

When we got outside a little over an hour later, I noticed that Dank's charcoal-gray Dodge Challenger was parked beside my ride. I glanced over at Daisha and held my car keys out to her.

"Go wait for me in the car, Ma," I told her.

"Who's that?" she quizzed as she took the keys from my hand.

I sighed. "Dank."

"Oh," she simply said and then walked off.

I had put our bags in the trunk a few minutes ago and was ready to peel out. What could that nigga possibly want? As I walked over to his car, I checked that my strap was where it needed to be. It was right there in the waist of my jeans, just in case that nigga Dank was up to no good. There was a chance that he was playing that shit off to help Mike.

"'Sup, man?" I asked, giving him a look to let him know that his timing was all wrong.

"I see you on your way out, but since you wasn't answerin' your phone, I figured I'd just come on over here."

All I did was nod. *Shit*. That was part of the reason why I wanted to leave for a couple of days. I'd even emptied my safe, because I didn't trust niggas. Something had told me they'd be on that pop-up shit, and I wasn't trying to be there. Not only did I want to get away to think, but I also didn't want to be bothered by Dank or Mike for a while. I didn't need them in my ears, trying to convince me of shit. At least not until I knew the truth. That shit had to be deciphered by me. I wasn't easily influenced. Instead, I investigated shit, weighed the facts, and drew my conclusions from there. The verdict wasn't in on those niggas yet. Not even on Dank's ass.

"Yeah, I'm on my way out. So what's up?" He had to know that I wasn't in the mood for that pop-up shit.

His eyes were on Daisha. He was probably trying to figure out if he'd seen her before, but I needed him to get back to the subject at hand. What the fuck was he at my spot for at seven in the morning?

"Who's shawty?" he asked. "You ain't said shit 'bout her, man."

"Uh, I think why you are over here so early is more important right now, man. What the fuck's up?"

"Oh shit. I came through to let you know that Mike's in the hospital and shit."

Had that nigga been shot too? Given how the streets were set up, it was a possibility. Shit, he'd just killed Mario. What if some inside bullshit was going down? That was why I didn't really fuck with a bunch of niggas or get down with a big crew. You could never really trust that niggas wouldn't turn on you.

"Did he get shot?" I asked.

"Nah, man. I found that nigga in the middle of the street in front of the crib, all broke up and shit. Somebody ran him over right there in the road. He's at Grady. They stabilized him, but he's unconscious. He's fucked up, man. They got that nigga in ICU. . . ."

"Who ran over him?"

"That's the thing, man. I don't fuckin' know."

"Is that nigga Rae still locked up?"

"As far as I know, he is."

I sighed, not knowing how to feel. Shit was getting more and more chaotic by the minute. As much as I had wanted to kill that nigga earlier, my animosity wasn't too deep at the moment. I needed more information, but this nigga here had none.

"That's fucked up, but you know I can't go to the hospital. Keep me posted, though, man," I said.

"Right, right. A'ight, man. I just hope bro pull through."

I spit on the driveway. "Yeah. Holla at me."

Walking toward my whip, I wondered who had done that shit to Mike. What bullshit was that nigga really involved in? I couldn't figure

out why somebody would try to run him over
with a car. Normally, niggas didn't handle street
shit like that. That shit was up close and personal. Most hood niggas handled street beef
with a few bullets.

Once I was behind the wheel, that nigga Dank
drove off.

"Everything straight?" Daisha's eyes were
searching mine.

"Somebody tried to kill Mike."

The way Daisha's eyes lit up when she realized where we were made me feel good as hell.
All I could do was smile at her, and that was off
the wall, since shit was chaotic as hell back in
Atlanta. The peace and serenity of the ocean was
a welcome distraction. Well, that and Daisha's
beautiful face.

"I always wanted to come here," she said, beam-
ing, before she jumped out of the car.

"You've never been to Myrtle Beach?" I asked
as I stepped out of the car.

I'd surprised my mother a couple of years
ago with a nice spot right there on the beach in
South Carolina, but she visited only from time
to time. It was a two-story, cottage-style beach
bungalow that sat right there on the oceanfront.
I whipped the house key out of my pocket.

"How many hideaways do you have?" She grinned at me as her hair whipped in the wind. "Shit, if I was you, I would've just come here instead of Atlanta."

"Then I wouldn't have met you."

"True," she agreed as she blushed.

I passed her the key and told her to unlock the door and go inside while I grabbed our bags. When I walked inside, she was giving herself the grand tour. The way she was oohing and aahing about everything was so cute. Her carefree spirit was one of the things I loved about her the most. She didn't hold herself back or act all reserved and shit.

"So you like the place?" I asked as I put our bags down on the floor.

"Oh my God. I love it. I didn't think anything could top your uncle's spot. We have to go get me a bathing suit. I can't wait to go on the beach."

"Okay. We gon' do that, but can I chill first, Ma?"

She put her hands on her hips. "I saw a gazillion shops on the strip. Gimme the keys. I ain't tired."

I reached in my pocket to retrieve my car keys. "Hurry back. I got plans for you."

"Yeah, yeah," she said.

I lay down on the sofa while she got ready to go. I was drifting off to sleep by the time I heard the door close.

About an hour later I awoke from my nap and saw that Daisha hadn't returned yet from shopping. I was a little concerned so I called her, but she didn't answer her phone. I tried two more times, but still no answer. When she finally burst through the door half an hour later and dropped her shopping bags, I grabbed her and kissed her deeply.

"Um, hey to you too," she said, smiling, after I finally pulled away.

"I was worried. . . ."

"Why, babe? We ain't in Atlanta. Rae and them ain't here."

I sighed. "I know. It's just . . . I'm an overprotective-ass nigga."

"No worries, babe. I got a few bathing suits, and I got you something too." She reached in one of the bags and pulled out a little red Speedo.

"Um, who the fuck is that shit s'posed to be for?" There was a smirk on my face.

"You." She giggled as she held it up.

"Nah, Ma. That ain't gon' happen."

She gave me a sly look as she laughed harder. "I'll suck your dick from the back if you wear it."

Suddenly, she was serious, and I was too. I'd never had a bitch suck my dick from the back before. At first I was curious, but that was just a little too close to a nigga's ass. I held her in my arms and gave her another kiss before I started removing her clothes.

"How 'bout I eat yo' sweet-ass pussy from the back?" I suggested.

"So, does that mean that you don't want me to suck—"

I covered her lips with mine. As much as I loved her head, the desire to taste her was overwhelming.

"How 'bout we please each other at the same time?" I said when the kiss was over.

She looked up at me and nodded. "Hell yeah. Sixty-nine. Let's see who taps out first."

I laughed. "Okay. So what will happen to the one who taps out first?"

"Uh, the one who taps out first will have to be the only one who performs oral sex for a week. No reciprocation whatsoever." She smiled slyly as she gave me the terms.

I shrugged my shoulders. "Sounds good to me. Shit, head for a week without having to serve you sounds like a plan. Although I love the way your pussy tastes."

Daisha playfully shoved me in the chest as she laughed. "Oh, okay. You act like you know you gon' win. Don't underestimate my skills, nigga. I was holding back on your ass at Chops."

I gave her a skeptical look. "Okay. We'll see, Ma. I mean, you got skills, but—"

"Nigga, shut up and just show me what that mouth do."

"I love a challenge," I told her in a low, raspy voice.

Her sultry eyes penetrated mine as I pulled her shirt over her head before helping her remove her shorts. Then I undressed, and she watched attentively. No more words were exchanged as we engaged in a passionate kiss. I lay down on the sofa first and darted my tongue out teasingly.

"Come put that thang in my face, Ma."

"Shit, you only gotta tell me that one time." Her face lit up as she stared down at me before straddling my face, positioning that fat pussy over my waiting lips.

My tongue and lips were working on her swollen clit in no time.

"Mmm . . . ," she moaned as she wrapped her lips around my engorged dick.

Damn, I was so hard, and her mouth felt so warm and wet. A trail of saliva streamed down my shaft to my balls, and she used her soft hand to jack me off as she sucked.

"Ma . . . damn . . . ," I gasped against her pussy and then sucked, slurped, and licked.

The sight of her thick, round ass cheeks right there in my face had me aroused to the fullest. I could feel the nut rising in my balls, but it was mind over matter. A nigga started thinking about shit that wouldn't make me cum. That was hard, being that baby girl was working that ass as she fed me straight pussy.

"You taste so fuckin' sweet . . . ," I whispered, then sucked on her pussy lips as I added one finger to stimulate her G-spot. Then, moving my tongue in circles around her clit, I started going in on that pussy.

"Ah, shit . . . fuck, Pistol. Damn . . . ," she moaned and then started sloppily deep throating my dick.

By now li'l mama's lips were on my balls; she'd taken that shit in so deep. My shit was tingling like a motherfucker. The pressure of her sucking and the sensual flicks of her tongue had me all fucked up. As she did her thing, I had to stop what I was doing and enjoy it. My eyes were closed, and I could feel the warm rush of my orgasm building. Then I thought about our little bet and went back to devouring that pretty pussy.

"Mmm, baby . . ." I started to twirl my tongue around and around between those thick ass cheeks. As I did, I slapped her fat ass over and over again, until her cheeks were red and I could see my fingerprints.

"Ohhh, fuck . . . ," she whispered around my dick. "Mmm . . ."

Hell yeah, I thought to myself and went back to concentrating on that clit. I went back in with no mercy on that ass. As I held her in place, she arched her back and started fucking my tongue. She moved her pussy around in small circles as her sugary juices spilled down my chin. I slurped up all I could, and then I felt her left leg shaking. Yup, I was winning. I was going to be served head on a platter for a week.

Baby girl then tried her best to lift her ass up and get away from the assault my tongue was inflicting on her.

"You see what this mouth do, Ma?" I taunted her, without missing a beat.

My fingers were working and grinding against her G-spot. I could feel her muscles twitching and squeezing my fingers. Damn, I was ready to have that shit wrapped around my dick. Her mouth felt good as fuck, but to me, the pussy was always the ultimate prize.

Suddenly she stopped moving, and her head flew back. "I'm fuckin' cumin', nigga. Shit! Uhhh . . ."

Her love came running down the side of my face like a waterfall. *Damn.* Shawty was squirting and shit. That was sexy as hell to me, and all I wanted was that pussy. *Fuck that shit.* I grabbed her ass cheeks.

"Sit that wet mu'fucka on my dick, Ma. Just like that. I wanna see that ass twerk while I'm up in it."

She looked back at me and blew me a kiss. "You're the champion, so you get whatever you want, baby."

I passed her a condom, and she put it on me with her mouth. My shit was still tingling, although I hadn't nutted yet. The plan was to nut up in the pussy. Part of me wished we were on a level where a condom wasn't a must.

Daisha positioned her legs on each side of my torso and then got on her knees, with her feet on the sofa. Oh, hell to the yeah. She was about to ride a nigga reverse froggy style, and I was ready to go deep. I place my hands on her hips, and then she lowered that tight, sopping-wet pussy down on my hardness.

"Fuck, yeah . . . ," I whispered. I wanted to close my eyes from the pleasure, but I kept them open. Watching her ride my dick like that was like my own personal, private porn.

"Oh . . . shit. Your dick is so . . . fuckin' . . . good. Mmm . . ." She leaned over and really started grinding on my shit.

My dick was up in her gushy tightness. The feeling was overwhelming, and the sound of me exploring her insides corresponded with our moans and groans.

"Yo' pussy got me fucked up, Ma. Damn . . ." I had to scrunch up my face and shit. *Wow.* She was working that ass like my dick wasn't as far up in her as it was.

I lifted my pelvis to meet her thrusts, and the sound of our skin slapping together added to the chorus of our incredible lovemaking. The sight of her ass rippling every time those walls crashed down on my dick was driving me crazy. I slapped her ass cheeks, then watched as they shook and jiggled out of control.

"Mmm, Ma. I love this shit . . . for real. Ride yo' dick. Uhhh . . . argh . . . fuck!" My toes started curling, and she looked back at me, with seduction written all over her beautiful face.

"Tell me how good my pussy feels to you, Daddy."

"Mmm . . . It feels better than good, Ma. That shit . . . mmm . . . feels like heaven. That juicy, tight-ass pussy's givin' a nigga . . . mmm . . . shit . . . It's givin' me fuckin' life right now. Oh, fuck. Work that shit. . . ."

She arched her back, leaned forward, grabbed my ankles, and started working me over. My eyes were glued to her on top of me, swirling her body like a sexy-ass serpent. The way her body was moving mesmerized me. It was like she was dancing on my dick.

"I'm 'bout to make you nut, nigga. . . ." She moved up to the tip of my dick head and then came all the way down, sucking my shit up with her pussy as she did.

"Ahhh . . ." I had to squeeze my eyes shut.

She kept doing that shit over and over again, and my dick started to jerk inside of her. The tingling feeling was becoming overwhelming. Then I started to shake uncontrollably. My body was overheating, and it felt like I'd lost control of myself.

"I'm cumin'. Fuck!" I yelled.

Chapter 20

Daisha

"Oh . . . yes, Pistol. Mmm . . ."

We were cumming at the same time, and the feeling was so damn powerful. It was like that shit had opened the floodgates. That sofa had to be soaking wet, because I was nutting all over that nigga's dick. Pistol was still trembling and jerking beneath me.

"I know my pussy's good, babe, but damn . . . ," I said.

I lifted myself up off the couch, and as I stood over him, I noticed that something was wrong. It was like he was convulsing, his body out of control, and I knew that it wasn't the orgasm anymore. It was something else.

"Pistol, baby, are you okay?" Tears stung my eyes as I stood over him.

Was he having a damn heart attack or something? *Damn. What the fuck?* Was it a seizure?

Okay, I remembered that my mother used to have seizures because of her drinking. If that was what it was, I had to do something. I used all my strength to turn him over on his side so that he wouldn't choke on his saliva or anything. My immediate thought was to call 911, but I knew that he wouldn't want me to do that.

"Pistol. Shit, baby. Please . . . God, let him be okay." Tears fell down my cheeks as I waited and prayed for it to be over.

Finally, after about ten seconds, his body was still, but his eyes remained closed. I checked his pulse and his breathing. He was alive, but I could tell that he was out of it. Suddenly, his eyes opened and focused on mine.

"Baby, what the fuck happened?" I asked him. "Can you talk?"

He cleared his throat. "Ah shit . . ." His voice was a whisper. "I ain't had a seizure in years."

"In years?" My heartbeat increased. "You've had one before?"

"I had the first one right after my father died. The doctors couldn't figure out why it happened. They never diagnosed me as epileptic, because the seizures didn't happen that much. I probably had, like, seven. Every time I had one, they didn't have any answers. I haven't had a seizure in ten years. I thought that shit was over. I guess not." With a sigh, he sat up.

"Hold up. Are you okay?" I was really concerned about him.

"Yeah, I'm fine." With that said, he leaned his head back against the sofa cushion. "Just get me some water, please."

"Okay." I nodded and did what he asked.

When I returned with the water, he was twisting up a blunt.

"Uh, you sure you wanna do that right now?"

Pistol looked up at me and shook his head. "This is the universal medicine of our generation. It didn't cause the seizure. That bangin'-ass pussy probably did." He laughed it off, but I didn't find it funny.

"There you go again, making light of a bad situation. You have to take meds for seizures even if you wasn't diagnosed with epilepsy, right?" Why was he downplaying that shit?

"Yeah, but, like I said, this the first time I had a seizure in a long-ass time, so I stopped taking medication."

"You need to go to the hospital, Pistol. This time it's not a gunshot wound. They won't have a reason to call the cops. I saw the name on your license. You can use that name."

He had to know that I was genuinely concerned about him and his well-being. I didn't want him dying on my watch. If the medicine would help, he should just swallow his pride and go get it. The cops weren't going to come get him. They wouldn't even know that he was there. It wasn't like his face was all over the news or anything.

"I don't need to go to the hospital, Ma. I'm fine. It's just stress. That's it. I'm good. Just relax." He lit the blunt and took a long pull.

"Are you fuckin' serious right now? You're fine? It's just stress? You could've died for the second time in a week, Pistol." The tears started against my will again, and I tried to wipe them away before he saw them. "I can't take losin' you, so I need you to do what you gotta do to get your medicine."

"I can probably get a prescription for phenytoin. Maybe I can find a way to get my moms to get some and bring it to me. I'd love to see her and my brothers. Then again, I don't want the cops to trace that shit back to me. I don't know if they know about my condition and will intercept the prescription."

"You have to take your chances, babe," I told him as I softly rubbed his back.

"I know, Ma. I know." He passed me the blunt. "I don't wanna chance bein' in nobody's fuckin' prison, though." That nigga was so stubborn and would do anything to stay out of prison, even if it meant risking his life.

After taking a deep pull from the blunt, I held the fragrant smoke in my lungs. Damn, that was some high-grade shit. Pistol was extra quiet now, and I wondered if he was really feeling okay. As concerned as I was for him, I decided not to keep bothering him about it. He had to feel like he was vulnerable, and I knew that men had their egos. I didn't want him to feel weak or like I was trying to run his life.

He broke the silence minutes later. "Don't worry about me, Daisha." His sexy, rich, deep voice sounded strong again. "I'm a man. I'm strong. I can survive anything."

I sighed, because he acted like he was invincible or something. Didn't that nigga know that he was human? After I passed the blunt back to him, I got up and quickly got dressed. The ocean was so close, and I decided to walk outside and let the sound of the waves calm me. Pistol was really stressing me the fuck out. Okay, so he hadn't had a seizure in years, but what if he kept having them now? Without a sure diagnosis and meds, his life was really in jeopardy.

My eyes burned as I walked outside and slowly made my way across the soft sand. The sun was setting, but the sand was still warm beneath my bare feet. I just loved the way it felt between my toes. Once I was right there by the water,

I watched the swells of the rising tide. As the waves rushed in, my tears fell. Then, suddenly, I was on my knees, letting it all out. Damn, it felt good. Like I was cleansing my soul.

Then I heard Pistol's voice behind me. "I'll make sure my mom brings me the meds tomorrow, Ma. I don't want you all stressed out over me. I'll risk it all for you."

Trying to get myself together, I stood up, turned, and wrapped my arms around him. "I just don't want anything to happen to you, Pistol. I . . . I finally found the man for me, and damn, look at what you're going through. You don't deserve any of it. It just hurts me so much to see a person that I care about suffer."

He squeezed me tighter, and I could feel him inhaling the scent of my hair. "Just bear wit' me, Daisha. We gon' get through all of this. I promise." He kissed the top of my head and just held on to me for what seemed like an eternity.

Eventually, we separated and walked back to the bungalow hand in hand. Once we were inside, we took a shower together and then got dressed to go out for dinner. I didn't know if he was really up for it, but he acted like he was okay.

"You sure you wanna go out?" I asked, feeling really skeptical about it.

"Yeah, I told you, Ma. I'm good. Now, let's go get some crab legs."

I let out a deep sigh as we headed out to the car.

The next day I was nervous as hell, because I knew that Pistol's mother was on the way over here. What if she didn't like me? I really hadn't had much luck with mothers, especially with my own. My anxiety was fucking with me hard, but Pistol kept trying to get me to relax about it.

"Baby, chill. Ma's gonna love you. My brothers will too," he assured me as we sat next to each other on the sofa.

His brothers, who were nineteen and twenty-one years old, were coming as well. That was because they had to drive. His mother had had chemo treatment the day before and was too tired to drive herself. According to Pistol, she'd been able to get his medicine. He hadn't taken it in years, but his mother had a close friend who was a pharmacist. The pharmacist hadn't even questioned it when his mom asked her to fill the outdated prescription. Now his mom had the medicine that Pistol needed, and I felt relieved. I hadn't had a wink of sleep last night, because I'd been up watching him. The fear of him having another seizure was overwhelming

"I hope so," I said. "I mean, I ain't never been close to any of my exes' mothers. I just don't really bond with women, for some reason. Whether they're old or young."

"This time you will. You'll see." He ran his fingers through my hair and then leaned over to kiss me. "Just don't look at me differently now."

I stared up into his beautiful eyes. "I don't. If anything, it just makes you more human to me, Superman."

We both laughed as he pulled me into his arms and held me.

"Oh . . . my baby!" Pistol's mother gasped as he took her in his arms as we stood in the living room. "I missed you so much."

Immediately, she started bawling, and I understood why. The reunion made me want to cry my damn self. I simply stood there, taking in the scene. Pistol's brothers looked just like him. They were tall and delectably milk chocolate, just like him. Neither of them had hazel eyes, though. His mother was beautiful, and I couldn't tell by looking at her that she was sick in any way. Her flawless milk-chocolate skin and her eyes were identical to Pistol's, and she had long hair that flowed to her shoulders. Pistol had already filled me in on the fact that she would probably be wearing a wig due to hair loss because of the chemo.

When she and Pistol finally separated, he gangsta hugged his younger brothers. The whole exchange made me wish I had a bigger family. I'd missed out on that.

His mother looked me up and down with a straight face before a genuine smile decorated her features. "You must be Daisha."

"Yes, I am." I nodded and smiled back at her.

Surprisingly, she enveloped me in her arms and held on to me. The gesture brought tears to my eyes, but once again, I willed them away.

"Thank you for taking care of my baby," she whispered in my ear.

My tears fell against my will, and I wiped them away quickly, before anyone could see them. "He takes care of me, so I wouldn't have it any other way."

"Bless you, baby." She separated from me and held on to my hands like we'd known each other forever. "He told me that you haven't known each other that long, but that doesn't matter. I'd known their father for less than a week when I fell deeply in love with him. Haven't loved another man since. It's hard to find someone that you can count on these days. I know you're aware of what he's going through."

I nodded. "Yes, ma'am, I am."

"You don't have to call me ma'am." She chuckled. "Call me Maddie."

"Okay, Maddie."

"These are my other two sons, Tyshaun and Tyrese. I named them all after their father. His name was Tyrone."

"Hi, Tyshaun and Tyrese." I shook their hands.

"You can call us Shaun and Rese, like everybody else," Tyshaun said with a cocky grin. He was the youngest.

Tyrese spoke up next. "It's nice to meet you, Daisha. You must really be something else if you got my bro's head gone."

"Shut the fuck up, Rese," Pistol laughed.

His mother passed Pistol a pill bottle and looked him in the eye as she spoke. "I know you're worried about me and everything's that's going on, but I need you to take care of yourself, Reek."

"I know, Ma." He lifted her up and spun her around. "It's so good to see you. I love you, woman."

She let out a hearty laugh as she beamed at her firstborn. "And I love you more."

The tears flowed down my cheeks as I absorbed the love in the room. How I longed for that, or at least something like it.

We all headed down to the beach. While Pistol and his brothers spread out a blanket on the sand and chatted, I spent some time talking to Maddie as we strolled along the water. She was all I would've ever wanted in a mother. In a short time, I told her a little about my own mother. She was very sympathetic, and I really was warming up to her. She then told me that her own mother had abandoned her when she was two, and she and her eight-month-old brother had been raised by their aunt. The entire time she'd thought her aunt was her real mother. And her biological mother had pretended to be her aunt, but they'd never been close. Now, that was fucked up.

"Bro, you said we was goin' paintballing next time we came down here," Rese reminded his brother as Maddie and I sat down on the blanket.

"We still can," Pistol said as he sat down on the blanket beside me and his mother. "You feelin' okay, Ma?"

She smiled at her oldest son. "I'm feeling better than I have in a long time. It's so good to see your face." With that said, she squeezed his cheeks like he was a little boy and then kissed both of them. All Pistol did was laugh, and I couldn't help but smile.

Tyshaun spoke up next. "So, we goin' paint-ballin' or what, man?"

"Uh, yeah. You gon' come, Ma?" Pistol asked his mother. At first I thought he was talking about me, because he called me Ma too.

She declined with a laugh. "Y'all young folks go ahead and have fun. I'm going to stay here and cook some dinner. I picked up some things before I got here from the grocery store. I'm cooking a pot roast with potatoes and carrots, homemade corn bread, and my famous baked mac and cheese."

Pistol rubbed his stomach, wearing a huge grin, as he licked his lips. "My favorite."

"I know, and of course, I'm going to cook a peach cobbler."

Pistol laughed. "You tryin'a make me gain 'bout twenty pounds, ain't you?"

"Right. That sounds so good, Miss Maddie," I interjected.

"Just call me Maddie, sweetheart."

"Okay," I agreed.

"And what do you care about gainin' a li'l weight, Reek? Look like you lost ten pounds since the last time I saw you," his mother said.

"Stress," Pistol admitted. Then he tried to make light of the situation. "I guess we should get ready to go. You comin' wit' us, Daisha?

That'll make it even. We can be like Bonnie and Clyde against those niggas."

His brothers laughed. I kind of wanted to stay there and bond with his mother, but I figured that she wouldn't need me in her way in the kitchen. Besides, I had never gone paintballing before, and it sounded like fun.

I nodded. "Uh, sure, I'll go."

"Can you cook, Daisha?" his mother asked out of the blue.

"Yes, ma'am. I mean Maddie."

She smiled and nodded. "I need you to put those ten pounds back on my baby. I ain't used to seein' him look so frail."

I glanced over at Pistol, and he damn sure didn't look frail to me. He was built like a Gladiator, and I didn't think he needed to gain ten pounds. However, his mother knew what she was used to seeing him look like, so I agreed.

"I got you, Maddie. I actually love to cook," I said, sensing that a friendship had sparked between me and her.

Pistol grabbed my hand and pulled me up from the blanket. After that, he gave me a quick peck on the lips. Then he helped his mother up, and we all chitchatted as we headed back to the house.

"Mama's 'bout to throw down," Pistol told me, with a smile on his face. "I sure have missed her cookin', but I gotta admit, you can burn too, Ma."

"Thanks, babe." I blushed as he pulled me closer.

"What is the world comin' to?" Rese asked. "I ain't never seen bruh like this."

"I know, right?" Shaun said, chiming in. "I thought it was an icebox where that nigga's heart's s'posed to be."

We all laughed as we made our way across the soft sand.

Chapter 21

Pistol

"Yo, that was so much fun," Daisha laughed as we headed back to my car.

"Yeah, it was," I said. Before I got behind the wheel, she gave me a look.

"Want me to drive?" Her eyes were full of concern, and I could tell that she was afraid that I would have a seizure behind the wheel.

"I told you not to act different toward me," I whispered in her ear as I leaned over.

She looked confused as she stared up at me. "I'm not. I just asked."

I shook my head, knowing that I was just being all sensitive and shit. That wasn't her fault. Having feelings for her was just turning me into a little bitch.

My brothers didn't say a word. They just climbed in the back seat and tried to lighten the mood.

"I hope Ma finished cookin'. Shit, I'm hungry," Rese said.

Shaun spoke up next. "Me too, man. I'm tastin' that damn roast."

I didn't say a word as I pulled out of the parking space and left Adventure Beach Paintball and Airsoft Park. Daisha was clearly pouting, and I wanted to apologize for getting all sensitive on her. Being a vulnerable-ass nigga was not my forte, and I'd never had to deal with a woman knowing about my seizures, since I hadn't had one in all my adult years, until now.

Instead of pushing the issue, I decided to wait until we were alone. My mother and brothers would be leaving the next morning, and we would have to talk when they were gone. Daisha just looked straight ahead, and I kept looking over at her, hoping to get her attention. She ignored me.

Rese's voice rang out from the back seat. "Turn that shit up."

"Hell, yeah, nigga. That's my shit," Shaun said.

I turned the radio up and realized that I also liked the song that was playing.

"Who's this nigga? I like this joint too," Daisha said.

I smiled, knowing that we were still connected.

"Bryson Tiller," Shaun answered. "The name of that shit is 'Don't.'"

Daisha continued to talk to my brothers, while I thought about our future. What the hell was going to happen once we returned to Atlanta?

The house was lit up with the delectable aroma of my mother's cooking. One thing I could say about her was she could throw down in the kitchen. I'd never tasted anything like her food in my life. I'd missed my mother's cooking just as much as I'd missed her. Now, Daisha's cooking was good as fuck, but she didn't have shit on Mama. I figured after a few years, she'd have the same skill level in the kitchen.

"Dinner is done!" Ma called out.

We scrambled from the living room, where we had been sitting in front of the TV for over an hour. Daisha still hadn't said two words to me. I was sure she would have a lot to say when we were alone. All I wanted was some food. I'd taken my medicine right before we went paintballing, and I needed to eat. My stomach had been growling out of control.

We all sat at the kitchen table and served ourselves some pot roast, potatoes, carrots, and mac and cheese. My mother then brought the corn bread over to the table, and we passed the plate around. As we grubbed, Daisha carried on a conversation with everyone but me. It was probably obvious to everyone too, but nobody reacted much. My mother just kept giving me questioning looks.

"Uh, son, can we talk alone?" my mother asked while Daisha cleared the dishes from the table.

I didn't know what she wanted to talk to me about, but I figured it was about the tension between me and Daisha. Maybe she had some motherly advice on how I should handle the situation. As I followed her outside to the patio, an uneasy feeling washed over me. Was she about to give me some bad news? Had the cancer spread? Was her condition getting worse?

"I can tell that you're overthinking this, but it's not about me, son. This is about you." She cleared her throat and sat down in the one of the patio chairs.

I sat down in the chair beside her and stared out at the sparkling pool as she continued.

"Daisha told me that you got shot."

Damn! Why the hell had she told my mother that shit? I didn't want her to worry about me any more than she already was.

She went on. "I know everything about how you met and about her ex Rae. Now, I want you to kill him. Don't get me wrong."

Let me find out my mother has a gangsta side, I thought. She was from the streets, so although she held it in check, that mentality was still there.

My mom made eye contact with me, and I was surprised by the look in her eyes. "There's a lot that you don't know, and there's a reason for that. As your mother, I chose to tell you what you needed to know."

I was silent, and she kept talking.

"I'm worried about you, son. I don't want you to end up like your father."

"Don't worry 'bout that, Ma. I won't—"

She cut me off. "I know you better than you know yourself, Pistol. You love the streets, just like your father did, if not more. Tyrone was hardheaded as fuck." She laughed. "You're just like him. I warned Daisha. I think she can handle you, though. Don't fuck up and push her away. I like her way better than those ratchets you usually mess with. She's a tough cookie. Reminds me of me. Been through a lot of bullshit she didn't deserve. She'll be okay, though. I can tell she got something that's rare, or you wouldn't love her like you do. You love her, don't you?"

I looked in my mother's eyes and decided to tell the truth. Clearly, she already knew. "I'm in love with her, Ma."

"You told her yet?"

"Nah. It's too soon."

She shook her head. "It's never too soon. Say what you feel, before it's too late. Tomorrow is not promised, son."

"You okay, Ma?" I studied her face, hoping that she wasn't shielding me from the truth.

"I'm good. Like I said, this is about you, not me."

I sighed and watched her closely as she went on.

"Like I said, you're just like Ty. He was determined not to go to prison. When I found out that he was facing all those charges, I nearly lost my mind. Drug possession, trafficking, three counts of murder . . . The list went on and on. He was facing life with no parole, and he couldn't bear the thought of being in a cage. Your father wasn't murdered, son. He killed himself. I found him in the bedroom, with a gunshot wound to the head. The Feds, the DEA, and the ATF had the house surrounded, and he wouldn't surrender. He would rather die than spend the rest of his life in prison."

She went on. "I know that you think the same way, Reek. Daisha told me. She doesn't want that same fate for you, and neither do I. I'm not saying you'll kill yourself intentionally, like he did, but you won't seek medical attention, because you don't want to be locked up. You could die too, Reek." Tears fell from her eyes. "I don't want to bury my child. You're supposed to bury me. I already saw your father put in the ground, and I refuse to sit back and watch the same shit happen to you or your brothers."

Damn. Her words were getting to me, and I had to fight to keep the tears at bay. Crying wasn't some shit I normally did, but she was my mother. She had made me feel things I didn't want to. The woman who gave me life had brought out so many emotions that I'd tried to bury. That shit was uncomfortable for me, but I had to deal with it.

It was really shocking to find out that my pops had committed suicide. When I thought about it, that shit was a selfish-ass decision. Why didn't he think about us, his family? That shit hurt like hell. He left three young boys and a wife behind because he didn't want to face time behind bars. Still, I could understand, because I didn't want to go to prison, either. Not having a wife and children made my situation different in my eyes, but I realized that my mother and brothers would be just as hurt. Maybe I didn't form attachments to others out of fear of having to detach. That explained why I'd waited so long to give my heart to a woman.

"Ma, I can't be behind nobody's bars. It ain't no life for me."

"Son, I can't visit your grave. That ain't no life for me."

Damn. Why did she have to say that shit?

"So you'd rather see me behind a piece of glass, then?"

"Hell yeah. Especially if seeing you dead or going to prison are my only options. At least I'd know that you're alive. I'll visit you as much as I can, and I got a feeling that Daisha will too. She loves you just as much as you love her."

I smiled all hard and shit, like we weren't just talking about something serious. My mother wanted me to turn myself in if it came down to my life being threatened, but I just couldn't do it. "She told you that?"

"No, but I can tell. I can see it when she looks at you." She wiped her eyes. "I got something else to tell you."

"Okay." I sighed and rubbed my temples. I was getting a headache, and I wondered if it was the medicine. When I used to take it before, I'd get the worst headaches, but they would go away once the meds got in my system good.

"I know you're in Atlanta, although you won't tell me. Your father used to do business with this guy named Diablo Perez back in the day. He can help you. You can't trust just anybody, but you can trust him. I wanted to tell you that before, but we couldn't really get into it over the phone. He and your father were really close. He always said to let him know if I needed him after your father died. I just don't know how to reach him now. I'm sure if you . . . dig deep enough, you'll find him yourself. He's the leader of a crew called the Cue Boys."

After she said that, I didn't hear anything else. The Cue Boys were even deeper and more ruthless than the Bankhead Mob. My pops had been connected to Diablo and the Cues Boys? *Shit.* I'd heard all about them from my cousins. They'd never met Diablo, but he was notorious in Atlanta.

"I heard he don't run the Cues no more, but I'll see what I can find out," I told her.

My mom nodded and then gave me a hug. "Good. I don't want you to be out there just dealing with Mike and Dank. They ain't as smart in the streets as Diablo must be. If he's still alive, he gotta be more resourceful than them."

How the hell did she know that? Had Daisha told her more than my mom was telling me? I didn't even bother to ask. I had a bone to pick with Daisha's ass later.

"I love you, Ma, and I'm gonna do my best to make you proud of me for once. I don't know how yet, but I'm gon' pull it off. I promise." My voice cracked, and I knew that all the emotions I'd held back were running to the forefront.

My mother grabbed my hand. "I'm already proud of you, son. You did what you felt you had to do for me and your brothers."

The fucked-up shit I'd done included paying both of my brother's tuitions at Johnson C. Smith University in Charlotte, North Carolina.

We hugged, and I held on to her tight as hell. "I love you, Ma."

"And I love you, Reek. More than you'll ever know."

My brothers and I said our good-byes as my mother and Daisha said theirs.

"A'ight, my nigga. Stay up," Rese said, trying to play all hard.

Shaun was a little bit sappier and shit. "Be easy. I love you, man." We hugged for the second time. "Take care of that beautiful woman," Shaun added.

"I will," I told him. "Love you too, man."

When it was time to say good-bye to my mom, that shit crushed me. I held on to her, not wanting to ever let go. It was like I was that little boy who had lost his father all over again. For some reason, I felt like I was losing her too. Maybe that was because I didn't know if either of us would survive much longer. What if cancer killed her or I became a casualty of the streets? I had an eerie feeling that we would never see each other again.

All I could do was hold on to what she had told me. I was determined not to mess up what I had with Daisha. We had one more night there at the beach bungalow, and we needed to have a talk that wasn't interrupted by anything, especially what was going on in the streets of the A. I thought about my father and what my mother had told me about him. Knowing that she was stressing out about what was going to happen to me had me all fucked up.

"Ma, look." I held on to her hand. "I want you to focus on gettin' better. I'm a man. I'll be a'ight. I need to know that you'll be a'ight too." I put my hand under her chin and nudged it so that she was looking up at me. For some reason, she wouldn't make eye contact with me, though. "What you hidin', Ma?" My eyes were on hers.

"Nothin'." She waved me off. "Love you, munch-kin."

Daisha laughed. "Munchkin and Punkin. Wow."

I stared at my mother as my brothers joined in on the joke.

"Ma, really?" I said. Pretending to be pissed, I shook my head, with a frown on my face.

My mom grinned and pinched my cheeks like I was three years old. "You'll always be my munchkin. Who's Punkin?"

"Punkin is my childhood nickname," Daisha said.

"Aw, that is too cute," my mother said as my brothers made faces behind her to taunt me.

"Punk," Rese interjected.

"Hell yeah. Nigga's sprung than a mutha . . ." Shaun had looked at our mother and cut his statement short. We all knew what he had meant to say, though.

"You gon' make me lose all my morals, li'l boy. Watch yo' mouth." My mom shook her head as she walked to the car.

I didn't want to watch her leave, so after I waved good-bye, I went back inside the bungalow. Daisha stayed outside, and I wondered what else she was telling my mother. The thought infuriated me. It was like she wanted to be accepted by my mom so bad that she'd sell me out.

Daisha came back inside a few minutes later, and I figured she could sense my mood.

"What's wrong wit' you?" she asked, with a frown on her face.

"Shit. What the hell's wrong wit' you? You the one who's been actin' funny since yesterday," I pointed out. "What's up?"

"What you talkin' 'bout?" The pitch of her voice told me she was exasperated.

"Do you have amnesia?"

She rolled her eyes toward the ceiling. "No. I remember shit just fine, nigga. I'm glad we can talk now. You've been actin' like shit ain't the same since you had that damn seizure. Why are so afraid to let me see the real you? I'm still here, Pistol. You can't scare me away. Don't you see that? What you think scares me away just draws me in."

I shook my head as I sat down on the sofa. She sat down beside me. "I don't want you to think I'm some weak-ass mu'fucka. If you think like that, how can you trust me to keep you safe?" I decided to leave out what my mother had said Daisha told her. For some reason, I didn't want to jeopardize their relationship.

"Oh my God. Are you for real? A seizure does not make you any less strong to me. I can't believe you think I see you that way." She caressed my cheek. "You have shown me more strength than anybody I've ever known. . . . You saved my life."

"And you've saved me just as much, if not more."

"So, what is that supposed to mean? Are we keepin' score now?" Her eyes shined with tears. "You're punishing yourself, just like I do myself.

We think we're not worthy of love, so we make up every excuse not to have it. I can't do that with you, Pistol. Don't you get it? I love you! Okay. I'm in love with you so deep that I don't know what to do. I'm sinkin' like it's quicksand. I want to fight it, but I can't. That's why I left after you helped me that night. I caught feelings for you too damn soon, and it fucked my head up. I thought I couldn't do it.

"The thought of losing what we have makes me want to run away again. How can I leave you, though? You're everything I've ever wanted. I can feel your love, baby. You don't have to say it. You prove it with your actions. Those say more than any words a man has ever told me. Every man who's been in my life, other than you, has told me they love me, but their actions tell a different story. You show me how you feel, and you don't have to say it. Which proves that actions speak louder than words, but that's just a cliché. Fuck clichés. I want something real. Fuck what you talkin' 'bout, nigga. I'm gon' hold you down, just like you hold me down. That don't make you weak. That makes you a lucky-ass man, if you ask me."

Shawty's words hit me like a ton of bricks, for real. For the first time, a mouthy-ass nigga like me was at a loss for words.

"Nah, that makes me blessed, Ma. For real," I said after a good minute had gone by. For the first time ever, I was close to tears around a woman other than my moms. I grabbed her hand. "I love you too, Daisha. This is the first time I've told a woman that, other than Madison Gordon."

Tears fell from her eyes, and she tried to wipe them away, but I stopped her.

"Don't hide from me." I wiped her tears away. "Let me see all of you. Please. I'm in love with you. I love everything about you, but I know there's so much more for me to love. Give me that chance."

"Damn! What the fuck? Where the hell did you come from? I've prayed for you all my life, and now . . . now you show up." She shook her head.

"Tell me about it." I pulled her into me and held her in my arms. "Didn't I tell you not to dwell on that? Shit, I found you right when I needed you. It just so happened that you needed me too."

That night I held her and didn't even try to get some ass. I needed her to know that it wasn't just about a nut with her. She needed to know that I could feel more with her than just an orgasm. My feelings for her were deeper than that physical shit. I wanted her to feel my love for her. She didn't need to just hear the words. They were so empty, without meaning behind them.

When I woke up at 5:00 a.m., Daisha wasn't in bed. It didn't take me long to figure out where she was. I slipped on a pair of basketball shorts and went outside. Just like I thought, she was on the beach. It was obvious that she found the ocean to be an escape from what was going on. Too bad we would be leaving soon.

After walking up behind her, I wrapped my arms around her waist and pulled her close. She looked back at me and smiled.

"I love the way you hold me," she told me in a breathless voice.

"And I love to hold you." I kissed her neck and then buried my nose in her hair, taking in my favorite aroma. Even the crisp, fresh scent of the ocean couldn't compare.

She spoke over the tranquil sound of the waves hitting the shore. What she said surprised me. "You're pissed at me for telling your mom too much, ain't you? You didn't say it, but I could see it in your eyes last night. I was waiting for you to bring it up, but since you didn't . . ."

"Nah, I ain't pissed at you, Ma. At first I was a little bit upset, because I didn't want her to know so much. I realize that you both are just worried about me, but you ain't got a reason to be." I kissed the top of her head.

"I'm gonna stop bringing it up, because obviously, I'm talking to you in circles. I keep on repeating myself, but you're so damn stubborn." She turned and looked me in the eye. "We do have a reason to be worried about you. As a matter of fact, we have several reasons to be worried about you. I wish you'd see that."

I shook my head in frustration. "If I stress about that, I won't be able to focus on what I need to do. I can't afford to worry, Daisha. I have to be confident that I'll come out on top, alive, and with my freedom still intact. If I don't, I'll fuckin' crumble, and all the shit I've been fightin' for will be for nothing. Do you want that?"

"No," she mumbled. "I just want you to be realistic."

"I am, baby." I pulled her closer to me, and she rested her head on my chest with a sigh.

That was the reason that I'd avoided loving a woman. My problems had become hers, and I had never wanted that for the woman I loved.

Chapter 22

Daisha

When we returned to Atlanta, I found out that Rae was still in police custody. I'd found this out only because I had visited Kevia's Facebook page. She'd posted pics of G's funeral there.

As I sat on the sofa now, a day after our return, I hurriedly logged off my own Facebook page so that I could get ready for my job interview. Pistol was out and about at the moment, and I assumed he was trying to find out all that he could about Diablo. On the way back to Atlanta, he'd asked me if I knew who he was.

"Of course I know who Diablo is. He's a living fuckin' legend in Atlanta. There was even a movie made about him called *The Forbidden Fruit*," I'd replied excitedly, filling him.

He'd said that his mom had told him to find Diablo, because Diablo had been close to his father. According to her, Diablo would be able to back Pistol up when he went after Rae. Going after Rae meant that Pistol may also have to take on the Bankhead Mob. Especially if they found out that he'd killed G. There was no way that Pistol would be able to take them on alone. He needed help, and I was hoping he'd find Diablo, because Mike and Dank were questionable as hell.

"I don't know how you gon' find him, though. He don't lead the Cue Boys no more. I heard he's outta the game. It might be hard to find him, since he's so low key now. You can't just be asking anybody about Diablo. Even if you do, I'm sure they won't tell you, since they don't know you," I'd told Pistol.

He had sighed as he looked over at me. "I'll find him, baby girl. Don't worry. I'm a resource-ful-ass nigga."

That was the day before, and I knew that things took time. One thing that I was learning was patience. Things were going to fall into place when they needed to, and I had convinced myself to deal with whatever happened. Even if it went left or right, life would have to go on.

I went into the bedroom to change into clothes for my interview, then hurried out of the condo. I got behind the wheel, backed out of the driveway, and headed to Buckhead. When I pulled into the parking lot of Beauty Land of Oz, my heartbeat quickened. My nerves were getting bad because I'd never had a job that utilized my mental skills, and so I felt uncertain. Instead, I'd always used my body and my looks to make money. Of course, I had worked at Wendy's, but being a cashier didn't take that much skill. I hated the fast-food industry and hoped that I would never have to go back to that.

I walked inside the salon/spa, and the atmosphere felt positive. The sound of house music with dramatic bass drops filled the air, and the sound of blow-dryers and chatter was like a hum in the background. A short, brown-skinned chick with a long, flowing weave and slanted eyes greeted me at the front desk.

"Welcome to Beauty Land of Oz. How can I help you?" she asked cheerfully, with a huge grin on her face.

"My name's Daisha, and I have an interview for the office manager position."

With a nod, she stood up. "I'll let Ozzy know that you're here." She pointed toward the comfortable-looking sofa and ottoman in the waiting area. "You can wait there if you'd like."

"Okay. Thank you."

"My name's Miranda," she offered. "I love working the front desk, but I'm about to go back to school to finish my BA. It's time to move on and focus on my career."

She looked like she was about my age, and it made me feel awful that I wasn't working toward my own degree. The shit was fucking with me, but I could only blame myself. Never again would I allow a man to dictate where my future went. If I'd had any sense, I would've left Rae alone a long time ago. All the time I'd spent with him wasn't even worth it. However, I had learned a lesson from being with him. I'd never settle again.

As I took a seat in the waiting area, the front door opened, and a beautiful woman with caramel skin, bouncy shoulder-length hair, and pretty hazel eyes walked in. Her aura let me know off the top that she was a "boss chick." That was obvious from how she held her head up high, exuding confidence. The Hermès bag she carried also proved that she was either holding it down on her own or holding a nigga down who was getting it.

Miranda came back to the front, with a pleasant smile on her face.

"Hey, hon. How are you today?" she asked the woman.

"I'm good, Miranda. How're you, boo?" They air kissed. "Ozzy told me that you're going off to school in Virginia. I lived in Virginia for a little while."

"Yup. I got an older sister in Norfolk, so I'm moving in with her while I finish getting my BA from Norfolk State. I hate to leave, though. I'll let Ozzy know that you're here."

"Thanks, love."

"Oh, I love that bag. You're always so damn fly," Miranda said, complimenting her.

"Aw, thanks, hon."

The woman sat down beside me in the waiting area, and my eyes scanned her outfit and her high-heeled pumps. They were obviously expensive. I could tell. She just seemed to be one of those women who had it all together. She seemed much older than me simply by how she carried herself, but she still looked young. Her body was banging too, and I wondered if all her ass was real. It was the norm to see fake asses in Atlanta, so you never could tell.

A minute later a dude walked out from the back. He had shoulder-length dreadlocks and chestnut-brown skin. His black slacks and black-button down looked like a uniform, but they were crisp and expensive looking at the same time.

"Ayanna, how are you? Lookin' gorge, as always," he said when he reached the woman sitting next to me. She stood. They hugged and then separated before he looked at me.

"Oh yeah. You must be Daisha. I'm Ozzy," he said.

I stood up. "Yes, I am."

Ozzy turned and looked at his client. "Uh, go on to my chair, boo," he said. "I'll be right over."

"Okay, boo," Ayanna answered, then walked off, with her hips swaying from side to side. Her confidence was enviable, and I wished I could carry myself like she did.

"Nice to meet you, Daisha." Ozzy shook my hand and smiled down at me.

He was fine as hell, but obviously gay. Still, he wasn't flamboyant with it, but he had a boisterous personality. I loved it and knew that I would enjoy working for him. Shit, I was already claiming that job.

"Nice to meet you too . . ."

"You can just call me Ozzy. We're all family round here."

"I love this place, Ozzy. It is so . . ."

"Lit, right?" He put his hand on his hip and laughed. "Y'all young 'uns and your slang."

His laughter was infectious, because I laughed too. "Yes!"

"See that chick right there?" He pointed at Ayanna. "She was one of my first clients. If it wasn't for her, I wouldn't be who I am today."

That piqued my interest. "Wow."

"So, let me go get her ready, and then I'll be back. Okay?"

I nodded. "No problem."

As I sat back down, he made his way over to his chair. I loved how he was the owner but still did hair himself. It showed his passion for the craft. Just because he was the owner of the salon didn't mean that he was too good to do what he loved. To be honest, with all the stations and the private spa rooms, he didn't have to. They did everything from hair to nails to facials here, so I was sure he was making that gwap.

A couple of minutes passed, and I heard Ozzy's laugh again.

"Girl, bye. You know damn well Diablo would kick your ass if you cut your hair! Not gon' do it. Bitch, you tried it," I heard him say as he walked away from his station and headed toward me.

Did he just say the name Diablo? I knew that there was a possibility that he wasn't referring to the same Diablo, but what were the chances that he was talking about someone else? A sneaky grin crept up on my face. I had to do everything in my power to get this damn job. If Ozzy was connected to someone who knew Diablo, I could find out some information for Pistol. Damn, it was so crazy how shit had worked out.

Now wasn't the time, though, to fish for information. I realized that Diablo lived the type of lifestyle in which privacy was a must. It wouldn't be that easy to get information about him. Ayanna had to be his woman. If I asked Ozzy about him right away, he'd be suspicious about my agenda. I wasn't trying to make him think I wanted to know about Diablo or anything. Once I got the job, I could work my magic. For the moment, I had to work that interview.

Well, as it turned out, Ozzy hired me on the spot, though the position wasn't quite what I'd expected.

"Office manager is really just a fancy name for receptionist," Ozzy told me with a chuckle. "You won't just be answering phones, though. You will be responsible for scheduling appointments, keeping up with inventory, etcetera. Miranda will train you for two weeks, so don't worry. You'll get everything down pat. I can tell."

I was glad that he had confidence in me, because lately I'd lost confidence in myself. Being surrounded by successful, ambitious people would be good for me. It would motivate me to want more, and eventually, I'd be able to go back to school like Miranda.

I couldn't wait to let Pistol know that I had a job, as well as a connection to Diablo. It was just a matter of time before I figured out a way to get them face-to-face. I left Beauty Land of Oz, and when I was back in my car, I was finally able to let it out. "Yes, yes, yes!" I did a little happy shimmy before putting on my seat belt.

The thought of Rae crossed my mind a second later, and I knew that the police might let him go soon. There was really no way they could hold him with no real evidence. The charges would be hard to prove in court with no physical evidence, no witnesses, and no murder weapon. They might think they had established a motive, but from what I knew from watching the ID channel, that wasn't enough to convict him.

Then I thought about the fact that black men were wrongfully convicted all the time simply due to their race. So it was also possible that they would hold him, and then Pistol and I would be able to go on with our lives without worrying about him or the Bankhead Mob. Nonetheless, we had to be prepared for anything. The fact that Pistol was running from federal charges was even more threatening to our love than a showdown with one of Atlanta's fiercest crews.

Well, at least I had a job, and my pay started at twelve dollars an hour. It wasn't much, but it would do. Soon I'd be able to move into some cheap-ass apartment somewhere. Even with my blossoming relationship with Pistol, I wanted my own place.

Just as I pulled off into the thick rush-hour traffic, my phone rang. When I looked down, I saw that it was Kevia's number on the screen. I immediately had a bad taste in my mouth. What the fuck did she want now?

"Hello," I answered, hoping she'd hear the animosity in my voice.

"Hey, Daisha. What you doin'?" she asked, as if everything was good with us.

"Nothing," I said simply.

"Look. I really need to talk to you face-to-face. There's . . . a lot goin' on, and I don't want to lose your friendship."

"I don't think that's a good idea, Kevia. To be honest, I forgive you and all, but I don't think we can save our friendship. Instead of thinkin' about me, you thought about your cousin. At this point, you're still helping him, after he supposedly slapped you in the face. I don't think hangin' out with you is a good idea, being that your cousin wants to kill me. I'm sorry, but it's best if we just—"

"Really? You're breakin' up our friendship over Rae? Wow. That's fucked up."

"No, I ain't breakin' up our friendship over Rae," I retorted. "It's your fault. I can't trust that when he gets out, if he does, that you won't sell me out to him again. As far as I know, you'll help that nigga kill me. Rae's like your best friend, and I know that. The fact that you knew that he was cheating on me the whole time and that you didn't tell me says a lot about what our friendship really meant to you."

"Bitch, I tried to tell you 'bout that nigga, but you'd always take him back. I was tired of bein' in the middle of y'all shit!"

"You know what, Kevia? You don't have to worry about it anymore. I shouldn't have been with him in the first place, and if you were any friend, you would've warned me about his psycho ass. I'm done talkin' to you, bitch. Good-bye, and don't call me no more."

"You ain't no good friend, anyway," Kevia snapped. "I can't help you're dumb as hell when it comes to a man. Don't blame me for wastin' your life with my cousin. That's on you. I don't tell a bitch shit 'bout a man. It's up to you to find out on your own. Even if I had told you about him, I'm sure you would've still fucked him and fallen all deep in love, like you always do. You be stuck on stupid for a piece of dick, so it's whatever, bitch. Fuck you. Good luck out there alone. I hope you can survive without me and my family protectin' your no-common-sense-havin' ass. You'll never make it in these streets. Watch your back, bitch! You never know when somebody'll run up on you."

She hung up, and I just sat there at a red light, not believing the things that bitch had just said to me. So, that was what she'd thought of me all that time? And when had she ever protected me? She hadn't tried to protect me from her fucked-up-ass cousin. It was good that I had finally realized that slut-bucket, dick-sucking ho was not really my damn friend.

A car horn blared behind me.

Oh shit. I hadn't even realized the light had turned green. Had that ho just threatened me, talking about how I had better watch my back? She had had the nerve to say that I didn't have common sense. *Wow.* She just didn't know that what I lacked, Pistol made up for. I wasn't a green-ass bitch, though, so she was wrong about that. I had plenty of common sense. Unlike her, I'd always been on my own. That heifer had always had her family to fall back on.

"Just wait till I get my hands on that bitch," I said out loud.

She didn't know that I'd committed a murder. That bitch also didn't know that I wouldn't hesitate to do it again.

Instead of going straight to Pistol's condo, I rode out to the hood, because I had a taste for some wings from one of my favorite spots. J.R. Crickets had the best hot wings, and my taste buds were dancing from the thought of that sauce hitting my tongue. The fries were the bomb. I figured it would be cool, since Rae wasn't around and so I didn't have to worry about him. Besides, I planned to be in and out fast, anyway.

I parked in a spot near the door, rushed inside the restaurant, and placed my order at the counter.

"Can I get a twenty-piece hot with a side of fries? All flats please." I thought about Pistol, so I got extra.

"That'll be a dollar more for all flats," said the chick behind the counter, acting like I didn't know that.

"Okay," I agreed with a nod.

After paying for my food, I grabbed my receipt and my drink, then sat down at a table to wait for my order. I spotted this chick from my neighborhood named Quita. That ho wasn't cool with me at all. All she had ever wanted to do was instigate and start fights. We'd gotten into it a few times because I'd called her out on her bullshit, but the ho had only talked shit and had not fought me. I guessed I had too much heart for her to try it. She stared at me now, while she talked to somebody on the phone. It was clear from her hand gestures and facial expressions that she was talking shit. All I did was shake my head and send Pistol a text.

Hey, babe. I got some good news for you. I'm grabbing something to eat, and then I'll be on my way.

I didn't expect for him to respond right away, but after ten minutes, when he still hadn't texted me back, I started to get worried. Maybe he just hadn't checked his phone or was busy or something. He had told me that he was going to meet up with Dank so they could talk. Of course, Mike was all fucked up in the hospital, and they were trying to find out who had run him over.

Something told me that it was connected to G's murder. Maybe Mario had said something to the wrong person, and the BHM had gone after Mike. What if they had run him over instead of shooting him, because that would have made it look like an obvious gang hit? They might have meant to make it look like something else.

"One twenty-one!" I heard the chick behind the counter call out.

Looking down at my receipt, I realized that was me. I was so glad that it hadn't taken long for my order to come up. That bitch Quita kept on mean mugging me, and I wasn't in the mood for any bullshit. Maybe I should've just grabbed something to eat in Buckhead, I thought. The thing was, the food in the hood tasted so much better.

I got up from my seat and walked up to the counter. Old girl behind the counter flashed me a pleasant look as she opened the Styrofoam box for me to check my order. Everything looked good, so I put seasoned salt on my fries.

"Ranch or blue cheese?" old girl asked.

"Both please. I like to mix them up," I confessed.

She laughed good-naturedly. "Now, I ain't never heard nobody say that before."

"I know. It's weird."

After she put my food in a bag, I left the spot and headed to my car. Once I was behind the wheel, I threw the bag on the passenger seat and then put on my seat belt. When I looked up, I saw that Quita was standing outside now, her eyes on me. She just stood there and stared at me as I pulled out of the parking spot.

If I wasn't so focused on getting away from the mentality of the streets right now, I would've asked that bitch what she was looking at. Instead, I headed back to Pistol's condo so that I could

grub and get some rest before my first day of
work. If only everything in Pistol's life would
start to fall in line. I wished his charges would
just disappear, but I knew better.

The music was blasting in my car, and I sang
along to Drake's "Hotline Bling." *Dang*. Was
the road bumpy, or was that my car? *What the
fuck?* I turned the music down and recognized
the familiar thump of a flat tire. The traffic was
thick as hell, so I decided to pull off on a side
road. *Shit*. I remembered that I had a spare in
the trunk, but I didn't have a fucking jack. *Fuck!*
It was dark as hell, and the road that I was on
didn't have many streetlights.

After pulling out my phone, I called Pistol.
There was no answer. My heartbeat quickened
when I realized that I was fucked. My next move
was to contact Uber, but I didn't want to just leave
my car there on the side of the road, only to come
back and find it gone or sitting on bricks. Why
hadn't I made sure that my roadside assistance
was up to date? Rae was supposed to have paid it
for me, but of course, he hadn't. I'd forgotten all
about that shit. *Damn*.

I called Pistol again. He picked up this time.

"Hey, babe. Sorry I didn't answer before, but—"

"I got a flat. I'm gonna need you to come help
me change it. I don't have a jack, but there's a
spare in the trunk."

After putting my gun in the waist of my jeans like a goon, I got out of the car and went to look at the back tires. I was in a bad neighborhood, so I had to make sure I was strapped. There was a puncture in my right back tire, and it looked like somebody had intentionally flattened it. I hadn't run over something, like I'd initially thought.

"Shit, babe. Where you at?" Pistol's voice broke through my thoughts.

"It looks like somebody stabbed my tire."

Just then a car pulled up, and its bright headlights temporarily blinded me. Maybe someone would be able to help, and I wouldn't have to wait for Pistol. All I needed to know was if they had a jack for me to use. I wasn't one of those chicks who didn't know how to change my own tire. Shit, I'd learned how to survive. Then I thought about the worst-case scenario. What if they were there to rob me or something?

"Get back in the car, Ma. Where you at, so I can come to you?" Pistol said.

The car's headlights went off; then the driver's-side door opened. After that the passenger-side door flew open. When I saw that bitch Quita walking toward me, I didn't know what to think. Then I spotted Kevia walking toward me too. When had those bitches started hanging together? Suddenly, I knew what it was all about.

It all came together. Quita must've called to tell Kevia that I was at the wing spot, which was less than ten minutes from where Kevia lived. That bitch had to be the one who flattened my tire. Those hoes were so damn dramatic.

"I knew I'd get your ass, but I didn't think it would happen so soon, bitch," Kevia said, with a smirk on her face.

"I had to call you, girl. I ain't never liked that prissy-ass bitch. Can't believe that ho didn't even support you after your brother died. Didn't even show up at the funeral. What kinda fuckin' friend is that? I knew I should've whupped that ass," Quita commented as they closed the distance between us.

"What the fuck's goin' on?" Pistol asked. I hadn't answered his question, and he could probably hear the women's voices.

Shit. I couldn't depend on him to get me out of this situation. It would take too long for him to get here. Not many cars came down that road, because it led to a subdivision. It was also pitch black outside without the glare of headlights. By the time somebody turned down here, I could be dead. Even if I wasn't, it was the damn hood. Those hoes could jump me or shoot my ass, and people would just drive right on by.

"Shit. Kevia and some other bitch are here to fight me or something. I gotta go."

"Where you at, Ma! Shit!"

"Off of Panola. It's a little side road not far from J.R. Crickets."

"Baby, why the hell would you go back over there?"

Honestly, because I didn't think Quita would be there to report my moves to Kevia. That ho didn't scare me, but she tended to let other people boost her head up. Quita was like fuel to a fire. She lived for that type of shit.

"Who the fuck you talkin' to, bitch? The police?" Kevia asked, thinking she was taunting me.

I hung up the phone and threw it on the driver's seat. Then I felt the weight of the gun. It reminded me that I was strapped, and I relaxed. Still, I didn't know if those hoes had guns too.

"That ho gon' get in the car and cry like a li'l scary bitch." Quita laughed, looking at Kevia. "You can't go nowhere. If you do get in the car, we'll just bust the windows out. Either way, we gon' get you, bitch!"

With what? I wondered. They didn't have anything in their hands to bust the windows out with. Then the thought of them both being strapped occurred to me. Two guns were definitely better than one. Still, I had to let them know that I wasn't scared.

"Fuck y'all lame-ass bitches," I snarled. "You could've fought me right then and there, Kevia. You didn't have to flatten my damn tire and shit!"

She was right in front of me. "I did that shit 'cause I ain't want nobody to save your life, ho! I'm gon' finish the job for my cousin. I can't stand a disrespectful-ass bitch."

With that said, the bitch pulled out a sharp-ass pocketknife. I laughed out loud as I pulled out my strap and pointed it at her. That ho knew I had a gun, but she had still come unprepared.

"You swear you hard, but you brought a knife to a gunfight," I said. I shook my head, taking in the shocked look on both their faces.

They had underestimated me, and they didn't know that what I'd been through had made it so that a bad bitch they didn't recognize was standing in front of them.

"Shit!" Quita gasped, not expecting for the tables to turn. "I told you to get the fuckin' strap outta the car!"

"This the second time you done pointed a fuckin' gun in my face, bitch," Kevia growled. "You gon' shoot me for real? Yeah, right! You ain't never shot nobody in your fuckin' life! There probably ain't even no bullets in that mu'fucka, you soft-ass bi—"

As if it was second nature, my finger squeezed the trigger, and four shots rang out before I even knew I'd fired the gun. They both fell to the ground, and I didn't even know where they'd been shot, because it was so dark. I jumped in my car and turned the key in the ignition. Getting very far away on that fucked-up tire was impossible, but I had to get away from the crime scene before the police came.

Chapter 23

Pistol

I'd talked to Dank earlier that day, and we were supposed to meet up at the pool hall. After waiting almost two hours, I realized that nigga wasn't going to show up. I tried calling his phone, but he wasn't answering. What the hell was going on? Did that nigga have something to hide? With Mike in the hospital, I had no other way to get in contact with him. I didn't know what to think.

Dank and Mike were my cousins on my father's side. Their mother, who was my father's only sister, had been killed four years ago by her husband, who had then turned the gun on himself. My uncle Quentin, whose house me and Daisha had stayed at, was my mother's only brother. He was a little younger than her and wasn't involved in the streets at all. He was a computer engineer and traveled a lot. My mother's mother had died years ago, and her father had never been around. My father's mother had let him and his sister go into the foster-care system when they were little. That was my family pretty much in a nutshell.

I guessed my finding Daisha and falling for her was right on time, because I needed somebody. The thought of something happening to her devastated me, and it hurt like hell just thinking about it. Why hadn't she just listened to me when I told her to stay away from her old hood? She thought that because Rae wasn't on the streets, she was good, but it was clear that the bitch she'd once thought was her friend really never was.

I called her phone for the tenth time since she'd called me, and it went to the voice mail again. The J.R. Crickets restaurant was right in front of me now, but I had no clue what side road to go down. *Shit!* Then my phone rang. It was her.

Letting out a sigh of relief, I answered. "Baby, are you okay?"

"Yes, but I . . . I had to shoot them. I don't know if they dead."

She told me the name of the apartment complex that she'd managed to drive to, and I went to Google Maps to find it.

"I'll be there in two minutes, Ma. Stay in the car."

Hopefully, she'd listen this time, with her hardheaded ass. *Damn.* My baby had had to kill again. That shit was fucked up, because I didn't want that life for her. Still, it was good to know that she did have the instinct to save her own life. What if she was feeling guilty because she knew her victims personally this time? That shit could've been the other way around, though, and then I'd feel like I was incomplete.

With everything that was going on, Daisha had given me a reason not to give up. If she was not in my life, I didn't know if I'd ever be capable of falling in love again. Being in love with a woman like her was actually a good feeling, and I wouldn't trade that shit in for the world. Thank God my baby girl was okay.

When I pulled up behind Daisha's whip minutes later, I didn't see her. That shit made me go into panic mode. After parking in an empty space a couple of spaces down from her, I got out and then walked over to her car. The sound of sirens filled the night, and I already knew what it was. I'd avoided the road on which the shooting had taken place. The cops and EMTs had got there fast, because I'd seen the lights from a distance.

Daisha was all ducked down in the driver's seat, as if she was hiding. I knocked on the window, and she looked up, with tears in her eyes. More than likely, she had heard the sirens too and was afraid that the cops would find her. She was clutching her cell phone in her hand, and when my baby spotted me, she looked so relieved. As she opened the door, I looked around to make sure that the coast was clear. We were going to have to get up out of there fast.

"C'mon, Ma. We gon' have to leave your car here for now. I'll get it taken care of later, okay?" I stared into her eyes, and she only nodded.

I picked her up and carried her to my car. She rested her head on my shoulder and started sobbing hard as hell.

"Why the fuck is this shit happenin' to me!" she wailed.

"Shhh . . . It's gonna be okay, baby," I said, trying to soothe her.

"No it's not! I had to shoot two people. I can't deal with this shit, Pistol!" she wailed, her words incomprehensible to anybody other than me.

After I put her in the passenger seat, I strapped her in and got behind the wheel. "Look, Ma. We gotta get outta here, okay? But I gotta let you know one thing. It was either you or them bitches, and if you had let them kill you, I wouldn't have forgiven your ass."

As she looked over at me with vulnerable eyes, she wiped her tears away and nodded.

Nothing else was said, but my head was full of thoughts. Why the hell had she chanced going out there?

"My wings . . . ," she whispered just when I was about to pull off. "Get my wings out the car."

"Where do you think he could be?" Daisha asked me when I told her that I couldn't find Dank.

"I don't know, Ma. That's the crazy-ass part about it."

We were smoking a much-needed blunt at the crib, and I was at a loss about what to do next. Then shawty dropped a bombshell on me when she let me in on the fact that she had a new job and the fact that one of the clients knew Diablo.

"But you don't know if it's the same Diablo my mom's talkin' 'bout," I commented.

Daisha's tears were finally gone. "That's not a common name, Pistol. I'm sure it's the same Diablo." She passed me the blunt and sighed.

"So, why didn't you tell me that you had a job interview?"

"I didn't want you to talk me out of going."

I nodded. "Yeah, I would've tried. Why the hell did you go to your old hood, Ma? I told you not to do that."

"It sounds stupid, but I was craving some damn hot wings. There's wing spots around here, but they ain't as good. I didn't expect that to happen. What if the police . . ."

"There ain't no evidence against you, Ma. They ain't got no weapon, you drove away from the scene, and I'm sure nobody saw shit. As long as you keep your mouth shut, you cool."

"Who do I talk to 'bout shit like that other than you?" she asked. "You ain't gotta worry 'bout that."

"Good thing your job ain't far from here, Ma. I'm proud of you, but be careful, though. You see, shit can happen that you don't expect. You never know. You sure your wanna take that job right now? You really don't have to."

"I have to. It's the only way to get to Diablo. I got a bad feeling that shit is only gonna get worse. We need him. At this point, I don't even know if those bitches are dead or not."

That was so true, and they could both identify her. Then the thought of Dank's disappearing act crossed my mind. What if that shit was more sinister than him just avoiding me?

A few days had passed, and I still hadn't heard anything from Dank. Dank's phone kept going to voice mail, and so I went over there earlier today, but he wasn't home. What the hell was going on? Had the BHM come after Dank and Mike, and if so, was I next? At that point, I didn't even know how Mike was doing. I decided to just go ahead and visit him. It was the only way I could find out if he was still alive or if he'd heard from Dank.

When I got to the hospital, the waiting room was full. With my head down slightly, I walked over to the front desk. Dank had told me that Mike was in ICU, and I was sure that it wouldn't be that easy for me to just go to his room.

"Hello. Can I help you, sir?" the front desk attendant asked politely.

"Hi. Yes. I'm here to see Michael Gordon."

She pressed some keys on the computer keyboard in front of her and then looked up at me. "Room one-twenty-eight. Just go through those double doors." She pointed. "He was moved out of ICU earlier today."

"Thank you." I guessed the fact that he'd been moved to a regular room was a good sign.

When I walked in his room, there was a short, brown-skinned nurse mopping his forehead with a wet cloth. He was obviously still out of it, but the constant beep of the heart monitor let me know that cuz was still alive. At least there wasn't a respirator or tubes everywhere, so that meant he was breathing on his own. He looked like he was banged up a little bit, but not as bad as Dank had made it seem.

"Hey. How're you? Nobody's been here to see him in days. Are you his brother, Darrick? He keeps asking for you," the nurse said with a smile.

"Uh, yeah, I'm Darrick." That was Dank's real name.

"I'm Alexandria. Your brother's awake, which is a blessing, considering how things started out for him. He has two broken ribs, a broken clavicle, and a shattered femur, and his spleen had to be repaired. He's a fighter, though, so although he's in a lot of pain, he's still here."

"Thank you for taking good care of him."

She nodded. "That's what I do. Now, I'll leave you two alone for a while."

When she walked out, Mike's eyes suddenly opened. "Where's Dank?" His voice was low, and it was like he was straining to talk.

With a sigh, I told him the truth, although I didn't want to. "I don't know, man."

His voice rose. "What you mean, you don't know?"

"He's been missin' for a few days. I thought the police was gon' be in front of your door and shit.

The only reason I even chanced comin' was that I wanted to know if you was still . . ."

"Alive?" He chuckled. "I know you wanna kill me, cuz. Join the club. Mario was lyin' like a mu'fucka, though. I just want you to know that."

I nodded, and he continued.

"Now, as far as my brother, you gotta find out what's goin' on. It ain't like Dank to just not show his face or not at least call and shit. No matter what you may think, li'l bro is a loyal-ass nigga. Don't let what that nigga Mario told you fool you, man. He had his own agenda."

"You got that, man, but who did this to you? Was it the BHM?"

He shook his head. "Nah, man. That bitch did it." His voice was a mere whisper, and I could barely hear him.

"Huh? What bitch?"

"My baby mama. We got into it 'cause she thought I killed G, and she ran me over and shit. I'm goin' kill that bitch and then get my shawty, yo."

I was stunned. His baby mama had done that shit to him over that nigga? She must not know what he'd done to their daughter, or she just didn't care.

"Are you fuckin' serious, my nigga? Yo' baby mama did that shit?"

"Hell yeah. I ain't say shit 'bout it, 'cause I'm gon' handle that shit myself. Now that I know something's goin' on wit' my bro, it makes me wonder. Now, the BHM probably got something to do wit' that. I tried to tell her about what G did to Kayla, but she ain't believe me. Right before she hit the gas and ran my ass over, that ho told me that I was lyin' on G and that those niggas suspected me. I'm sure they thought that goin' after Dank was the next best thing after she'd already done that shit to me."

Mike shook his head and cast his eyes down. "I'm sorry for gettin' you into this, cuz. I know you don't trust me, and you think there's some truth to that bullshit Mario sold you. Believe me, man. There ain't. I need you to find out what's goin' on wit' Dank."

I nodded as I grabbed my cousin's hand. He held on the best he could, but his grip was weak. "I got you on that, fam," I assured him.

He nodded and closed his eyes. I figured that was because of the pain medication that was dripping through his IV at timed intervals. For some reason, I thought they'd keep him protected in the hospital. What if those BHM niggas came up in there to finish what his baby mama had started? Without even a second thought about it, I left the hospital, on a mission.

***

"That bitch Kevia is still alive," Daisha told me right after I walked through the door.

"How you know?" I asked, sitting down on the sofa beside her. Leaning over, I kissed her before she continued.

"I saw all the prayers and well wishes for her to get better on her Facebook page. That ho Quita's dead, though. I saw 'Rest in peace' on hers. From what I read, Kevia's still unconscious, but if she comes to, she's gonna tell somebody that I shot her. Whether it be the cops or the BHM, I'm fucked."

Baby girl was shaken up, and I held her in my arms, attempting to calm her down. "You don't know how shit's gon' turn out, Ma. Okay?"

Daisha pulled away and shook her head as she stared over at me. "Let's just leave. I don't want this life anymore, Pistol. How can you? Ain't you tired of looking over your shoulder, waiting for the cops to get you? Rae's locked up, and nobody knows you killed G. Let's just go!"

Tears fell from her eyes, and I was at a loss. I had no idea what to do to soothe her, but I couldn't leave. "I can't. . . . I wanna leave, but I can't. I gotta make sure I find out where my cousin is. Then I gotta merk that nigga Rae. I got to."

"Well, what am I gonna do? I don't know about you, but I'm scared. What if the cops come after me? That could lead them to you too. Then what?"

"I seriously doubt that Kevia will tell the cops if she comes to."

"But she'll tell the BHM. I'm sure they still got her back, even although her brother's gone. Shit, her boyfriend, Rock, is part of the BHM too. She's covered. We're not. I still don't have any info on Diablo. We don't stand a chance, Pistol. They got your cousins, and if they're coming for you next . . . that means they may come for me too."

"Nah, Mike's baby mama who was fuckin' G ran him over. The BHM didn't do it. There's a chance them niggas got Dank, though. I already told you I'll protect you. Don't worry."

Daisha stood up and started nervously pacing the floor. She had been working at the salon/spa for a few days but still hadn't had the nerve to ask Ozzy about Diablo. According to her, she just didn't know how to bring it up, and I didn't blame her. At that point, though, desperate times called for desperate measures.

"You gotta ask Ozzy about Diablo tomorrow, Ma. You were right. I can take on Rae, but I can't take on the BHM by myself. I need some backup, and I need it fast."

"But how am I supposed to . . . ?"

"Tell him the truth. Well, part of it, anyway. I mean, what's the worst that could happen? All you gotta do is tell him that my father knew him and I've been lookin' for him. He don't have to give you an address or nothing, just a number, and I'll handle the rest."

With a nod, she agreed. "Okay, bae. I'll try."

We sealed it with a sweet kiss.

Chapter 24

Pistol

The next morning I hit the streets early as hell to find out what I could about what had happened to Dank. I needed to know if he was alive and running from something or if the BHM had done something to him. First, I hit Wesley Chapel up to talk to the niggas who trapped with Mike and Dank. They didn't know shit, of course, so my next stop was to holler at the corner dope boys. Those niggas had nothing for me, so I headed to Dank and Mike's crib. Mike had given me his key to check on the spot.

Once I was parked at Mike and Dank's, I turned the engine off, grabbed my strap, and headed to the door. I opened it, not even knowing what the fuck I was looking for, but I was hoping to find some evidence to lead me to where Dank was. Everything seemed normal as I took a look around. Nothing seemed out of place or anything.

I sighed as I stood there in deep thought. Where could I possibly look next? I was at a loss. My eyes drifted down to the floor, and I noticed a cell phone right there by the door. It was crazy, because there were no signs of a struggle. The door had been locked, but the cell phone lying there was out of place.

Picking the phone up, I wondered if it was Dank's. I noticed that it was an iPhone, and Dank had a Galaxy Note. There was a pattern code to unlock it, and of course, I couldn't figure it out. I had only six attempts before the phone would be set back to factory settings. I damn sure didn't want that to happen, so I put it in my pocket. I'd figure out a way to crack it later.

As I put my hand on the doorknob to leave, I heard a noise. By the time I turned around, it was too late. I was hit on the head with something. The impact from that shit made me stagger, but it wasn't enough to knock me out. Blood dripped into my eyes, temporarily blinding me. With my shirt, I wiped it away. When I looked down at the floor, I noticed the broken shards of a lamp. My eyes moved up to see the culprit. That nigga was brown skinned, with long dreadlocks. He was about my height but a lot slimmer. I didn't know who the hell he was, but something told me that he was affiliated with the BHM. Then I spotted the tattoo that let me know that I was right. As I got ready to pull my strap out, my eyes focused, and I noticed that he already had his pointed at me.

"Who the fuck you is, nigga?" he asked, chewing on a toothpick.

"Who I am don't matter. Who the fuck you s'posed to be?" I spat, mad as hell that he'd pulled his strap out on me first.

"That don't matter, either." He glanced at a broken window on the side of the house.

So that was how he'd got in here. "Why the fuck you here?" I ice grilled that nigga as my mind came up with some way to reverse the situation.

It was clear that he was here looking for something too. I needed to know what. First of all, he didn't even know who the fuck I was. Maybe I could convince him that I was here for the same reason as he was, although I had no idea what that was.

"I'm here for a good-ass reason, nigga. What you here for?" he said.

"Shit, I'm lookin' for the niggas who live here. They owe me some money."

"Hmm. Who you wit', nigga?" He acted like he wanted to lower the gun, but he didn't.

"I don't claim no set. I'm a one-man army."

That nigga nodded. "Damn. We need a nigga like you on our team. Those niggas who live here owe me their lives. I heard that nigga Mike's fucked up in the hospital, but his bitch-ass brother, Dank, is bein' taken care of."

My heartbeat increased. He knew where Dank was.

"I heard about Mike, but I thought that nigga Dank was here. Fuck! I was gon' pop that nigga, get my money, and get the fuck outta here. Damn." I tried to throw him off. "I know where the safe is, but I don't know the combination and shit. Maybe we can figure out how to open it together."

"Together?" He tilted his head to the side like he was confused. "Who said I was gon' share that shit wit' you?"

"Uh, I just figured that since I know where that shit is and you don't, I'd get a cut."

He nodded and then smirked at me as he cocked the gun. "I ain't got no reason to trust you, mu'fucka."

"True, but if you lookin' for money, you won't find it without me."

"Who said I was lookin' for money, nigga?"

"You don't have to be. Who don't want free money? I mean, I'm willin' to share wit' you since you handled Dank for me. One less nigga for me to kill."

"Real shit. He's still alive, though . . . for now."
He nodded. "A'ight. Show me where this damn
safe is, nigga."

I was relieved to hear that.

With the gun, he gestured for me to lead the
way.

"So why you wanna kill Dank and Mike?" I
asked as we went. I needed to know if he was
really with the BHM or if those niggas had beef
with somebody else.

"They the reason the leader of the BHM is
dead, and there are consequences for that shit."

I tried to act surprised. "What the fuck? Them
niggas gotta be crazy. I'd never go against the
BHM."

Without skipping a beat, I led the way down
the stairs to the basement. All I wanted to do
was get my hands on a gun. I walked straight
to the spot and pulled out three floorboards.
There the safe was, right where it had been the
last time I was here.

"How'd you know where that shit would be?"
Dude asked behind me.

"I watch shit when niggas don't think I am," I
simply said.

Although I wanted to know where my cousin
was, I had to go ahead and kill that nigga. If I
didn't, he was going to kill me. At least I knew

that the BHM had Dank for a fact and that he was still alive.

"Uh, I need something sharp to pry this shit open with," I said.

"Pry it open?"

He asked too many damn questions.

"Hell yeah. A screwdriver or something, nigga. I done this shit before. Have you?"

I looked up at him, and he shook his head.

"I'll go see if I can find one. If you move, I'll kill yo' ass," he said.

"Uh, we on the same team, man. Ain't no need for all that," I told him.

A few minutes later he returned with a screwdriver. How he'd found it that damn fast, I didn't know.

He stood behind me, pointing that gun, as I pretended to try to open the safe. The thing was, I knew the combination. And I used the combination when he walked off to peek out the basement window. He must've heard something. The whole time he kept his strap aimed in my direction.

I wanted to whup that nigga's ass, but I had to play it cool with a gun in my face. One thing about me was, I could think fast as hell. My plan was to use Dank and Mike's strap hidden inside the safe. Although I had my gun on me, it was too damn risky to pull it out. I definitely didn't want him to shoot at me. I wanted to be the only one doing the shooting. And killing that nigga seemed like the only way I would get out of there alive.

"I got it open . . . ," I announced. Then I grabbed the Smith & Wesson inside the safe and turned toward that nigga and emptied the clip. The loud pops filled the silence.

I raced up the basement steps and out the front door. As I scrambled to get to my car, I looked around to make sure that there weren't any witnesses to me leaving. The nosy old lady next door was peeking out her blinds. That let me know that she had heard the gunshots and was probably on the phone with the cops. *Shit!* I peeled out of there so fast, hoping my license plate was blurry. She'd seen me before a few times, so I was sure she could describe me. *Damn!*

As I reached in my pocket and grabbed my phone, my heart thumped erratically. Then I realized that the phone I'd pulled out of my pocket was the one that had been dropped on the floor of my cousins' crib. I had no idea at that point if this phone belonged to Mike, Dank, the nigga I'd just killed, or whoever had my cousin. I retrieved my phone from my other pocket, then checked to see if Daisha had called. Getting in contact with Diablo was a must, especially if I wanted to save Dank. It was already after five, and she hadn't called yet. *Shit*. She was about to get off work, and it was possible that she still hadn't talked to the dude who owned the salon.

By the time I made it to the highway, I was able to exhale and relax a little. I was just pulling up to the crib when my phone rang. Looking down at the screen, I expected to see Daisha's number. Instead, it was a Georgia number I didn't recognize.

Something told me to answer my phone, although I didn't usually answer calls from strange numbers.

"Hello?" It was more of a question than anything else.

"This Pistol?" It was a man's voice that I didn't recognize.

After an awkward pause, I asked, "Who wants to know?"

"Diablo," he stated in a deep, powerful voice. "I remember your pops, Ty G. Your girl was tellin' Ozzy 'bout him and what I told your moms after he . . . died. Ozzy called me, and now I'm callin' you. I heard you got some shit goin' on that you need help wit'. A promise is a promise. So, when can you come meet me?"

"Uh, some crazy-ass shit went down, but I can meet you in 'bout an hour." I needed to clean up the blood from when dude had hit me in the head with the lamp.

Baby girl had come through for a nigga again. There I was, about to walk up in the Doll House, the strip club Diablo and his son Zy owned. During our phone conversation, Diablo had filled me in that his son was about my age. He'd also said they were both trying to leave the streets behind. But I felt that Diablo would make a comeback for me.

This guy who was head of security frisked me at the door, and I felt naked as hell without my strap. Especially after what had just gone down at Dank and Mike's crib. Still, I had had to let that shit go and take my chances. I already knew they weren't going to let me in with a weapon.

After I was cleared at the door, I was led through the club. My attention lingered on the stage. Some thick-ass bitch was working the pole. It was early as hell, and that joint was packed. Damn, I was impressed. Obviously, Diablo and his son knew what they were doing. Even the bartenders and waitresses were sexy as hell. This was so many steps up from the Blue Flame. I was led to the back of the club, where I figured the offices would be. A set of double doors was opened for me, and I was given the go-ahead to go inside.

When the doors closed behind me, I was face-to-face with the person I figured was the one and only Diablo Perez. His skin was the color of a bronze sculpture and was smooth, as if he was the same age as me. Of course, I knew that he wasn't, since he had a son who was about my age.

With eyes the color of butterscotch, he stared at me like he'd just seen a ghost. As he stood up from the seat behind his desk, I closed the distance between us.

He shook my hand, then said, "Come sit down, Pistol." He used his hand to gesture toward the chair on the other side of his desk.

After I took a seat, he sat back down at his desk. There was a cocky aura about him, and I figured that it had been earned. From what I'd heard about him, he wasn't to be fucked with. That nigga had a line of bodies that could stretch way across the East Coast. Not only that, but he had eluded the cops for years and lived as a totally different person in Miami. How he'd avoided having those charges stick, I just didn't know. I did know that I wanted to learn from the master. Not only did I need backup, but I also needed him to teach me how to be on the run without getting caught.

"Diablo, man, this . . ." I was at a loss for words. "This shit is crazy as fuck. My moms just told me about you, and then my girl ended up gettin' that job and . . ."

"Here we are. . . ." He flashed a crooked smile. "I remember Maddie and Ty G. Ty wasn't just a nigga I did business wit'. He was a loyal-ass mu'fucka for sho'." With that said, he poured what looked like cognac into two shot glasses. "You look just like both of them." He pushed one of the glasses toward me. "I heard you need my help wit' something. What's up, young buck?"

After we took a shot, I filled him in. As I did, his face pretty much stayed the same. He didn't seem to be fazed at all. I figured that was because he'd seen and done it all. None of what I told him either scared or surprised him one bit.

"The BHM." He shook his head. "A bunch of sloppy, unorganized ghetto-ass mu'fuckas. Bringin' them down'll be easy as fuck."

After he poured two more shots, his eyes rose up to meet mine. The wrinkles in his forehead let me know that he was contemplating something hard as hell. He held his shot glass up like we were making a toast, and then took it back. I took my shot too.

"I gotta move fast, though. At this point, my cousin's still alive. I just committed a murder, and I think I was seen. You get why I'm in a hurry, right?" I said as he poured shot number three for us.

Damn. I was buzzing already. What the hell were we drinking? That shit couldn't be no cheap shit.

"Yeah, I see why you're in a hurry." He pulled out his cell phone and made a call while I sat there, looking dumbfounded.

"Yo, Ju. What's up, man?" He paused for a second and continued. "I need you to send a car and pick up one for me. Chop it up." "Yeah, I'm at the club. One."

After he hung up, he nodded at me. "You gotta get rid of your car, just in case the neighbor did see you."

I agreed. "Right. Thanks." He was on point, being that I didn't know how to contact the dude Mike had taken me to, to get a car before.

"No problem, young buck. Now, what do you know about where your cousin is?" Diablo intertwined his fingers together on top of the desk. His stare was intense.

"I don't know where he is. I didn't get that information out of dude. Something told me to go ahead and kill him before he killed me. All

I know is the BHM got him somewhere. They keepin' him alive for a reason," I explained. "Oh, but I do have this phone I found on the floor in his house. I can't crack the pattern to unlock it."

Diablo put his hand out. "Give it to me. I got somebody who can. Maybe he can find out where they holdin' your fam. Hopefully, he'll still be alive when we do. If not . . . which is a possibility, we'll just merk all them niggas."

Damn. I was intimidated by another human being for the first time in my life. I could tell that Diablo was very powerful, and I felt confident that he would have my back. His loyalty to my pops was evident, so I had a feeling he'd make sure shit was handled.

I took the phone out of my pocket and handed it to him. "A'ight. Thanks, Diablo."

"Don't mention it." He pulled out a baggie of weed and a blunt. "I'm 'bout to fill you in on some of the shit I've been through. You know that there is no statute of limitations on your charges, so they can get you anytime. You have to take on another identity and believe it. Don't worry. By the time I'm done wit' you, you'll be a pro. The Feds won't be able to touch you."

He rolled the blunt up, and silence filled the room. All of a sudden, I could feel my father's presence. It was like he was protecting me from the grave.

For the next hour, Diablo spoke with me. I learned a lot from him in that short amount of time. At the end of our conversation, he assured me that he'd handle everything.

"Just go home, make love to your girl and shit, and I'll have something for you as soon as possible," he said.

I left his office and was led back to the front of the club, where I was shown the car that had been brought there for me. It was a simple black Nissan Altima. Of course, it wasn't my style, but I had something to drive. Diablo had explained that it was best for me to have a car that wasn't flashy or old school. The cops always made assumptions when they saw black men driving either. All I wanted to do was get my ass to the crib, and what I was driving didn't matter.

Thirty minutes later, I had my key in the front door, ready to set my eyes on the woman whom I'd fallen in love with so quickly. When I opened the door, the smell of something good cooking greeted my nostrils and led me straight to the kitchen. Daisha had no idea about what had happened at Dank and Mike's, and I didn't want to tell her. She had enough shit to worry about.

"Mmm. You must've known a nigga would be hungry."

She turned around, and I wrapped her up in my arms. It was automatic for my lips to find hers, and when our tongues touched, I felt an overwhelming desire to eat her pussy right there on the counter. Then I remembered our bet. She was the one who was supposed to be giving me head. I decided to wait for her to keep up her end of the bargain.

"So glad you're home," she whispered in my ear.

When I leaned over to look in the pots on the stove, her nosy ass noticed the gash on top of my head.

"What happened to you?" she asked, concern clear in her voice and eyes.

"Nothing."

"Uh, that wasn't there the last time I saw you, but nothing happened?" Her skepticism about my short answer was evident.

"No."

She shook her head. "Did you have another seizure? Are you takin' your medicine?"

"No, I didn't have a seizure, and yes, I am taking my medicine. Don't worry." I softly kissed her lips again. "Thank you for puttin' me onto Diablo. I got a feelin' shit gon' fall into place now."

She turned to tend to the food. "You're welcome, babe. Now, go get cleaned up. The food's almost done."

I hurried out of the kitchen. My mouth was watering for the blackened tilapia, asparagus, and rice that she was preparing.

As I got cleaned up, I thought about how the shit that was going on around us was a distraction, but not a hindrance. Daisha and I both felt strongly enough for one another that we were able to shut out all of that. When we were together, it was all about us. Nothing else in the world mattered.

Chapter 25

Daisha

"Ohhh . . . mmm . . ." As I stared up into Pistol's eyes, I saw something there that I'd never seen before. It wasn't just love. It was deeper than that, but I didn't know exactly what emotion was showing through.

He bit his bottom lip, letting his eyes linger on mine. His hands were on my ass cheeks, and his lips were now on my neck, setting my flesh on fire.

"Damn, Daisha . . ." He exhaled, and the heat from his breath sent tingles down my spine.

When he grabbed my breasts and started to suck on my nipples, I gasped. "Shit . . . ," I hissed, moving my hips with his rhythm.

I had kept my word about our little wager and had given him some superb head right before our lovemaking session.

"I love you, Ma. Mmm . . . ," Pistol moaned as he thrust deeply, filling me up to the brim.

It was as if I had to try to open up for that nigga, so I spread my legs wider. The sound of my juicy pussy popping was like the sexual soundtrack that Pistol needed to motivate him to work that dick.

"I . . . fuckin' love you too. Oh . . . Pistol. I'm 'bout to cum. . . ."

"Cum for me, baby. Cum all over this dick. . . ."

"Uh, yes . . . fuck, yes . . ." I wrapped my legs around his waist and really started throwing it back to his ass.

Then, suddenly, I remembered him having that seizure, and I pulled back. My nut had disappeared too. The sweet tingling sensations that were traveling over my body had ceased. It was like the fire of passion had just fizzled out.

Pistol stopped moving and stared down into my eyes. I was sure they'd suddenly dimmed and he could tell that something was wrong.

"What's up, Ma?"

I didn't want to say anything, so I raked my fingertips up and down his back in silence. That cut on his head had me wondering what had really happened to him. What was he not telling me? I'd noticed that he had pulled up in a totally different car. Shit, why was I thinking about all of that right now?

"Nothing," I told him, just like he'd told me. "Why'd you stop?"

"'Cause one second you tellin' me you cumin', and you puttin' it down on a nigga, and then the next, you just shut down on me." He rolled off me and pulled me into his arms. "What's up?"

I snuggled up close to him. "Nothing, Pistol. I swear."

He shook his head and propped himself up on his arm to look at me. "I don't believe you."

"And I didn't believe you earlier, when you said nothing happened to you today."

Letting out a sigh, he tightened his grip on me. "If I tell you what really happened, will you be honest wit' me?"

I nodded and waited for him to explain. He let me know all about what had happened when he went to Dank and Mike's to check up on things. My eyes were wide with shock.

"And you wasn't gonna tell me that?" I punched him in the chest. "What the fuck is wrong wit' you?"

"Ow! Shit. I didn't want you to be all stressed out over me. I done put you through enough. . . ."

"Fuck that, Pistol. Why keep shit from me when I'm still gonna be stressed trying to figure that shit out? I was all into it at first, but then the thought of you havin' another damn seizure, and it . . ."

"Turned you off." He finished my sentence for me, but that wasn't what I was going to say.

"No, it . . . scared me, and then my nut just . . . went away."

"Damn. I'm takin' the medicine, baby. It's not gonna happen again."

"But you don't know that."

"So, you ain't gon' fuck me no more, 'cause I had a fuckin' seizure?" He looked pissed off. "You didn't have no problem suckin' my dick. I didn't have a seizure then, did I?"

"Don't get mad, Pistol. It's not that . . ." Damn, I was getting frustrated. "It's just . . . I . . . wasn't thinkin' about it then, and suddenly, it popped up in my head like I was having a flashback."

Pistol got up and walked off to the bathroom without saying a word. Damn, I felt bad as hell. He didn't deserve to think I felt sorry for him or thought he was weak. I didn't. He was the strongest man I knew. I was just concerned about him. There was enough shit going on to stress out the average man to the point of giving up. There was no way I wanted to endanger his life any more than it already was. We'd been having sex when he had that seizure, so I couldn't help but associate sex with it.

When he returned to the bedroom, he threw on a pair of boxers, some black basketball shorts, and a white T-shirt. After that, he walked toward the bedroom door like he was leaving.

"Where you goin'?" My eyes burned with tears. I didn't want him to feel rejected.

"To watch TV in the front."

It was a relief to know that he wasn't going anywhere. "Okay." I sounded meek, because I really didn't know what to say to him.

He left the room, and I just lay there under the covers, thinking, as those tears finally fell. Was I going to go through that every single time we had sex? The thought made me sad. What kind of relationship could we have without a healthy sex life? Eventually, he was going to go out to get it elsewhere. I had to push his seizure out of my mind. There was a chance that it would never happen again. Shit, at least I hoped not.

When I woke up the next morning, I reached out to feel for Pistol, but his side of the bed was empty. I figured he'd fallen asleep on the sofa watching TV, so I popped up to brush my teeth. It was only eight in the morning, and I was off work today. It was a Sunday, and of course, the salon was closed on Sunday and Monday. Maybe Pistol and I could talk about the awkward moment the night before.

After washing my face and brushing my teeth, I jumped in the shower and then got dressed in a pair of shorts and a tank top. I walked into the living room and noticed that Pistol wasn't asleep on the sofa, nor was he in the kitchen or the hall bathroom. He wasn't there. Why didn't he wake me up before he left? Was he that mad?

I dialed his cell number, and after only two rings, it went to the voice mail.

"Really? You're mad or nah?" I said into my phone. Shaking my head, I added, "You're really actin' childish, Pistol. You could've said something to me before you left this mornin'. Call me back . . . please."

Ending the call, I had to sigh in frustration. Why were men always so damn difficult? His behavior wasn't called for. He knew that I'd be worried about him out there, and he hadn't even bothered to let me know that he was leaving. That shit was fucked up. Damn. Did he want some pussy so bad that he didn't see that I wasn't into it only because of my concern for him?

Instead of moping and dwelling on what was going on, I decided to prepare myself a light breakfast of eggs, toast, and turkey sausage. After that, the plan was to work out. I'd noticed that my clothes seemed to be fitting a little bit tighter lately. I used to go to the gym twice a week, but of course, with all that was going on, I wasn't keeping up with my workout routine. Damn. I couldn't wait until things got back to being even semi-normal, so that I could get back to me.

The sound of my phone ringing more than two hours later startled me. I was hoping it was Pistol finally calling me back, but it was Megan.

"Hello," I answered, wondering what she could want so early in the morning.

"Hey, Daisha. What you doin'?" she said. It sounded like she was crying.

"Not much. What's wrong? Are you crying?"

"No, I'm just . . ." She sniffed. "Okay, yeah, I was crying, but I'm good now."

"What's wrong?" I asked again, because she still hadn't answered that question.

"It's a long story. I got into it with my boyfriend. You know how it is." It sounded like she was blowing her nose.

I scrunched up my face and shook my head. "Uh yeah. I know, girl. You wanna get away and come hang out over here with me? If not, we can go somewhere. It's kinda early on a Sunday mornin', so I don't know what's . . ."

"Can you come over here? I don't really feel like driving or going anywhere."

I didn't really feel like driving, either, but I figured she needed a friend. Besides, I needed to be gone when Pistol got back. He needed to see how it felt for me to wonder about where the hell he was.

"Okay. Text me your address."

I headed right over to Megan's place. She lived in a cute brownstone in Decatur. It was close to downtown, which was a nice area. I'd seen white folks jogging and walking their dogs, so it was all good. You never saw shit like that in the hood. If a person took their dog outside, it was just to shit or piss. When you saw someone running, it meant that they were getting away from the cops, they had committed a crime, or they were trying not to become the victim of one.

When Megan opened the front door, she was looking all miserable in a white, fluffy bathrobe, with her hair all over her head. I was hoping my face didn't show my true feelings. She was taking her relationship crisis way worse than I did. I wasn't with all that "being all down in the dumps" bullshit. Life went on. The few times I had seen her before, she hadn't looked anything like she did now. She was a damn makeup artist.

Hugging me, she said, "Thank you so much for coming over, Daisha. C'mon in."

I walked inside, and she closed the door behind me.

"Damn, girl. What happened? I'm being a friend, so I'm being honest. You look a hot mess," I said.

Megan plopped down on the sofa in her living room and shrugged her shoulders. "I don't even care right now. I'm always caring about how I look, and right now, I don't."

All of a sudden, I understood how she felt. There were times when I just didn't give a damn, either. I guessed this was one of those moments for her, so I cut her some slack.

"I'm sorry, boo. I feel you. It be like that sometimes. For real." I sat down on the opposite end of the sofa.

As if her butt was on fire, she suddenly jumped up from her seat. "Shit, I forgot the mimosas. I wanted a drink, so what better shit to drink this damn early?" She managed to smile a little before she left the room.

Shaking my head, I checked my phone to see if Pistol had called. He hadn't. What the fuck was that nigga's issue with me? He'd been all pressed about us dealing with each other, and now it was just that easy for him to ignore me? Or *was* he ignoring me? What if something had happened to him? What if the BHM had figured out that he was the one who had killed G? And if so, how?

Megan returned with glass flutes filled with champagne and orange juice. Before I took a sip, I had to ask, "Uh, what kinda champagne is this?" Cheap champagne gave me a headache, but I didn't want to tell her that.

"Ace of Spades," she simply said as she sat back down on the sofa.

That was impressive. How could she afford such expensive champagne? Then again, she was probably lying. I mean, I didn't think it was impossible for her to get a bottle of Ace, but maybe she was being sarcastic because I'd asked.

Without responding, I took a sip of the drink and then placed it on the coaster she'd put on the coffee table.

Megan looked over at me. "My sorry excuse for a boyfriend left it over here this morning. I wouldn't spend that much money on champagne. I get paid pretty good, but not that damn good. We were supposed to have brunch with mimosas on the terrace, but he's such an asshole."

I was wondering what her boyfriend did for a living, but I didn't ask. Something told me that she would tell me everything she wanted me to know eventually. I wasn't there to ask her questions. I was there to listen. Taking another sip of my drink, I waited for her to tell me more, and she did.

"So, we broke up a few months ago because he'd cheated on me with this skank I was cool with. During that time, I had a weak moment and fucked my ex. How 'bout my ex took pictures of me in his bed, naked, and sent them to BJ? That's my sorry-ass boyfriend. Mind you, that was months ago, and it only happened once. He wanted to come over here with the damn Ace, like everything was cool, only to show me the pictures and rub that shit in my face. We got into a really fucked-up argument. I put all the clothes he'd left here in the tub and bleached them. He was throwing all my shit off the balcony, talking 'bout he'll throw me out, 'cause this is his shit. I don't have time for it. . . ."

Uh, I had to ask her one question. "Is this really his place?"

"It's mine. It's just in his name, and he pays the bills."

That meant it was really his. I couldn't judge, because Rae wasn't shit, but my spot was in my name. It had been up to me to leave. He hadn't kicked me out. I wanted to go back to get my things, but even though I knew that he was gone, I was afraid he'd just pop up.

"You're living in some man's place, and you're not married to him. Do you really think he won't kick you out?" I said. That was why I wanted my own place. I didn't want Pistol having that kind of control over me. Then if he got locked up or killed . . . what was I going to do?

I didn't intend to be in her business, but she'd invited me in, and I was curious.

As she took a long sip from her drink, her eyebrows shot up at me. After she put the glass down, she answered. "That nigga ain't gon' do shit. I know too much about all the illegal shit he does. I told him I'd tell the cops where he keeps his kilos, and he left here all mad."

My heart pounded. "When did he leave?"

So, she was into those damn thugs too. No wonder we'd clicked so easily.

"About an hour before I called you."

Oh shit. Their argument was still fresh.

She continued. "He was supposed to come over last night, but I guess he was all in his damn feelings when he saw those pictures. Talking 'bout he gon' go kill Dalvin. I mean, he's capable of murder, but I don't think he'll do it. Dalvin's my ex-boyfriend. Now that I think about it, I should've stayed with him. He ain't a damn street thug. He actually works a legal gig as an X-ray technician at Emory. He just works so much and doesn't have the money that fool BJ has. He couldn't spoil me like him, but now that shit don't even matter." She sobbed and then put her face in her hands.

My reaction was pure lack of know-how. The ability to comfort another woman was foreign to me. Kevia had been my only friend, and I'd hardly comforted her when we were close. I guessed not having my mother around to hug and kiss me as a kid had affected my ability to express emotions toward other women.

"Money's not the most important thing in a relationship. I mean, it's important, but not the most important. A lot of couples break up over lack of finances, but you can't stay with a person who treats you like shit because of money, either. I learned that I couldn't keep lettin' my ex treat me any kind of way. People do what we allow them to do to us. Obviously, you went back to your ex for a reason. Was he a better boyfriend? Was your ex's lack of time and money the only reason you ended up with . . . BJ?"

"When Dalvin did have time, he was a better boyfriend, much better."

We were still talking about our past relationships and sipping on our second round of mimosas when the door burst open. A tall, caramel-complexioned dude with close-cut waves was standing there, with an angry scowl on his face. I assumed it was her boyfriend, because he had a key.

"BJ, what . . . ?" Megan spluttered.

"Didn't I tell you that you better be outta my shit when I got back, or I was gon' fuck you up? Who the fuck is this bitch?" He turned to look at me.

Damn. Why the fuck was he mad at me? I didn't have anything to do with what was going on with them. I should've just stayed my ass at Pistol's. I had had no clue that shit was that serious. Why had I thought her boo would be some square-ass nigga she had a simple-ass argument with? It was my fault for trying to be a friend to a strange bitch.

"I was just leavin'." I slid up to the edge of the sofa.

Megan's eyes pleaded with mine, and I saw her desperation. The thing was, my gun was in my car. If he did anything to her, I wouldn't be able to help physically. Maybe I could leave and call 911, just in case. I'd send someone to check on her. She hadn't said that dude was violent, but Rae hadn't been violent toward me in the past, either.

"Yeah, I think you should leave, yo. Me and Megan got some shit to talk about . . . in private," he growled.

I stood up. "Okay. Megan, I'll call you."

"No, Daisha. Please don't . . . ," she begged.

"Shut the fuck up, you cheatin'-ass bitch! You tell yo' friend 'bout that? I bet you made me out to be the bad guy, like your shit don't stink. How you gon' cheat on me wit' that lame-ass nigga? Huh? How the fuck you think you gon' fuck that nigga and just end up back wit' me like ain't shit happen! Then you think I'm just gon' let you live in the place where I pay fuckin'' bills?" He started walking toward us, and I noticed that he was holding something behind his back.

My first thought was that this nigga had a gun, so my instinct was to get the hell up out of there. How could I just run out and let him kill Megan, though? I had to try to do something, but what?

When he got closer, my eyes almost popped out when I saw what he really was holding on to.

The sounds of my and Megan's screams could probably be heard all the way across town.

"Aah! Aah!" Megan yelled.

"What the fuck!" I screeched.

That nigga was holding up a severed head, which, I assumed, belonged to Megan's ex Dalvin. Blood dripped down to the floor, creating in a small red puddle. There was a bullet hole in the middle of his forehead, and his empty, dead eyes, which were wide open, were freaking me out.

An evil smile spread across BJ's face, and he let out a wicked laugh. "You should've gone on and left, shawty." He stared at me with a deranged look on his face. "Megan got you mixed up in her bullshit. Now the both of you gon' die."

He looked familiar as hell, and then, when I saw the tattoo on his neck, unfortunately, I knew exactly who he was. My heart raced. I wanted to be anywhere else on the earth than where I was at the moment. *Damn. Damn. Damn.* All I could do was hope and pray that Pistol would swoop me up and save me once again.

Chapter 26

Pistol

"Meet me at the J. Christopher's on Peachtree Street. It ain't far from your spot. I don't know about you, but I'm hungry. The missus is still asleep and ain't makin' breakfast, 'cause the kids ain't up yet. Plus, I don't feel like cookin'," Diablo had told me over the phone.

I had got back in bed a little while after Daisha fell asleep. She was sleeping so soundly that she didn't wake up when I got in bed or when I got out very early the next morning. Not wanting to wake her up, I didn't even bother to tell her where I was going. The thing was, I wasn't mad at her at all. It was more disappointment in myself. For some reason, I felt like things had changed between us. She had seen me at my most vulnerable, and no man wanted his woman to see him like that. If she viewed me as weak, how could she trust me to protect her? Honestly, it wasn't just about sex, like she might think.

Of course, I wanted her to let go with me and let me please her like I had before the seizure. The only thing that bothered me was the issue of how long her reservations were going to last. There was no way that I wanted my woman to be afraid for me. The feelings between us were so damn real that I couldn't just turn my back on her. It was up to her to deal with me and my issues. All I could do was hope she'd be able to come to grips with it all.

When I walked up to Diablo's table at J. Christopher's, I noticed a younger version of Diablo sitting next to him. That had to be his son Zy. The resemblance between them was startling. I greeted them both as pleasantly as was possible at such an early hour of the morning.

"You two look just alike. It's crazy," I commented as I took a seat.

Diablo had told me all about how he'd first met his son five years ago. Zy had become a Cue, although at the time he had thought Diablo was dead. Diablo had faked his own death due to some criminal charges that he didn't want to face and had fled to Miami. When Zy found out that his father was alive, he had planned to kill him for not being there for him over the years. He'd even gone as far as pulling a gun on him. Of course, he hadn't gone through with it. Diablo hadn't even known that Zy existed, but when he'd laid eyes on him, he felt something. He still hadn't figured it out on his own, though. That was a shock to me. It should've been like he was looking in a mirror.

"Yeah, that's all me," Diablo chuckled.

Zy sipped his water. "For real. Like father like son."

"So, y'all got something for me?" I quizzed anxiously as my eyes scanned both their faces. Seeing them together made me really miss my father.

"Yeah." Zy looked up. "But I'll tell you all about that after we order."

The server was standing right beside me, and I realized that Zy was looking at him. We all ordered our food and then got back to business.

"So," Zy continued and pulled the phone I'd given Diablo from his pocket. "It took me all night, but I finally cracked it."

My heart pounded at the news, and I hoped it wasn't too late to find Dank alive.

"Whoever took your cousin must've dropped it. There're a few text messages detailing their plan, but it's in code." Zy showed me the phone.

I skimmed the text messages, which were just a bunch of gibberish, but I could read between the lines. The plan was to kidnap Dank, because they were suspicious about him and Mike being involved in G's murder. The thing was they knew the two of them didn't actually do it. I was sure Rae and the nigga he was with had confirmed that.

"BJ's one of the BHM enforcers, and he's a cold-blooded killer. If Dank's still alive, there's a reason. From what I can tell, they got Dank 'cause they tryin'a find out what he knows. They wanna get whoever merked G. Once they find out, they gon' kill him. I hope he's holdin' out and he's still alive, but none of the messages say anything about where they holdin' him at," Zy explained. "I figured they went after Dank because they knew that your other cousin was fucked up in the hospital. Guess they figured he was gonna die, anyway."

I nodded, getting the same thing from the messages that had been sent by the contact known as BJ. If Dank was still alive, that meant he hadn't put them on me. He was either trying to stay alive or just didn't want to give me up. Then again, it was probably a mixture of both.

"Ain't no address or nothing in the texts. How do we know where they got Dank at?" I had to ask.

Before I got an answer, our food arrived.

Zy spoke up once the server was gone. "Don't worry. We're already workin' on that. I do know that the BHM got a stash house out in Lithonia, close to Redan Road. It got a basement, so it would be the perfect spot to hold somebody."

"I nodded. "So, we gon' try that place first?" I put a forkful of eggs in my mouth. They were delicious, or maybe I was just hungry as hell.

Whoever the phone belonged to was smart enough not to take a bunch of pictures or selfies. We had no clue what he looked like. It really didn't matter, though. We would be going for the BHM as a whole. The plan was to kill all of them that we came in contact with.

Diablo and Zy had brought down plenty of crews before. From what they'd told me, those crews were even bigger and badder than the BHM.

"Strength ain't just in numbers, young buck," Diablo told me as he poured syrup on his waffle. "Strength is in the mind. If you've ever read one of Aesop's fables, you'll know that it's all about strategy."

He was right, and I was so ready for them to lay out the master plan.

Zy's phone rang, and he looked down at the screen. "It's the wife. Hold on." He put his pointer finger up.

Damn, that was a surprise. He was my age and was married already. That shit really impressed me, and the way he talked to his wife showed his affection toward her. I had visions of Daisha becoming my wife one day. But first, I had to

make sure that we both survived the threats
around us.

After Zy ended his call, we discussed the plan
to hit up the BHM's stash house. Then I left
the restaurant alone. Daisha had called me a
few times, and I listened to her voice mail as I
headed to my car. I could tell from the voice mail
she'd left that she was pissed. Before pulling out
of the parking lot of the restaurant, I decided to
call her back. That time my call went to voice
mail. I left her a message.

"Babe, I'm sorry I didn't answer your calls. I
had to meet up with Diablo and his son. I'm
on my way home now. So, I'll see you in a few.
Hopefully, we'll be handlin' business tonight. I
got some shit to tell you. No more secrets, babe.
I promise. Love you, Ma."

I hung up and headed toward my crib. Diablo
would be calling me in a few hours to tell me
where to meet him and Zy. We would be hitting
up the BHM's stash house while the Cues went to
Bankhead to take them on at their headquarters.
I was hoping we'd find Dank at either location.
From what I'd learned, BJ was next in line to
lead the BHM, and not Rae. That was interesting.

Before I got to the crib, I decided to stop at a
floral shop to pick up some orchids for Daisha.
She'd told me they were her favorite flower. I
also decided to stop at a jewelry shop to pick her

up something special. After such a tense night, I wanted to make up with her. Besides, I had no idea how shit was going to turn out later that night.

When I pulled up in one of the parking spots in front of my building, I noticed that Daisha's car wasn't there. It wasn't like her not to tell me where she was going. Being that it was so early, I didn't really worry. Maybe she just wanted to get out on her day off.

Still, a feeling in my gut told me that it was more than that. She was probably pissed at me for not answering my phone and had left so that she wouldn't have to be there when I returned.

I grabbed the vase of flowers and the bag from the jewelry store and made my way inside. Once I was inside the condo, I put the vase on the coffee table and tried calling Daisha for a second time. Again, I got her voice mail. What the hell was going on?

Something told me that she had probably gone out to get a bite to eat. I didn't want to think the worst. Maybe my baby girl just needed some time to herself. We had been together a lot lately, and with the tension between us, she may have wanted a little space.

Almost thirty minutes passed by, and I just had this anxious feeling that I couldn't shake. I was starting to really worry about Daisha at that point. She should've seen that I was calling her, and I couldn't imagine her being so upset that she wouldn't call me back.

When my phone rang, I grabbed it, just knowing that I'd see Daisha's number on the screen. Instead, it was a number that I didn't have in my contacts. I had saved Diablo's number, but not Zy's. Maybe it was him. I answered the call.

"Yo."

"Yeah, nigga. You won't answer when I call from my number, so I had to use somebody's else's phone."

I didn't even recognize the bitch's voice, and I was not in the mood for no bullshit.

"Who the fuck is this? I ain't got time for games. I'm a grown-ass man," I growled.

"Oh, so you don't know my voice, huh? That's fucked up, Pistol." The way she said my name like it was poison in her mouth showed me her disdain for me.

So, obviously, she'd called the right person.

"Nah, I don't know your voice, so that gotta tell you that you don't mean shit to me." The venom I spit back had to get under her skin.

She sucked her teeth like the truth pissed her off. "Well, damn. I knew you wasn't all in love wit' me or nothin', but if you would've let me in, it could've got to that point. You know you loved how I was suckin' that dick, Daddy."

"A'ight, shawty. If I loved how you sucked my dick, thank you. I appreciate the favor and shit, but I ain't tryin'a fuss wit' you over my dick bein' in yo' mouth. That was your choice. I don't owe you shit. You act like I begged you to suck my dick. No worries, Ma. That's covered now. My baby girl got that. I gotta go. . . . Bye."

Before I could hang up, she started screaming erratically. "It's Kendra, nigga, and I don't appreciate you dissin' me for that li'l bitch you fuckin'! I'm gon' show you that you shouldn't go around messin' wit' people's feelings and—"

"Bitch, please! You sound silly as hell. I ain't never messed wit' your feelings, yo. You knew that all I wanted to do was fuck. I got a text to prove it. Don't keep playin' yourself, shawty. Just go ahead and hang up 'fore you get yo' li'l feelings hurt."

"Get my feelings hurt? Really? You think that's what this shit is about?" She laughed loudly, sounding ignorant as hell. "You can't hurt my feelings, nigga. It's just . . . I'm tired of y'all niggas thinkin' I'm a damn play toy." It sounded like that bitch was crying. "Like you can just fuck me when you want and put me back on the fuckin' shelf."

What was that ho talking about, and why was she crying? We hadn't even fucked. All she had done was *start* sucking my dick. She hadn't even got to finish that shit. So, there was another crazy bitch out there, ready to complicate things for me. If only I hadn't been thinking with my dick head. It was like the situation with Niya all over again. At least I knew that she didn't have a key to my spot. This ho didn't even know where I lived.

"If you got issues wit' yo' sperm donor, you need to take that shit up wit' him, not me. We didn't even fuck, baby girl. Get that fantasy outta yo' head. It didn't happen, and it'll never happen. I just let you get a small taste of this dick, and you couldn't even handle that. Get yo' mind right, shawty. Then some nigga out there might just fuck wit' you like that. Won't be me, though."

I hung up and immediately blocked the number she'd called from. A nigga had other shit to think about, and fussing with some bitch on the phone was not on the list. Knowing where my girl was at was way more important.

The phone rang again. That time it was Daisha, and I sighed with relief. At least I knew that she was okay.

"Hey, baby . . . ," I said into my phone.

She spoke in a whisper. "This nigga's gonna kill me. You gotta get here . . . quick."

"What?" Did I hear her right? "What nigga? Rae . . . ?"

"No, it ain't Rae. It's Megan's boyfriend . . . BJ. I came over here 'cause they got into an argu-